Trouble at Cl

Lou Elliott Mystery Adventure Series: Book 4

By

George Chedzoy

GEORGE
CHEDZOY

LOU ELLIOTT MYSTERY ADVENTURES:

1. Smugglers at Whistling Sands
2. The Missing Treasure
3. Something Strange in the Cellar
4. Trouble at Chumley Towers

To:

Our nieces, Charlotte and Sally

Trouble at Chumley Towers
Lou Elliott Mystery Adventure Series Book 4
© George Chedzoy MMXV

First published by George Chedzoy, 2015 in eBook format
First edition in paperback, 2016
This book: First edition, first print

CONTENTS

CHAPTER ONE

Lou is fed up

THE wind blew like iced vapour into Lou's face. She pulled her scarf tighter and quickened her step. The High Street in Church Stretton bustled with chattering shoppers and twinkled with festive lights. It was a pleasant, cheerful scene – which she could not wait to escape from.

Louise Elliott's school in rural Shropshire had broken up for two weeks the previous day. Christmas was a week away. At thirteen years old, she ought to be excited and happy. She was neither. December 25th was a painful reminder of how different her family was from other people's. It was at this time of year that she yearned for the brother and sister she didn't have, and a mother and father willing to make their daughter feel special. If only.

In the living rooms of her classmates, heaps of presents would sit beneath sparkling fir trees; dining room tables would groan with food. Lou could expect a couple of badly-wrapped, cheap, unimaginative gifts – if she was lucky. As for Christmas lunch, there was no reason to hope that things would be any different from last year, namely a microwaved turkey dinner with ready-made sachets of gravy. On Christmas afternoon, her mother would hit the brandy and her father would fall asleep in front of some soppy film on TV. Lou would find herself alone with her books and her thoughts.

So it was with relief that she reached the top of the high street and crossed over to the steep, winding lane beyond. The teeming hordes, struggling under the weight of their shopping bags had gone, replaced by high garden walls and long drives to grand old houses. Within five minutes or so, these vanished too and Lou found herself surrounded by a tussocky, undulating wilderness. This was Shropshire's Long Mynd – acres of gloriously unspoilt hillside a stone's throw from the village centre. In mid-winter, when it often snowed heavily, it was like stepping through the back of the wardrobe into C S Lewis's Narnia.

There was no snow on this occasion, although the rolling clouds in the west threatened to deliver some. But just then, the ground and boughs of the trees were encrusted with frost, glistening under a weak sun.

Lou passed through the gate to the stream threading its way between towering ridges. It was reasonably sheltered here. With the exertion of brisk walking, she soon warmed up. But a chill remained in her heart. Usually, she was perfectly content roaming this idyllic spot on her own. In fact, she preferred it that way. Yet it was becoming unbearably lonely as Christmas drew closer.

Her thoughts strayed to Jack, David and Emily with whom she had made friends on holiday earlier in the year. She wished they were with her right then; sharing the rugged beauty of the landscape and the music of the gurgling stream. No doubt they were aching for Christmas, counting the days down. Lou slipped off the path and found a flat rock to sit on between a couple of ragged trees. She gazed hypnotically at the flowing water and imagined life at the Johnsons' house with their jolly mum bustling to and fro and their dad cracking daft jokes. She could picture them in a week's time in their party hats gathered round the dinner table, a huge turkey with crispy skin waiting to be carved.

Lou recalled the fun times they had shared – in August at the Welsh seaside resort of Abersoch, then camping in Staffordshire a few weeks later, then back at Abersoch at autumn half-term. She had pushed her luck to clear off to her parents' holiday cottage on her own – most youngsters wouldn't have dared. On the other hand, she wasn't most youngsters. But it was sad, on reflection, that her mum and dad had not been unduly concerned that their twelve-year-old daughter, as she was then, should give them the slip and disappear. In her dad's defence, he had been up to his neck with work. He was a freelance journalist and had got a week of shifts on the *Shropshire Star* newspaper standing in for one of their reporters while he was away. At least dad did what he could to keep the family solvent. Times were tough. Every week was a struggle. Her mother, meanwhile, preferred an easy ride through life. Any displeasure she might have felt at Lou's behaviour would have been outweighed by the satisfaction of having the house to herself.

She'd pack me off to boarding school if she could afford it! Never mind, I'll just have to clear off by myself more often, mused Lou. It will be great! I can be gloriously free to do as I please!

A tear rolled down her cheek, dried instantly by a breath of wind. Lou looked about her. The place was idyllic, yet its winter bleakness was becoming oppressive; amplifying her feelings of isolation. She got up, aware that she was becoming stiff and cold. She walked briskly to the top of the ridge and gazed down at the expanse of countryside all around her, gloved hands thrust firmly into fur-lined pockets.

Far below, spires of smoke rose from matchbox homes. In her mind, happy children were inside gathered round a roaring fire; their mother emerging from the kitchen with mugs of hot chocolate and plates of buttered crumpets.

Forty miles away in the Cheshire village of Malpas, Jack Johnson tapped out a text message on his mobile phone – his most prized possession, given him by his parents on his twelfth birthday in March. It was childishly cheery: *Hope you're all set for Crimbo. I can't wait. David's got his head buried deep in a book and Emily's flicking through a magazine. I'm off for a long walk over some frosty fields. Wish you were here – we could go together. Get in touch soon and tell me your news. Hope you have a great hols. We're all missing you, Jack x.*

It was to Lou, Jack's best friend in all the world, even if he did only get to see her in the holidays. Her phone duly beeped a few seconds later. She dug it out of her pocket and smiled wistfully as she read the message. Good old Jack. He had no idea what sort of Christmas was in prospect for her.

Lou typed a reply: *Yes, all fine here – great to finish for the hols. Looking forward to two weeks off with no school. Hope you have a good Christmas too. Should be lots of fun.*

She was about to send it when a black wave of unhappiness swept over her. Who was she kidding? Not herself, at any rate. How about a bit of honesty for a change? She deleted the message and wrote in its place: *Christmas here will be as grim as ever. It's the worst time of year for me. Can't wait for it to be over. Glad you enjoy it so much – have a good one. Missing you all loads too. Hope we can meet up next year, Lou x*

She regretted sending it as soon as it had gone. It was not right to make Jack and the others feel bad or guilty about enjoying Christmas simply because hers was sure to be miserable. Quickly, she fired off another text: *I'm sorry, feeling a bit fed up at the moment. Christmas is just a really bad time for me especially with my mother the way she is. I'll be thinking of you all and imagining I'm there with you, which will cheer me up! Let me know what Santa Claus brings! x*

There was no immediate response from Jack, who usually replied within seconds. Lou looked again into the valley below, now filling with slowly-rising mist. She hoped she had not upset him. It was out of character for her to be so self-absorbed and self-pitying. And wasn't she great at coping on her own? Hadn't she been doing so for years already?

A light sleet began to descend. The weather was worsening. Lou turned for home. She was getting cold, not that being inside their draughty and poorly-heated house would make much difference.

She walked through the back door and into the kitchen. Nobody was about. She went through to the living room, expecting her mother to be sprawled out on the sofa surrounded by empty crisp packets and sweet wrappers. There *were* a couple of scrunched up salt & vinegar packets – her mum's favourites – and a plate strewn with toast crumbs. A half-drunk cup of coffee and yesterday evening's wine glass with congealed ruby stains down the side were stuck fast to the coffee table, but that was it. No mother, no father.

Lou was reasonably indifferent to their absence but had thought they just might have shown a passing interest in spending time with her on the very first day of the holidays. She sank into an armchair and stared through the living room window at the greying sky.

A silent gloom hung thickly, resonating from all four corners of the spartan room. No Christmas tree stood proudly to brighten things up; no tinsel glimmered from behind a picture frame. There were no sprays of holly decorating the mantelpiece or window ledge, even though a holly bush with bright red berries stood prominently in the back garden. Not a single Christmas card was on display. Possibly, none had been received.

The wicker basket on the hearth, which should have been full of logs, was empty so Lou could not light a fire. Most likely her father had not got round to ordering any, preferring to shiver rather than shell out a hundred pounds or so for a delivery which would have kept them warm through the winter months. He was, at least, sensible with money and knew its value. The same could not be said for her mother.

Lou was hungry. It was well past lunchtime after all. Her parents must have gone out for a pub lunch or something. How typical that they hadn't troubled to ask her. She went into the kitchen and opened the fridge. It was almost bare, but on closer inspection, a bar of fruit and nut chocolate could be seen peeking out from behind a fat yellow jar of Hellmann's mayonnaise. Had her mother deliberately sought to conceal it from view? Probably. Lou took it out and ran her fingers along its wrapper. It wouldn't hurt to have a few chunks, surely her parents couldn't begrudge her that. She checked the cupboards first for stray tins of baked beans or something vaguely worth eating. They were empty too. So she wolfed down half the chocolate bar, leaving what remained on the kitchen table. It didn't seem right to re-hide it somehow.

Still in her coat, she took herself upstairs to her bedroom and wrapped a blanket round her shoulders like a shawl. Through the window, the sleet was turning to snow and sticking, dusting a line of fir trees with a seasonal sprinkling of feathery flakes. Mother Nature looked determined to celebrate Christmas at least – even if her own mother couldn't be bothered to. Lou picked up a book and climbed on to her bed, seeking to immerse herself in it as quickly as possible.

Half an hour later, the front door was opened and slammed shut. Her parents were back. Her mother's shrill voice echoed along the hall. They were arguing about something – money most likely. Their voices grew more distant as the row moved off into the kitchen. Then, a shriek of anger, followed by a shout up the stairs.

'Louise Elliott! Have you been at my chocolate?'

bawled her mother. 'How *dare* you – you've scoffed half of it. And you left it out on the table so it's gone warm. Come down here now, I want to speak to you.'

Warm? The house was so cold they barely needed to run a fridge. She was surprised her father hadn't un-plugged it to keep the electricity bill down. She ignored her mother's order. At that moment, she heard a muffled beep from her phone, buried somewhere in her coat pocket. She pulled it out. It was Jack, asking her what she thought, and how chuffed he, David and Emily would be if she said 'yes'.

Yes to what? Lou stared in bafflement. Whatever did he mean? Her mother yelled up the stairs again. Lou had had enough. She threw open her bedroom door and stormed down.

'So what if I ate your chocolate!' she shouted, her vivid green eyes blazing. 'It was lunchtime and there was nothing else to eat in the whole house. I was hungry, what was I supposed to do, starve? It's all right for you and dad, going out to lunch, spending money you can't afford while I have to make do with whatever scraps I can find. So I helped myself to a few chunks of your fruit and nut, get over it.'

'Don't you be so insolent! You had no right taking what doesn't belong to you,' snapped Mrs Elliott, glaring at her daughter. There's bread in the bread bin if you'd looked and jam in the cupboard.'

'The bread is stale and I daresay the jam will need the mould scraping off the top of it,' retorted Lou. 'By the way, have you ordered us a turkey this year, or aren't we going to bother? Perhaps you and dad are going to clear off to the pub for Christmas dinner and leave me here on my own?'

'You mind your manners and your sharp tongue, young lady, or it might come to that,' snapped her mother.

Lou looked tearfully at her father but he was in no mood to back her against his fiery wife. He was a pleasant, if rather weak man, with a pale, puffy complexion and tired eyes. His brow was furrowed from the stress of trying to make ends meet and keep his demanding wife happy.

'I'm sure we'll all have a lovely Christmas,' he said, limply, looking far from certain that he meant it.

'Oh come off it, dad,' said Lou. 'You know mum can't cook to save her life – she'll burn the turkey or forget to take the giblets out or something and then get in a foul temper and blame everyone else – hence why we had a supermarket ready meal last year. Christmas will be the disaster it always is.'

'Right,' said Mrs Elliott, screwing up her long fingers as if she wished they were clasped around Lou's neck. 'I've had enough of this. If our daughter doesn't want to spend Christmas with us then she can clear off and find someone else to spend it with, and jolly good riddance, too.'

Lou stared hard at her. 'Hang on a minute,' she said.

Her mother's cruel words had got her thinking. She dashed back upstairs, grabbed her mobile phone and clicked on her messages. Jack must have sent her some sort of invitation in an earlier text that she hadn't seen, or why text her saying he hoped she would say 'yes'? Sure enough, there *was* an earlier message. It must have come as she walked back and she hadn't heard her phone beep. She clicked on it eagerly and for the first time that day, a broad smile crossed her striking face and she kissed the phone with delight.

She bounded back downstairs and into the kitchen. 'Mother, I would like to take you up on your kind suggestion to clear off and spend Christmas somewhere else. Listen to this.' She read out Jack's message, which said: *I'm sorry you're feeling unhappy. Can't bear to think of you having a miserable time when we'll all be having such fun. Look, I hope you don't mind but I asked our mum and dad if you could spend Christmas here and she said you'd be very welcome. Her exact words were, tell Lou to get the next train. So what do you think? David and Emily want you to come as badly as I do and our parents would love to see you – they say you're like a second daughter to them.*

Lou's father looked rather shamefaced. 'Come on, Lou, it won't be so bad. Perhaps we could all go out to a restaurant for Christmas lunch – there's one close enough to walk to if the weather's fine. Your mother and I really do want you to have a good Christmas, don't we, love?'

'Let her plough her own furrow and stay with her friends if their parents are keen to have her. She won't be any trouble, will you Lou?' said Mrs Elliott, appearing to brighten up. 'Actually, I do rather like the idea of the two of us going out for Christmas lunch, darling. It would save an awful lot of work.'

Lou rolled her eyes in disgust, then turned to her father. 'Dad, I *would* like to spend more time with you – but you know how busy you get over the festive period. You're always covering freelance jobs and doing shifts for the local newspapers so their own staff can take time off. You'll be rushed off your feet and mum clearly doesn't want me here. Let me go and stay with the Johnsons, please!'

Mr Elliott sighed. It was times like this that he really wished he was a better father to his only child. But Lou's absence would certainly free him up a bit to earn a few vital extra pennies and make for a more peaceful household.

'Very well, ring the Johnsons now – speak to Mrs Johnson, please, not just Jack – and make sure it's okay with her.'

'Of course,' said Lou, trying hard not to grin too much. Deep down, she regretted that it should come to this. On a good day, her dad was reasonable company but she had endured too many disastrous Christmases to believe that this one would be any different. For the first time in her life, she was to spend this special occasion at the heart of a loving family – in a warm, comfortable house!

CHAPTER TWO

Off to the Johnsons

T HE following day, Lou felt strangely churned up as the train pulled out of Church Stretton railway station. Her father stood on the platform cheerily waving her off. She waved back and blew him a kiss and her eyes moistened.

But as the train increased speed and the scenic Shropshire countryside rolled by, she felt a growing sense of anticipation. It was thrilling to be unexpectedly heading off to see Jack, David and Emily again – and to actually stay in their house and spend Christmas with them! As for her parents, they would be free to mark the occasion in their own unique way – by more or less ignoring it, without feeling under pressure to 'entertain' their only child. They would go out somewhere for Christmas lunch – the village pub most likely – and feel relieved that they could stagger back home with no washing up to do.

Lou's phone beeped from inside her smart dark suede jacket. It was another text from Jack. She gazed at it with mystified amusement. Someone had been stealing valuable items from Chumley Towers – a nearby stately home – and the thief was suspected to be local. It was on the front page of the *Whitchurch Herald*. Jack would show her when she arrived. Everyone in Malpas was talking about it and speculating on whom it might be. Nobody had a clue, however, including the police. Fair enough, thought Lou, there would be a mystery for them to investigate as well, which should make her stay even more interesting.

Lou was getting peckish. She pulled out the remaining half of her mother's chocolate bar from the outside pocket of her rucksack and nibbled hungrily on it. Her mum had given it her as she went through the door. Possibly she was feeling guilty about her unpleasantness the previous day and, as her daughter was going away for Christmas, had been willing to indulge in a rare display of generosity.

It was a cold day and the train carriage was poorly heated. Lou pulled her coat tighter around her. Despite the chill, she enjoyed the journey. She loved trains, especially when travelling through such scenic country-side. She wondered if it would snow in Malpas. It was not uncommon where she lived but that was high up, nestling amid the hills. Somehow, at her place, snow rarely seemed particularly jolly and festive, but now that she was off to the Johnsons, a good thick blanket of the stuff would be perfect. Certainly, the sky looked grey and heavy, so maybe she would be in luck.

Lou checked her watch. It was nearly 11am – she would be at Whitchurch station in a few minutes, where Jack was due to meet her. A moment of insecurity shook her. Jack definitely wanted her to come but did the others really feel the same way? Christmas was such a special, family occasion, she hoped her presence wouldn't be an imposition. After all, if her own mother treated her with indifference, how could she expect warmth and affection from someone else's? Either way, it was too late to back out now. The train was slowing down and, in the dis-tance, she could see the railway station platform. Await-ing her arrival was a very eager-looking 12-year-old boy – Jack, of course!

She waved at him through the window. His face lit up when he saw her. He waved back manically. Lou picked up her rucksack and queued impatiently for the doors to open. Why were some people so slow? As she alighted, Jack reached out a hand to take her rucksack. She gave him a hug, and looked around her.

'Welcome to Whitchurch,' he said, grinning broadly. 'We'll have to get a bus from here, but it's not far. There's one in seven minutes. The stop is just round the corner. I can't believe you're actually here, it's amazing! I never thought we'd set eyes on you again until next Easter or something.'

'I thought the same,' said Lou. 'Are you sure it's okay though, Jack – with the others, I mean? Do David and Emily really want me to stay, and your parents?'

'Everyone's thrilled about it. As I said in that text, my parents think of you like a second daughter and they know that you haven't got a – you know – very good home life. They loved the idea of you coming and having a proper Christmas with us.'

'That'll do for me,' said Lou, smiling. She felt more relaxed now. 'I can't tell you how pleased I am to be here. Let's go and queue up for that bus. Then when we get on board, I want to hear all your news. Our week together at autumn half-term seems like an age ago now.'

On the short journey to Malpas, Jack told her about life at the village's Bishop Heber school and who was getting on with whom and who used to be good friends but had since fallen out. At times, Lou had to stifle a yawn when he went into rather too much detail but she felt very content to be in his company again. After all, it was Jack whom she had met first – on the rocks just below her parents' holiday home at Abersoch.

'A word of warning about David,' continued Jack. 'He's been having a bit of a tough time of it at school. There are a few bigger kids in his year who have started picking on him and bullying him. So he's a bit sensitive at the moment.'

Lou's face fell. 'That's a shame. I thought he was much more confident than he used to be.'

'Yes but that was partly the problem. He went back to school brimming with tales of our adventures and some of the other boys didn't believe him and thought he was trying to show off – which he was, to an extent. Anyway, he has sort of gone back into his shell a bit. It will do him good to see you again. Oh and you must meet some of my schoolmates, I've been telling them all about you. My best friend in the village is Tony Bounderton – usually known by his nickname of Bounder. He's the sort of leader of our gang.'

'Okay,' said Lou, doubtfully. 'Not the most complimentary of nicknames, but I suppose it's based on his surname rather than his character. But if I were you, I would be careful what I said about our adventures. David should be, too. Oh, talking of which, what was that about stuff going missing from a stately home near you?'

'Yes, at Chumley Towers! How could I have forgotten! Here, take a look at this – it's a newspaper article in the local paper, giving all the details. Malpas is buzzing with it. No-one knows who on earth it can be. At first it was assumed to be a tourist. But there have been several thefts since, which has made the police think it might be someone local.'

'They have no idea who it is?' asked Lou, her vivid green eyes scanning the newspaper article quickly. 'Goodness me, they seem almost to have given up. Read what Detective Sergeant Simon Walker says half way down: "North Mercia Constabulary are appealing to anyone with any information on these thefts to contact them immediately. We need members of the public to be our eyes and ears on this one. In particular, we are keen to hear from anyone who is offered these items for sale."

Lou curled her lip scornfully. 'Can't the police use their own eyes and ears? That's what they're paid to do, isn't it? I bet we could solve this little mystery if we put our minds to it.'

'Hey that would be great, Lou,' said Jack, his eyes shining. 'I was hoping you would say that.'

'Or, plan B, we could concentrate on simply enjoying Christmas. I'm so looking forward to spending a few days with you all. Our house is as silent and cold as a tomb at the moment and my mother is her usual sour-faced self,' said Lou.

'What about your dad?' asked Jack, gripping the seat in front to steady himself as the bus took a bend rather too sharply. 'Surely he is reasonably good fun at Christmas?'

Lou shrugged her shoulders. 'He's infinitely more fun than my mother, but he still doesn't bother much with me, mainly because he spends almost every moment either feverishly trying to make money, or worrying himself about not earning enough. I don't what he'd do if ever he actually had some – hoard it under the bed, probably.'

'So what were your plans, if you hadn't come to stay with us?'

Lou looked at Jack and he saw traces of sadness behind those vivacious, cat-like eyes looking out from beneath her dark fringe.

'Let's put it this way, have you got festive decorations up?' she asked. 'And Christmas cards everywhere and a turkey on order and your mum made the plum pudding weeks ago? That sort of thing?'

'Almost,' said Jack. 'We're having goose this year, if that's ok. Dad says that although it's not as big as a turkey, a goose will feed six and there'll be five of us with you, so you'll probably be able to have an extra helping.'

Lou smiled. That was a classic 'Jack' thing to say.

'But yes,' he continued, 'there's a lovely real fir tree which we bought from a chap in the village who grows them in his field. There are decorations all over the house, but no gaudy, flashing lights on the outside. My parents think that's rather vulgar. Don't worry about the cold, we've got a wood-burner in the living room and an open fire in the dining room and a coal bunker full of coal and a wood store full of logs. You'll be as warm as toast.'

'At my place,' sighed Lou, 'you will not find a Christmas tree because my parents don't bother to put one up, even though we've got a misshapen artificial one in the loft somewhere. You won't find any tinsel or decorations of any kind and no Christmas cards. I'm not sure my parents actually receive any. We have a wood-burner with no logs to burn in it. My dad's like Scrooge trying to keep warm on a single lump of coal. As for Christmas Day, I think their plan is to go to the village pub for a turkey roast, and that will be that. It's dismal, Jack.'

For a fleeting moment, Lou looked close to tears. Spontaneously, Jack grabbed her hand and gave it a squeeze. Then he blushed and took his hand away. 'We'll give you the best Christmas you've ever had,' he stuttered.

'Hey, that's not going to be a tough challenge,' said Lou, with a grin. 'I'm thrilled to be here – oh in fact, we *are* here. Isn't this Malpas high street? The bus has just pulled over. Come on Jack, ping the bell to let the driver know we want to get off, before it's too late. You really are a dope at times.'

'Oh yes, you're right,' said Jack, who would have cheerfully remained on the bus with Lou right the way to Chester or wherever it was bound, given the chance. The two of them clambered along the aisle. Jack gallantly took Lou's heavy rucksack, managing to bump it into several outstretched legs along the way.

'Come on, you pair, I haven't got all day,' growled the driver with an amused glance in his rear-view mirror.

'So here we are,' said Jack, proudly, as they got off. 'Our house is all the way up the high street on the left, then left again. Shall we go straight there, or walk about a bit?'

'Let's explore,' said Lou, enthusiastically. 'Show me around, I've been wondering what your little village looks like. It seems an interesting place. Hey that sky looks dark. I bet there'll be snow later on. I hope so.'

Jack beamed. 'Come on then, we'll start at the bottom end and work our way to the top, then head home. Mum's got some hot chocolate and crumpets waiting for us.'

CHAPTER THREE

The snow sets in

THE festive lights of Malpas shone bright against the menacing clouds above. Its attractive high street thronged with villagers on Christmas shopping sprees, their breath smoking in the crisp air. The scene was reminiscent of Church Stretton the day before, only it felt different somehow.

At first Lou could not work out why, but then it occurred to her. This time she was with her best friend Jack. Yesterday she had been on her own. She was part of the merriment, not merely a solitary onlooker. Jack twittered away at her as they walked, pointing out the elegant Georgian and Victorian buildings as if conducting a guided tour.

Lou listened courteously, content to absorb the atmosphere. She had fallen in love with Malpas and its mediaeval layout and historic architecture instantly. Old-style russet-coloured bricks, black and white timbers, towering chimney stacks, sash windows, quaint gabled roofs – *this* was the sort of place to celebrate Christmas in!

The village felt homely and welcoming and its residents seemed a decent, friendly lot. No wonder the thefts from the nearby stately home had caused such a stir, especially since a local person was suspected. Looking all around her, it was hard to imagine that any of these people could be responsible. They had an air of intelligent respectability, although looks could be deceiving, of course.

'Cross over,' said Jack, suddenly. Lou followed him, wondering what had suddenly alarmed him.

'See that old woman ahead, with a black shawl

wrapped round her shoulders? That's Mrs Mary Armstrong. She's mean-spirited and as bitter as a crab-apple. She can't stand children – although she doesn't like other grown-ups much either.'

'Really? We'll have to look out for her!' said Lou, interested.

'Oh and here comes another eccentric oldie – much nicer than Mrs Armstrong though. He's on the committee of the history society that my mum is chairman of.'

A strikingly well-dressed tall, lanky man was strolling down the pavement towards them. He wore a dark frock coat extending almost to his knees and a top hat. As he approached, he tucked his walking cane underneath an arm, pulled a gold pocket watch on a chain from inside his waistcoat, shook his head and tutted.

'Good morning, Mr Whortlebury,' said Jack.

'I will bid you good afternoon for my part, young sir, since the hour is twelve noon, precisely,' replied Mr Whortlebury, looking vexed. 'More to the point I am already late for my meeting with the Malpas and District Women's Institute. I am giving a lecture to them on Malpas as it looked in the nineteenth century.'

'May I introduce my friend . . .' began Jack, but he was gone, striding purposefully down the road. 'Oh dear, Mr Whortlebury looks to be in something of a flap this morning, or rather, this afternoon.'

Lou stared down the road after him. 'My goodness, he looks exactly like a character out of a Charles Dickens novel. I suppose he's dressed in costume because it's from the era he's going to talk about.'

'No, that's quite normal,' said Jack, matter of factly. 'I've never seen Mr Whortlebury wear anything modern. Usually he sports a silk cravat, you know, a sort of baggy-looking tie, but as it's cold he's obviously gone for a thick scarf. My mum has dated him at around the mid-1860s, or thereabouts.'

Lou chuckled. 'He must get a few funny looks going about like that.'

'Not really. You see, he's well known around here and well liked and this is quite a traditional village where no-one minds anyone dressing old-fashioned, so long as you're smartly turned-out. Funny looks are reserved for ripped jeans, hoodies and tracksuit tops – that sort of thing. Old Whortlebury is considered rather elegant and charming. The ladies in particular all love him. He's eccentric but harmless enough and mum says he's a very hard-working member of the history society committee. He's very knowledgeable about the world. Well, how it used to be, anyway.'

Lou smiled. 'You seem to have some real characters in Malpas. We have, too, around where I live. I think you get them more out in the countryside. I really like this place, it intrigues me. The buildings have a sort of olde-worlde feel and there are lots of quaint little shops. I'd love to have a browse round them sometime.'

'I thought you were all for roaming hillsides, not going shopping,' teased Jack.

'It depends,' said Lou. 'I don't like the huge, shiny modern shopping complexes you get in city centres. I keep well away, but I like small, independent stores with a friendly shopkeeper behind the counter, selling unusual items that you couldn't get in the big chains.'

'That's Malpas for you. I was hoping you'd approve. It's great at Christmas, don't you think, with all the lights and decorations up. And look, there's a huge fir tree by the Cross monument over there,' said Jack, pointing. 'There's a street stall next to it on the cobbles selling baked potatoes with lovely crispy skins and hot dogs. We'll have to try it sometime.'

Jack glanced upwards. 'All we need now is for some snow to fall, and it will look perfect.'

'Any minute,' said Lou, lifting her hands up. 'I can tell.'

Lou was right. She seemed to have an instinctive knack of predicting the weather. As she and Jack went up the hill, a few flakes tumbled from a tungsten sky. Then a few more.

'Snow! Jack, look at it, coming down all round us. Isn't it wonderful?'

Lou's face, blotchy pink in the cold, lit up and her emerald eyes danced. Jack, his tousled mop of brown hair now speckled with dabs of white, gazed upwards, exultantly. Christmas was always one of his favourite holidays but this year would be really special. He felt extraordinarily happy. School was over for two glorious weeks. Christmas Day itself was just four days away and astonishingly, Lou had come to stay. Even the weather had been perfect – cold, bright days and now the start of what looked like a thick fall of snow. Rooftop tiles were already whitening.

'It'll be prettier than a Christmas card before we know it,' exclaimed Lou. 'I can't wait to have snowball fights with you and the others.'

'Hey, we better get back,' said Jack, glancing at his watch. 'Mum will be wondering where we've got to. We'll probably look like snowmen by the time we arrive.'

They dug their hands into their pockets and walked briskly up the hill. Swirling flakes nuzzled their faces. It was getting colder. Lou put on her woollen hat, pulling it down over her ears.

Suddenly out of nowhere, a pale, rat-like face appeared, with lank dark hair parted in the middle and extending to his shoulders.

'Hello, hello,' he said, giving Jack a hearty clap on his shoulder.

'Oh hi Bounder. Lou, this is Bounder, my best buddy from school who I was telling you about.'

Bounder grabbed Lou's hat and yanked it off.

'Couldn't see you under all that wool,' said Bounder, a greasy smile breaking out over his pallid face. 'Hey, smart-looking lass. How you doing, Lou, nice to meet you. Jack's been telling me all about you and your adventures. He never let on you were coming to stay for Christmas though, the sly fox. Wants to keep you all to himself, does he?'

Lou backed away and shot Bounder a withering glare which he appeared not to notice.

Jack's face, already reddening from the cold, turned a shade deeper. 'We only arranged it the other day. We'll have to catch up over the holidays, if you're free.'

'Yeah sure,' said Bounder, winking. 'I can't wait to find out from Lou here whether all your scrapes were real or just you and your baby brother blagging it. Must say, I didn't believe a word of it. Well Lou, great to meet you, look forward to us all ganging up soon.'

'Yeah, that'll be great,' said Jack. Lou didn't respond.

'Sorted. It's a deal. Nice chatting, Lou. See you again soon,' said Bounder, giving her a cheery punch on the shoulder. 'I'll send you a text, Jack, let you know when I'm coming round. Or you can come to our place if you like. We've just had an extension put up – house is massive now. New taps fitted and everything, made of solid gold.'

Jack caught the tail end of Lou scowling fiercely at Bounder when he glanced at her after his friend had disappeared.

'Hey, you'll get used to him, he's just a bit larger than life and boisterous but he's good at heart,' said Jack.

'He's your best friend around here, is he?' said Lou, stonily, wiping a melting snowflake off her nose.

'Absolutely. He and I are best buddies,' said Jack en-thusiastically. 'With any luck he'll text us later on to sort out coming round. He's never actually been to my place, it will be great.'

'Brilliant,' said Lou, flatly. She shivered. 'Talking of your place, Jack, let's get back there. Even I'm getting cold now.'

'Of course,' said Jack, 'it's just up the road. We'll be there before you know it.'

The wind got up and started to whip snow into their faces. They walked the remaining five minutes in silence, partly because it was difficult to talk in a near blizzard but also because Lou was cross. Jack could sense that she had taken an instant dislike to Bounder but thought too highly of his friend to apologise for his behaviour. He was sure she would feel better once they got home.

CHAPTER FOUR

Puzzling mystery

'LOU!' yelled Emily in delight as she walked through the front door after Jack. The ten-year-old girl threw her arms around her. It's sooo great to see you again. This is going to be the best Christmas ever!'

Lou grinned. 'Hey, I think you've grown, Emily. I'm sure you look taller than in October. It's great to see you again and I'm really relieved you're pleased to see me.'

'Of course we're pleased, why shouldn't we be, silly!' exclaimed Emily. 'David's really looking forward to you coming, too.'

David was sitting on the sofa, his head in a book. He looked up as Lou arrived and smiled. 'Hello,' he said. 'Jack's been unbearably annoying since you agreed to come and stay. Hopefully he'll calm down a bit, now you're here.'

'Don't worry,' said Lou. 'I'll keep him in check.'

The back door opened and in walked Paul and Liz Johnson – Jack, David and Emily's parents. Mrs Johnson gave Lou a bear hug. 'Hello again! Hey you won't believe how excited our three have been about you coming to stay. They've been absolutely maddening! It's lovely to see you, we hope you'll enjoy yourself here.'

'Thanks ever so much, Mrs Johnson,' said Lou, feeling a little overwhelmed. 'Are you definitely sure it's okay for me to spend Christmas with you, it's just that I don't want to be in the way or anything.'

'It's more than okay, we're delighted to have you,' said Mrs Johnson. 'And we all felt so sorry to hear what a miserable time you were having at home.'

Lou looked a little sheepish for a moment. Then she

shrugged her shoulders and smiled. 'That's my parents for you,' she said.

'I'm sure they mean well,' added Mrs Johnson, hoping she hadn't upset Lou.

'No, they don't,' replied Lou, briskly.

'Well you make yourself at home here,' said Mr Johnson. 'But just remember, Lou, while you're under our roof, we'll treat you like you're one of our children, okay? Which means you have to obey our rules and not get up to too much mischief. Hey don't look worried, our rules aren't very strict. But no plunging our lot into any adventures, is that understood?'

'I promise,' said Lou, noting the twinkle in his eye. 'I'm sure nothing untoward ever happens in a nice, respectable village like Malpas anyway.'

'Well we like to think not,' said Mrs Johnson, folding her arms and looking earnestly at her husband, 'but there does seem to be someone a little light-fingered in our midst at the moment, doesn't there, Paul?'

'Light-fingered, what does that mean?' asked Emily.

'Someone who can't keep their hands off other people's things – in other words, the thief who's been carting off stuff from Chumley Towers,' said David. 'The police believe he may be local, but haven't got a clue who he is.'

'Jack was telling me all about it on the bus,' said Lou. 'It does sound intriguing. What do you think, Mrs Johnson, have you got any thoughts whom it might be?'

'Now, Lou, what did I just say about keeping out of adventures?' said Mr Johnson, with a reproving air. 'Anyway, if the police can't solve this mystery, I hardly think a group of children will have much joy.'

'Oh you never know what might happen when the four of us get together,' said Lou with a wicked gleam in her eye. 'Hey, I was only joking. All the same, I would be curious to find out a bit more.'

'Lou, take no notice of my husband,' said Mrs Johnson. 'Personally, I feel very sorry for Lord and Lady Somerset and surely any help the community can give is all to the good. They have suffered the loss of numerous treasured and irreplaceable possessions from Chumley Towers. They have been struggling to make ends meet as it is and, from what I gather, have been considering selling up and moving out. That would be a great pity since it is such a lovely place to go and visit. And it's part of our history – Chumley Towers has been in the Somerset family for several centuries and no-one wants to see that change.

'Anyway, you must be hungry after such a long journey. Let me get you something to eat and drink. How about a nice hot chocolate and some buttered crumpets, and do let me take your coat. Why don't you pull up a chair near the fire and warm yourself up a bit. Oh, hasn't the weather turned rotten – just look at the snow coming down!'

Lou looked at Mrs Johnson gratefully. It was nice to be made a fuss of. The others were lucky to have such a wonderful mother. She handed over her coat and sat down in the wicker chair close to the fire blazing in the wood stove. The others gathered around her and Jack pulled out the newspaper article he had kept.

Mr and Mrs Johnson disappeared into the kitchen, aware that their children would probably like to be left alone with Lou to swap news and chat. Jack was pleased that Lou seemed bright and animated now. He hoped she hadn't taken too much of a dislike to Bounder. She was most likely feeling a little nervous about coming to stay, he concluded.

Lou glanced around her. The Johnsons' home was a fairly modern, spacious detached house, bright and airy with huge windows. The living room was deliciously warm thanks to the wood stove. Alongside it was a burnished copper pot full of logs. In the far corner, an evergreen tree festooned with silver and gold tinsel and exquisitely pretty baubles reached almost to the ceiling. Countless dozens of Christmas cards jostled with each other on every available flat surface and hung on ribbons down the walls.

Everything was such a gloriously welcome contrast to her own home that feeling homesick was simply not an option. She hadn't taken to Jack's brash friend Bounder and hoped not to see much of him but she wasn't the sort to dwell on such things. She felt happy and at ease in the company of her three very best friends and their hospitable parents.

In a few minutes, Mrs Johnson reappeared as promised, with hot crumpets oozing with melted butter and mugs of steaming chocolate.

'It's so, I don't know, strange but in a good way, to see you here, Lou,' enthused Emily, licking butter off her fingers. 'It's almost like it can't possibly be mid-winter at our place with snow falling. I keep thinking we must be back in Abersoch again, or camping in Staffordshire yet we're actually at our home in Cheshire and it's Christmas! Isn't it amazing?'

'I know, it does seem odd, doesn't it?' said Lou. 'It's actually not that long since we met up though, when you think about it. Autumn half term was less than two months ago. No, David, there's no need to work out exactly how many weeks, days and minutes it's been,' she added, as David opened his mouth.

He scowled. 'I wasn't going to try and work it out that precisely, for your information. Although I could if you want.'

'Nooo!' yelled Lou, and they all laughed, including David. He had been getting much better at being teased although suffering bullying at school during the past half-term had not helped his self-confidence. He was as pleased to see Lou as the others, even though he found it a little unsettling for a friend to join them and stay over at Christmas. He did not easily cope with change and the idea took some getting used to.

The four of them chatted for a while about what they had been doing and school-life. Emily was keen to know from Lou what Christmas would have been like back in Church Stretton.

'Grim,' said Lou with a rueful shrug. 'I've never had what I'd call a proper Christmas.'

'What about all your presents?' asked Emily. 'Have you brought a few with you or will you open them when you get back? I suppose it wasn't practical to carry them on the train.'

'Presents? I doubt I'll get any, especially now that I've cleared off,' said Lou, with a trace of bitterness. 'There might be a box of Quality Street for me when I get back, if I'm lucky – probably still sitting in the carrier bag it was bought in.'

She glanced under the Johnsons' Christmas tree at all the carefully-wrapped presents in varying shapes and sizes, each tied with colourful ribbon. 'Hey, don't worry about me – I shall enjoy seeing you unwrap all of yours. Don't feel bad that I haven't got anything, believe me, this is going to be the best Christmas ever. I couldn't wish for any more than to be here.'

'All the same, it would be good if Father Christmas brought you something,' said Emily. 'I'm sure he will, you know.'

'You've done enough letting me come and stay,' said Lou, keen to change the subject. 'Now come on, I'm dying to know, tell me more about this scandal at Chumley Towers – what exactly has been taken and is there any clue at all who it might be? Let's have another look at that newspaper article again, Jack, the bus was jolting around so much before it was hard to read it.'

Jack fished out the article, headed *Thieves strike again at Chumley Towers* and passed it to Lou. She read it out loud:

Several more precious artefacts have gone missing from Chumley Towers – the second raid on the stately home this month, leaving their distraught owners a step closer to selling up.

This time, the haul included a silver teaspoon set, a Victorian rosewood music box, a silver hip flask and a silver condiment set. The thieves are believed to have struck sometime on Friday. In a previous raid around the turn of the month, offenders made off with items including a trinket box, a silver tankard, an antique set of drawers and a gold-plated carriage clock. The total haul is believed to be worth around £1,000.

The Marquess of Chumley, Lord Somerset, said he was at a loss to know who was responsible for the thefts. Casual visitors are suspected and Lord and Lady Somerset are now considering closing the Towers to the public as a result.

Lord Somerset told the Whitchurch Herald yesterday: "We are enormously upset by the loss of these items. Quite apart from their financial worth, they are of great sentimental value to this family. They are an integral part of the estate and are not only part of our heritage but that of the Malpas community at large.

"We can only assume that a visitor or visitors to the Towers are responsible and we are now seriously considering closing to the public altogether. However, if we do then we will lose a vital source of income without which we will struggle to meet the running costs of a huge building like this. We were already worried that we might one day be forced to sell the place and this is making a bad situation worse. Should that day ever come it will be terribly sad, since our family have lived at

Chumley since Norman times."

Detective Sergeant Simon Walker said that the culprits were believed to live locally since the raids both occurred within a short space of each other. Furthermore, the weather was very poor on Friday and travel warnings had been in force advising people not to make unnecessary journeys.

He added: "North Mercia Constabulary are appealing to anyone with any information on these thefts to contact them immediately. We need members of the public to be our eyes and ears on this one. In particular, we are keen to hear from anyone who is offered these items for sale."

CHAPTER FIVE

Interesting discussion

LOU stared hard at the newspaper article. 'Hmm, how interesting. I should imagine the police are right – it is more likely to be someone local, although they clearly haven't anything solid to go on.'

'The talk in the village is that the police haven't made much effort at all and quietly told Lord and Lady Somerset to write it off as an insurance claim,' said Jack. 'In other words, the insurance company coughs up for the value of the items taken and that's that. But it's believed that the Somerset family no longer have all their belongings fully insured because it was proving too costly. And if the only way they can prevent more thefts is to close the place to visitors, then they will lose income they rely on to stay afloat.'

'Mum says there's a real possibility that Chumley Towers will be sold,' said Emily. 'Wouldn't that be terrible? Local people are very worried about it. Chumley is part of our history. Malpas wouldn't be the same without it and the Somersets. Also, she's worried that it might be divided into flats or turned into an old people's home or something. Or even worse, the place might be bulldozed altogether. Mum says that's happened to a lot of stately homes in Britain over the years.'

David had been listening intently but saying nothing. Lou glanced at him. He looked troubled. Were problems at school bugging him, or was it simply that he too feared for the future of Chumley Towers? After all, he had a great love of history. He would hate to see something so precious put at risk. His face, which had become freckled and pink under the summer sun, seemed paler again and somewhat vacant. His manner was diffident and stiff, reminiscent of the first day she had met him in the caravan at Abersoch.

'Are you okay, David? What are you thinking about? Tell me,' she said to him, her piercing green eyes fixing on him.

David knew Lou was very good at reading people's facial expressions and working out what was going on in their minds. He attempted hurriedly to jolt himself out of his musings. 'I'm fine,' he replied, stoutly. 'I just wish we could do something about Chumley Towers, I'd hate to see the Somersets forced to sell it off cheap and have to move into a bungalow or something.'

'Is there any possibility that they could knock it down, as Emily fears?' asked Lou.

'Hopefully not,' replied Jack. 'It's a listed building but they could easily strip away its contents so that all that remains is a shell, and who knows what it might become in future?'

'Okay,' said Lou, scratching her chin. 'So the Somersets need to keep the place open to the public to raise money towards its upkeep. But there's a thief, posing as a visitor, walking round quietly helping himself to precious items. The only way to protect their valuables is to prevent the public from entering, but if they do that, they lose vital revenue without which they can't keep going.'

'Also, the Somersets have a long tradition of welcoming visitors, which is one reason why they are so popular. They don't want to shut out the local community,' said Jack, downing the last of his hot chocolate.

'Is there anything we could do to help catch whoever's responsible, Lou?' said Emily, her cornflower blue eyes looking beseechingly at the older girl whom she believed capable of almost everything.

David snorted. 'If the finest brains of North Mercia Constabulary can't manage to track down whoever's responsible, I hardly think the likes of us are going to have much luck,' he said, peevishly, staring despondently out of the window.

'You really aren't in a very good mood today, are you?' said Lou, sharply. 'Are you cheesed off because I've come to stay? Say if you are, I'll understand.'

'No, of course not!' said David. 'It's not that at all. I'm really chuffed you've come, we all are. I just don't think we can shed any light on this when, like I said, the top dogs of the local police are completely foxed.'

'Who says they're top dogs or possessing the finest brains?' said Lou, 'or local, for that matter? We four might be mere children but we have one great advantage over them – we *are* local, at least you three are, and we can poke our noses in and ask questions and size people up without anyone thinking anything of it. People clam up when a police officer in a helmet and navy blue uniform pops up and starts asking questions, whereas we can be as inquisitive as we like and get away with it.

'You know my dad's a journalist – he says that the police, these days, sit in their head office in some faraway town and they haven't got their ear to the ground the way they used to when there was a police station in every village and a bobby walking the beat. I'm not saying we're likely to find out who's responsible but it might be fun to try.'

'Anything is worth a go,' said Jack, rising to his feet. The fire was getting a little too hot for him. He went to the window and looked out. The snow was still falling and the garden, table and chairs and greenhouse were all crowned with a sturdy layer of solid white. It looked wonderful.

'I feel so alive,' he said, turning round. 'It's the Christmas holidays, our best friend Lou has come to stay, we've got an exciting mystery to solve and everywhere is absolutely smothered in snow! Isn't life brilliant!'

'Well, I'm not sure how the Somersets would feel, knowing that you think their ordeal is a form of entertainment,' said David, sourly.

'Oh David, lighten up,' said Jack, frowning at him. 'I hope they would feel pleased that we were concerned enough to want to look into it. You may be in a bad mood but I'm not. Hey, guess who Lou and I bumped into earlier – Bounder! He'll probably help us out with this little mystery as well. He's keen to gang up with us all over Christmas.'

'Great,' groaned David. Lou said nothing. She had not the slightest wish to gang up with Bounder.

'Right,' she said, clapping her hands together, briskly. 'Let's not fall out – it is the season of goodwill after all. Why don't we make a start at tracking down the thief of Chumley Towers, and see how far we can get?'

'Definitely,' said Jack. 'What should we do first, do you think?'

Lou tutted in amused frustration. 'Does it always have to be me who comes up with the ideas?'

The others fell silent – each of them desperately seeking to say something useful but without success.

Lou sighed. 'Okay, fair enough. I'll get the ball rolling. The obvious thing to say is that if the police are right that the person responsible is from round here, we need to draw up a list of possible suspects. That's what a detective would do – he would seek to establish a motive. You've lived in the village most of your lives and it's a close-knit community. Off the top of your heads, do any names spring to mind of folk with bad reputations – people willing to act dishonestly? Someone, for instance, who has been done for shoplifting in the past or possibly fallen on hard times, or perhaps even someone with a grudge against the Somersets?'

'Hey Lou, you've given me an idea!' cried Jack. 'What about an unscrupulous property developer who hasn't necessarily got anything personally against the Somersets but who wants to force them to sell up – and then buy them out? He steps in with a poor offer which they feel they have no choice but to accept. Developers in the area are keen to get their hands on large empty buildings and convert them into flats and bedsits. It makes them a lot of money. For instance, there's a builder's yard the other end of the village and the chap who owns it, Reginald Whitehouse, is very wealthy. I know for a fact that he has bought a number of houses already in Malpas that he lets out to tenants. What's more, he tried to buy a parcel of vacant land a few months ago, hoping to put houses on, but the owner refused to sell to him.'

'I remember,' said Emily, tugging at a lock of her blonde hair which Lou noticed had grown longer and noticeably curlier since autumn half term. 'The owner's daughter had kept a pony in a paddock there for years but then she went away to university. It wasn't being grazed and became wild and overgrown. But the owner hated the idea of it being swallowed up by housing so when Reginald Whitehouse asked him to sell, he refused.'

'That's right,' said Jack. 'And what's more, Whitehouse has been sniffing around the village trying to find other plots where he can stick his houses. I overheard mum and dad talking about it a while ago. They were quite worried but apparently the local council aren't willing to give him planning permission because they don't want the character of Malpas to be damaged by any more sprawling housing estates springing up. So, perhaps, Whitehouse decides that his best hope is to buy a huge building like Chumley Towers, carve it up into separate flats and make a fortune from all the rent he could charge. But he would struggle to afford the asking price, so his strategy is to force the Somersets to sell at a knock-down price.'

'Oh what nonsense,' interjected David. 'Firstly, I

doubt Whitehouse is wealthy enough to buy Chumley, even at a knock-down price, and he may be many things but I'm pretty sure he's not a crook. It's a very far-fetched idea.'

'Have you got any better ones?' asked Lou. 'Find a pen and paper someone and let's draw up a list of possible suspects, starting with this Reginald Whitehouse. Now, how about someone who might be tempted to steal simply because they're very poor and struggling to make ends meet? Or are there a few villagers who simply enjoy taking what isn't theirs? There must be a few dodgy characters about – every town and village has them.'

Jack went over to the wood-burner, opened it and threw a log inside. The flames, which had been sinking lower, licked up gratefully. He watched for a moment or two, as if mesmerised then span round, clicking his fingers. 'There is a woman, around dad's age I would guess, who might fit the bill. She's a freelance journalist, Lou, like your dad. Her name's Philippa Swift, usually known as Pippa, and she has most definitely fallen on hard times recently. Years ago, she used to work for a newspaper in Birmingham – the *Evening Telegraph*, I think. But she got bored with the local Press and became mad keen on working for TV. A colleague of hers was good friends with a presenter on Central News – it's the TV news channel for the Midlands, which we don't get it here, and he put in a good word for her . . .'

'*We* get Central News,' said Lou, interrupting. 'Her name rings a vague bell. You get North-West here, presumably.'

'Yes,' said Jack. 'Anyway, so Pippa went to work for Central for several years and began to swan around the village as if she was a big star – however, with most of our aerials pointing northwards, very few of us ever got to see her reading the news. So Pippa certainly wasn't having to sign many autographs around here. The trouble is, so our mum reckons, she was absolutely desperate to be a famous TV star. Her career as a journalist was just a means to an end. So after a while, local TV news wasn't enough for her, especially if her own neighbours didn't even know who she was. In the end, she went freelance and tried to get her foot in the door of the national TV stations. She eventually got a few temporary contracts working for Sky News and This Morning on ITV, but recently, work has apparently dried up and she's at home most days with her flashy white sports car parked in the drive.'

'Can I say something, Jack,' said Emily, eagerly. 'Don't you remember, mum said that Pippa was up to her neck in debt and she was struggling to keep up with the repayments on her house and car?'

'Mum said she was "up to her eyeballs in debt", re-marked David, dryly, not "up to her neck". I remember quite distinctly, she was in the kitchen at the time preparing the Sunday lunch. You were in there with her supposedly peeling sprouts only mum had to take the colander off you and finish them herself because you were doing more chatting than peeling. Meanwhile I was sitting at the dining room table trying to concentrate on my Welsh Teach Yourself book. Incidentally, Lou, I'm now on lesson twelve, if you remember in August I was only on lesson five.'

'Have you quite finished, David?' snapped Emily, looking scornfully at her brother as he flicked the last crumbs of crumpet around his plate. 'Perhaps Lou would like to know which particular point of grammar you're now studying and how many tenses you've mastered?'

'There's no need to be sarcastic,' responded David, scowling. 'However, on that point, I'm well clear of the perfect and imperfect tenses and am now trying to master the future tense. Apart from verbs, I'm learning various Welsh prepositions, which don't always match their

English equivalent.'

Lou fought the urge to smile. She wasn't willing to join in the baiting of David, tempting though it was. She felt concerned about him, and hoped that his ill humour and aloof manner weren't anything to do with her coming to stay.

'Hey David, sounds like your Welsh is really coming on,' she said, brightly. 'Next time we're back at Abersoch we'll all have to go for a bike ride to Mynytho and seek out the old Welsh lady, Mrs Owen so you can practise on her. It would be nice to see her again anyway.'

'Poor old thing,' said Emily. 'Wasn't it a terrible ordeal that her great nephew, Idwal, put her through? Thank goodness we were able to help her at autumn half-term. I wonder what happened to him?'

'Oh I should have told you, sorry,' said Lou. 'Mrs Owen wrote to me about a fortnight ago. He admitted the charges and was ordered to do two-hundred hours' community service. He should have gone to prison, if you ask me.'

'You know, Lou, if we could solve that little mystery, maybe we're the sort of people who can solve this particular one,' said Jack, enthusiastically.

'We can certainly try,' said Lou, 'although I think this will be a harder nut to crack. Do you really think that Pippa Swift is the sort of person who would actually help herself to other people's belongings? Many people fall on hard times but it doesn't mean they become thieves.'

'It's just that she's gone very sullen and hard-faced,' said Emily. 'Being in the limelight meant everything to her and she feels rejected and left with nothing. Mum's theory is that she feels she gave her best years to journalism and hasn't got anything to show for it. She never settled down and is now pushing forty with no husband and no kids. Oh and didn't her father pass away last year? Mum thinks she's very fed up.'

'Hey, why don't we send David round to cheer her up,' said Jack, winking. Emily hooted with laughter. Lou put her hand to the back of her mouth and bit hard, desperately trying to stop a chuckle from escaping. But her shoulders shook with mirth and gave her away. David looked from her to his brother and sister and back again, scowling ferociously.

'Right,' said Lou, briskly, desperately seeking to compose herself, 'we've made some progress. We've got two possible suspects but we could do with a good few more.'

'We ought to speak to Emma Bennett,' said David, suddenly.

'Oh really?' said Lou, pleased at his sudden contribution and determined to take it seriously. 'Is she the thieving kind?'

'No, I don't think so, but she might have an idea who is. She's the village gossip. She loves to know everyone's business, the more scandalous the better. Also, she loves children. We could maybe call round her place sometime and ask her what she thinks.'

'Excellent idea! Well done, David,' said Lou. 'We must be discreet though, it's better if people don't know we're trying to track down the culprit – for a start, we don't want whoever it is to find out that we're on his or her trail. Now, are there any more leads to go on at the moment? Any more possibilities?'

The children continued to mull over the details of other Malpas residents who just might have a few skeletons in the cupboard but it was hard to escape the feeling that they were grabbing at handfuls of thin air.

David, pleased that Lou was impressed with his idea to speak to the village gossip, made another sensible observation, namely that anyone connected with the antiques trade might have a keen interest in historic artefacts from Chumley – and furthermore would be perfectly placed to sell them.

Immediately, all the children chorused the same name at once: 'Mr Creepy!' More properly known as Dr Malcolm Finchfield of course.

'Yes!' said Lou, 'why didn't I think of that? He lives around here, doesn't he? And bearing in mind the unscrupulous way he tried to get his hands on the missing Anglo-Saxon treasure last August, I would guess he would not take much persuading to slip a few valuables into his pockets on a visit to Chumley Towers!'

'Oh and what's more, he owns M. Finchfield Antiques Emporium on the high street,' said David.

'It's an antiques shop,' added Jack. Creepy runs the place with a fellow boffin, Duncan something or other. 'They sell all sorts of bric-a-brac from centuries past in there.'

'Fantastic!' said Lou. 'It's too much to hope that Creepy's actually selling the Towers' wares in there, assuming he is the thief, because that would be far too obvious, but nonetheless, I think we can make him our prime suspect for now! She underlined his name twice. The others all stared down at the list of suspects which had now grown to three. Lou's dramatic double underlining of Creepy's name seemed almost to confirm his guilt. They looked at each other excitedly, had they already got their man?

'Come on,' said Lou, getting up from her seat and stretching. 'I could do with some exercise. I've been stuck on a train for half the morning, remember. The snow appears to have stopped, so shall we go out for a walk while it's still light?'

Emily glanced at Lou, admiringly. Lou looked leggy and athletic in her sequinned jeans, blue top and white cardigan. Emily was sure she had grown an inch or two taller since they had last seen her. She loved her bobbed dark hair with her trademark fringe. She wished she looked more sporty and grown-up like Lou. Emily still felt rather shy and babyish although was much more outgoing and confident than she used to be.

David yawned. 'Judging from the colour of the sky, I should imagine it'll be snowing again shortly and in any case, will be rather slippery underfoot. I think I'll stay behind if that's okay. I'm half-way through quite an exciting book.'

Lou looked hard at him. 'You'll do no such thing. I'm half-way through an exciting book too, but that can wait. Let's make the most of the daylight while we can. You can read all you want later when it's dark. I don't think it will snow for a while and if it did, it wouldn't harm us. Come on, David, isn't it beautiful when it's so soft and white and untouched? Let's go and run about in it! I promise I won't throw snowballs at you or anything.'

Not even David could resist an order from Lou and the four of them headed for the door just as their parents were coming in from the garden. Jack promised his mother that they would be back before dark and with that, they set off down the street.

CHAPTER SIX

Footprints in the snow

THE scenery had been transformed into a winter wonderland. There was no other way to describe it. The snow lay like a shaggy carpet, rucked up here and there into drifts by icy gusts of wind. The roofs and treetops crouched low beneath slabs of pure white. A bank of heavy cloud threatened further snowfalls. The children ran gleefully down the lane, slithering and sliding.

It wasn't long before the first snowball was thrown – by Jack, straight at David of course. It was perfectly aimed, catching David bang on the nose, much to his annoyance. Lou sidled up close to Jack and fired a huge snowball right at his forehead. Jack gasped, then went after her with a couple in each hand but she darted nimbly out of the way. Emily contented herself with watching the proceedings, deciding that was the best way to ensure she wasn't hit herself.

'Hey,' cried Lou, after a while. 'Never mind about snowball fights, have we got time to walk to Chumley Towers? Just to have a snoop around the outside? I'm dying to see it.'

Jack, glanced at his watch. 'Yes I should think so,' he said, panting, 'just about.'

David, eager to call a ceasefire, began strolling briskly up the road.

Lou ran ahead to catch him up. She was determined to keep his spirits up if she could.

Jack and Emily bounded up to both of them and the four children sauntered along in the middle of an empty, snow-filled road, climbing steadily higher until the last house in the village was some way behind. They took a left turn onto a narrow lane which began to circle up to the summit of the hill. Towards the top they came to a pair of ornate but rusting wrought-iron gates, set in tall pillars of granite, topped with brightly-lit lanterns. They went up and peered through. Beyond lay a grand, formal garden bordered on the right by fir trees.

To their amusement, they noticed that shiny baubles had been tied to the tree closest the gate and tinsel draped over its branches. The handiwork of the Somerset children, possibly. In the distance rose a sprawling stately home built in the style of a castle, with Gothic arched windows and tall towers topped with turrets. The snow lay flawless and untouched all around it like a newly-fitted carpet; its colour mother-of-pearl under a pinkish-grey sky.

The children gazed through the bars in awe at the imposing building, austere and menacing amid a wintry wilderness.

'Like looking back in time, to centuries past,' said Jack, slowly.

'Chumley Towers was built two hundred years ago, so that's not surprising,' muttered David.

Lou smiled. David was right, of course, but she knew what Jack meant. Furthermore, it still operated very much like a country house of yesteryear, presided over by Frances Somerset, the elderly Dowager Marchioness, her son Henry, the ninth Marquess of Somerset, and his wife Jane. To outward appearances, this was an aristocratic family of enormous wealth and yet the reality was different. Their money was tied up in land and buildings. Income from tourists and from the sale of produce grown on the estate was a vital lifeline they could ill afford to be without.

'Is it open to visitors today?' asked Lou. 'It doesn't appear to be.'

'Yes, I should think so,' said Jack, 'it just doesn't look it because so few people will have ventured out in this weather, at a guess.'

'Can we go back soon?' said Emily, digging her gloved hands deep into her pockets. 'It's getting chilly and it will be dark before long.'

'Yes, of course,' said Lou. 'Oh look, a light has just gone on, do you see on the upper floor?'

What looked like the wizened face of an old woman appeared at the window, although it was too far away to be sure. The mighty Dowager Marchioness? They turned away, feeling perhaps that their presence had been noticed. Then Lou spotted something interesting: footsteps in the snow, appearing to lead down the slope and into the broadleaved trees flanking the northern side of the estate.

'Look over there,' she said. 'Do you see those footprints? They must have been made this afternoon, since the snow began to fall. I wonder who they belong to?'

Emily shivered. She was far more interested in getting back inside their cosy home than tracking footprints, especially since her own feet were starting to feel like blocks of ice. 'I'm sure there's a perfectly reasonable explanation,' she said, her teeth chattering. 'Let's not take too long, Lou.'

'We won't, I promise,' replied Lou. 'I just find it very odd that on a day when no-one seems to be about, we come across a solitary set of footprints leaving the Towers from an obscure exit.'

The four of them trudged through the snow down the side of the walled garden to take a closer look.

'Look,' said Lou. 'There's a small arched gate set into the stone. Someone has come through there this afternoon, and then walked down the hill into the woods. Jack, what lies beyond?'

'You'd end up back in Malpas,' he said. 'It's only a

small woodland, criss-crossed with paths. It makes for a longer route than walking down the lane as we did. You come out at the end of a cul-de-sac a few streets away from us.'

'Why would someone choose to walk that way, rather than down the lane?' wondered Lou, puzzled.

'You could say it was the scenic route, I suppose,' said Jack, 'although everywhere looks scenic at the moment. Also, I should have thought it was difficult to follow the path with the weather like it is.'

'I suppose if whoever it was lived down that cul-de-sac or close by, it would make sense to go that way?' asked Lou.

'Yes,' said Jack, otherwise it makes no obvious sense, save for the fact that on a normal day you would be walking through woodland and not down a lane with cars passing every now and then. But with the roads all blocked with snow that isn't an issue today. Certainly, going through the woodland would allow you to return to the village from the Towers with less chance of being spotted.'

'Hmm,' said Lou, deep in thought. 'And that might be exactly what you'd do if you had something to hide. The route through the trees is not an obvious short-cut, nor is it any more scenic, as you say, on a day like this when everywhere is covered with snow and there is no traffic.' She turned to the others. 'Is there any chance that this could be our next suspect, do you think?'

She knelt down and looked at the prints closely. 'These were made by a man, I'm sure. It's someone with big feet anyway, wearing outdoor boots with a deep tread and a distinctive pattern. Hang on, I'll take a photo of them, just in case it might prove useful.'

Lou took out her mobile phone and used it as a camera to take the shots. 'Now, why don't we follow the prints back through the wood and see where they lead to?'

The others nodded. Lou really was needle sharp. Not only had she noticed the prints in the first place and thought they were strange, but she'd analysed them, photographed them and was now about to track them. She would make an excellent detective one day!

Lou and Jack led the way, with the others following. They felt excited – even Emily, although she was still trembling with cold. Where would these prints lead? It was easy to follow them, since there were no others at all, save for the fragile twig-like claw-prints of birds and the characteristic paw-marks of a cat.

'Do you know what this reminds me of?' chirruped Emily, determined to shake off her anxiety, 'going through the woods at Abersoch to your den, Lou.'

'Yes, except that everywhere is covered in snow, and we've never once seen snow along the Lleyn Peninsula,' said David, reprovingly. 'Which is hardly surprising of course, since we can never go in winter and, due to the influence of the Gulf Stream, the peninsula rarely ever gets any snow.'

'Why can't you go in winter, out of interest?' asked Lou, quickly, before Jack or Emily had the chance to tell David off for being pompous.

'The site is shut from November 1st to March 31st inclusive,' announced David, 'although the chap from the council who came to remove the wasps' nest under the eaves of the caravan roof said that there was some talk about allowing caravan and chalet sites to open all year round in future.'

Lou chuckled. 'I bet the poor old Welsh won't be chuffed, having to put up with us English descending on them twelve months of the year. We can go to our cottage, of course, all year round. We rarely do go in winter though.'

Jack grabbed Lou's arm. 'Could the four of us go and stay in your cottage all by ourselves one winter? Maybe next year perhaps? I would love to be back at the seaside in January or something, I've never done that before.'

'Possibly,' said Lou. 'Depends what the grown-ups say, of course. My parents would be fine with it – my dad because he trusts me and my mum because it means she gets rid of me for a few days. I'm not sure your parents would allow it, though.'

'Hey Lou, it's getting rather dark in this wood, don't you think?' said Emily.

'It's fine,' said Jack. 'I know my way through here, it's not far now.'

The footprints continued steadily onwards, as if guiding them, although with the light fading they were less easy to see. It was a rather surreal atmosphere threading their way beneath the snow-topped trees. In places, where branches reached across the path, the snow thinned and patches of bare soil could be seen. Mostly, it was like a jagged streak of white through the damp, musty-smelling woodland, marked only by a single set of footprints.

'We're nearly out now,' said Jack, after they had trudged onwards for several more minutes. It had actually taken longer than he had thought.

Street lights glowed orange ahead of them. Suddenly, they emerged to find two rows of houses ahead separated by a broad white ribbon.

'We must be very careful not to lose those footprints,' said Lou. 'Several other people have walked along here and we could easily mix them up.'

The children walked slowly along behind the prints, which meandered down the middle of the road and then onto the pavement as the walker, whoever he was, turned left into Overton Avenue. The road sign was flecked with snow but still visible.

They tried hard not to look as if they were tracking anyone's prints, lest it appear odd. Certainly, they did not want their target to have any inkling what they were up to. Where would the trail lead? It was hugely exciting, although Emily and David were both privately willing the pursuit to end sooner rather than later.

Eventually, the footprints swung decisively left, down a long drive to one of the larger and more expensive houses in the avenue, barely visible behind a thick laurel hedge.

'Bingo!' exclaimed Lou, her eyes shining. 'We need to know the name or number of that house, or we'll find it difficult to remember exactly where it is, especially if the snow clears by tomorrow. Everything always looks so different after a snowfall.'

They looked around. The nearest house opposite could be seen more easily. It had a name clearly fixed to the outside: Beechwood Cottage with the number twelve alongside.

'If that's twelve, then possibly this might be a number eleven or a thirteen,' said Jack, 'because streets are usually numbered with odds along one side and evens down the other.'

'However,' piped up David, 'many houses are not numbered with a "thirteen" because it's considered unlucky, so often it's missed out, or houses are known as 12A or something. Personally, I don't understand this irrational superstition about the number thirteen. It's known as triskaidekaphobia, I believe.'

'Of course, some people suffer from CPS – chronic pomposity syndrome,' quipped Jack to a glare from his brother. 'By the way, Lou, I'm pretty certain that the woodland route we have followed is actually longer than if you were to walk by road. It's certainly no shortcut.'

'Really? That's interesting. Right, what to do now?' said Lou, half to herself. 'Can we be sure that we'll locate this property again? Trouble is, Beechwood Cottage is not directly opposite. I think the only way to be absolutely sure is for one of us to slink along the drive and take a peek. Even if we can't see the house name or number, we could take down the registration number of any car parked outside.'

Neither Jack, David nor Emily appeared at all keen to 'slink along the drive'.

Lou sighed. 'It's always me who gets the best jobs, isn't it? Fair enough, I don't mind taking a look. I shall just have to hope no-one comes out of the house at the wrong moment.'

'We'll wait for you here and keep a look-out,' said Jack, matter of factly, trying hard to sound as if he was offering to do something useful.

'Fine,' said Lou, 'see you in a minute.'

Lou began to walk softly down the drive. Occasionally, the snow squeaked underfoot but that was preferable to the possible scrunch of gravel. It was a long drive, befitting a large, impressive house typical of this particular neighbourhood. Whoever owned it was doing all right for themselves, she surmised. That said, the Somersets appeared fabulously wealthy, but that would only be true if they were to sell their home and extensive grounds. One could never be sure about these things.

Now, what's my action plan if the front door suddenly opens?, mused Lou as the house loomed into view. The main door was partly obscured behind the columns of a grand portico. It looked almost like something from a Greek temple. To the side was a large double garage. Unfortunately, there were no cars on the drive itself.

A hand grasped at her shoulder! Lou froze. But it was only Jack. He whispered into her ear, 'sorry to make you jump, but I decided that it wasn't fair for you to go up to the house alone.'

'That's fine,' whispered Lou, 'now look natural and we'll walk up to the door normally, as if we were calling for someone. I think the house name or number will be on the door but we can't see properly with that portico in the way.'

As they approached, the door began to reveal itself. It was solemn navy blue or black with a sturdy brass doorknocker; its name in bold brass letters below: The Oaks.

'Great,' said Lou. 'Let's go. That's all we needed to know.'

But to her dismay, as they were about to turn back and rejoin the others, the front door slowly began to open!

CHAPTER SEVEN

Unexpected encounter

SOMEONE was coming out! They were tempted to run for it, but it was too late. They had to stay calm and claim they had come to the wrong house.

To Jack's complete astonishment, the figure who appeared in the doorway was all too familiar – it was Bounder!

'Hello, Jack!' said Bounder. 'And Lou, isn't it? Well, this is a surprise. Fancy you two coming round. I didn't think you even knew where I lived.'

Jack reddened, as he often did when embarrassed. He would never have had the cheek simply to turn up on the doorstep without being invited first. In fact, Bounder had never once asked him to come round while Jack, on the other hand, had begged him repeatedly to come to his place for tea. Those offers had never been taken up. Now Jack found himself in an awkward position he was unprepared for. He stood there, tongue-tied and uncertain.

Lou sensed that Jack was floundering inwardly. She had better say something quickly. 'Hey Bounder, we happened to be walking this way and Jack pointed out where you lived. I suggested we drop by and say hello. Jack felt a bit uneasy about just turning up, so it's my doing, I'm afraid. Hope we haven't caught you at a bad moment!'

'Not at all, that's great,' said Bounder, suddenly looking pleased. 'Well, are you going to come in? I was going out to build a snowman but you both look pretty cold so maybe you don't fancy doing that.'

'That would be good,' said Lou, happy to seize this

unexpected opportunity to view the inside of the house. 'We *are* pretty cold, to be honest. Actually, do you mind if we just pop back and scoop up David and Emily, we left them at the top of the drive. We just felt it was a bit rude for all four of us to turn up on your doorstep at the same time.'

It was a poor excuse and Lou knew it but Bounder didn't appear to notice. 'Yes, go and get them,' he said. 'Scoop them up and then we'll all have a drink. I'll get Gisela to fix us up some hot chocolate and cake, shall I? Gisela's the maid, by the way.'

Lou and Jack quickly returned with David and Emily, who were unimpressed by this strange turn of events. They had no wish to spend time in Bounder's house making small talk, especially as it was now starting to get dark outside. Their mum would be wondering where they had got to.

But Lou was determined to take advantage of an unexpected situation. As Bounder led them through the hall into the living room, she looked to see if any pairs of boots matched the footprints they had diligently followed. They might still be on the feet of the person to whom they belonged, of course, but Lou didn't think so, somehow. The carpet was plush and expensive and Bounder had immediately asked them to remove their shoes in the hall. No doubt his mother did not appreciate muddy footwear tramping through her clean, smart house.

'Hey Bounder, it's a great place you've got here,' said Jack, enthusiastically.

Bounder flopped himself down on a large leather sofa. His dark hair, which had appeared lank and slicked back in the snow earlier, was now lustrous and wavy. Bounder repeatedly pushed his fingers through his locks, in a rather girlish manner.

'Yes,' he said, proudly, 'looks good, doesn't it? I'll

show you the extension my parents have had built when we've had our drinks. It's amazing. The taps in the bathroom are solid gold and there's a built-in Jacuzzi in the bath.'

'Er, what's a Jacuzzi?' asked Emily.

Bounder eyed her rather disdainfully. 'Jets of air piped into the water to make them bubble like a whirlpool.'

Lou glanced around the lounge. It seemed an odd house to her. Old and grand in some ways; brash and modern in others. A large fake coal fire sat beneath a chimney sending up hissing, blue-tinged flames. Ludicrously, an antique copper bin sat alongside brimming with useless real logs.

On the mantelpiece were several China figurines which looked Victorian or older. Could any of these have been pinched from Chumley Towers? It was impossible to know for sure, but they were the sort of things that the thief, whoever he was, would be likely to find appealing. Lou decided to discreetly photograph them given the chance.

Gisela came in with a tray of steaming drinks and plates of cake and biscuits. The tray was heavy and it touched down on the coffee table with a slight bump causing a couple of the over-full mugs to slosh over.

'Oh I'm so sorry,' she said in a foreign accent, looking upset.

'You careless girl,' snapped Bounder, seeming both cross and amused at the same time. 'I'll get my parents to send you home to Romania if you do that again.'

'I am from Dresden in Germany,' said Gisela, wearily. 'You know that.'

'Vell clean up zat mess quickly,' replied Bounder, mimicking her accent.

Lou's cat-like eyes fixed on Bounder. It took great self-control to prevent her lip from curling. She guessed that he was trying to show off rather than be deliberately offensive but it was crass, smug behaviour which Lou disliked. However, she was keen to prowl around and find out who owned the shoes matching the prints in the snow. His father, presumably. It would also be an interesting experience to meet him. She would have to pretend to appear impressed by Bounder and enjoying his company.

'Where are your parents, Bounder?' asked Lou after an awkward silence.

'They're out,' he replied, airily. 'They've been out all day.'

'What, both of them?' asked Lou.

'Yes, why, I am thirteen now, after all and Gisela's here if I need her.'

How strange. A man with fairly large feet, whom Lou expected to be Bounder's father, must be here some-where, unless he'd gone back out in the time it had taken them to trail him, which was possible. Yet Bounder claimed not to have seen him all day. Was that just a boast, to show how tough and independent he was? She glanced at Bounder's own feet lolling off the end of the sofa. No, his were far too small, as you would expect.

It occurred to her that she had not, in fact, noticed the footprints going all the way to the front door. Had the chap in question gone round the back?

'So does anyone else live here?' she asked, doing her best to sound friendly. 'Do you have any brothers or sisters?'

'Just me, my parents and Gisela over the holidays,' said Bounder. 'My brother Lucas would normally be here but he's gone to Switzerland for a school ski-ing holiday. He's sixteen – he's in the sixth form.'

'It's a lovely house,' fibbed Lou, draining her mug. 'Perhaps we could have the guided tour now. I'd like to see the rest of it.'

Bounder was flattered by Lou's apparent interest in

their expensive family home and duly showed her all the numerous rooms, including the new extension they had had built, complete with its gold taps. He seemed animated and intense, although without the exuberant bravado he had displayed in their first encounter in the high street.

Underneath the extravagant showman's chatter, Lou detected an aloof remoteness about him, cold and not particularly pleasant. He seemed to forget all about the others, including his supposed best friend Jack who tagged along patiently behind him. David and Emily remained downstairs, seeking to make their hot chocolate last as long as possible.

'As you can see,' announced Bounder, with a regal wave of his hand, 'we now have four master bedrooms and two single bedrooms, two living rooms, a playroom, a study, four bathrooms, five toilets and, would you believe, a whopping eighteen radiators – plus four coal fires. Well, they're electric but they look just like the real thing.'

'Wow, that's amazing,' said Lou, woodenly, trying hard to appear impressed.

A couple of times, Lou managed discreetly to take a photograph of interesting items and artefacts strewn about. In a guest bedroom she noticed several antiques which might conceivably match those taken from Chumley. Jack, noticing what she was up to, shielded her as she held her phone at waist level to take a snap. But nowhere did they find the owner of the footprints in the snow.

'May I take a peek at the garden?' asked Lou, after they had returned to the lounge, aware that the light was fading fast.

'Erm yes, I suppose,' said Bounder, hesitantly. 'Actually perhaps we better not go out there, my dad doesn't much like people tramping around without his permission. He's very protective about his garden.'

'You know, Lou, we really ought to be going. Mum and dad will wonder where we've got to,' said Jack.

Right on cue, his mobile phone beeped. It was Mrs Johnson asking exactly that question.

'Fair enough,' said Lou, 'you're quite right, we ought to be heading back.'

Just then, they heard a rear door opening and steps coming down the corridor. In walked a big, slightly hunched man with thick eyebrows sprouting from a clever face. His greying-black hair was swept back, extending beyond the edge of his collar, rather like his son's, lending him a somewhat disreputable air.

'Hello dad!' said Bounder, turning round. 'I didn't know you'd got back. Dad was off to Chester earlier, doing some Christmas shopping. He always leaves it to the last day or so. Oh by the way, dad, these are friends of mine. They were passing this way and dropped by.'

His dad nodded to them all before turning to his son. 'I've just got in,' he said. 'I went straight down to the shed with a bagful of presents and you know me, once I get inside my shed . . .' Mr Bounderton grinned slightly knowingly as if there was more to that simple explanation than met the eye.

Lou felt certain he was hiding something – and more than just Christmas presents. She glanced at his feet. They looked quite large; possibly a promising match for the footprints. However, he had taken his shoes or boots off so it was difficult to be sure. In fact, it was difficult to be entirely sure about anything regarding both Bounder and his father. Both appeared to be showmen of sorts – pleasant in a superficial sort of way, but without any real substance. What went on beneath the façade?

It really was time to leave. Lou gave Jack a nudge and tapped her watch. Jack got to his feet.

'Well thanks very much for the drinks and biscuits,' said Jack. 'We must be off. We'll have to catch up again soon, Bounder.'

The others got up. 'I left my boots by the kitchen door earlier,' said Lou, 'I'll just pop and fetch them.'

Jack grinned inwardly, guessing that Lou had deliberately moved her boots from the hall to the kitchen door hoping that Bounder's dad would come in that way.

Her plan paid off. Alongside her own boots were another sturdy pair. As she crouched down to pull on her own she discreetly turned one of them over to check the pattern underneath. It looked exactly the same as those footprints in the snow! She slipped her mobile phone out and took a picture to compare it with her shot of the footprints earlier. She returned speedily to the others, busily lacing up their own boots in the hall. No-one seemed to have noticed the slight delay in her return from the kitchen.

'Come on Jack, your mum's going to be furious with us if we don't get a move on,' said Lou, as he chatted away to Bounder on the doorstep.

'Catch you all soon,' shouted Bounder with a wink, shutting the door behind them. It was dark as they trudged away but a security light came on, illuminating their path back to the road.

Jack's phone beeped again. It was another indignant text from his mum, asking whether they were on their way back yet because she didn't want their evening meal to burn. The time was now pushing half-past six. They had been out for ages. They had not, of course, bargained on accidentally calling on Bounder.

'We're going to be in trouble,' said Jack, matter of factly, as they slipped and slithered along the road. The snow crunched beneath their feet and their hot breath plumed out into the cold winter air. Misty streetlamps bathed everywhere in a surreal orange glow.

'You don't sound particularly bothered, Jack,' said Lou, shooting him a grin.

'Mum will cluck around us and wag her finger but that will be all,' he predicted. 'So long as her gingered beef casserole hasn't been entirely ruined, she won't mind too much. She's used to us getting up to mischief when we're with you.'

'Oh, so it's my fault is it?' chortled Lou. 'Well fair enough, I don't mind taking the blame and I actually think we've done rather well today.'

'Really?' said Jack. 'I thought we'd drawn a blank. We obviously lost sight of those footprints we were following at some stage, and ended up following the wrong prints all the way to Bounder's house.'

Lou knew for a fact that they were the *right* prints, but did not want to offend Jack by suggesting there might be something untoward about Bounder's father just yet. 'Who knows?' she replied. Anyway, let's not talk about it now. We're all cold, tired and hungry. I'm fed up of playing detective – I just want to get in the warm and sit down to a lovely plateful of beef stew.'

'Casserole,' corrected David. 'Stew is when you cook on the hob, casserole implies that you've cooked your meat dish in the oven.'

'You'll make someone a lovely housewife one day,' said Emily, with an impish grin.

The others hooted at that and David, determined to wipe the smile off his brother's face in particular said, slyly: 'it's a pity about Bounder's dad, isn't it – who would have thought that he might be the thief?'

Now it was Jack's turn to look sullen. 'David, I'm not falling for it, you're just trying to wind me up.'

'Listen, David,' said Lou, cutting in quickly. 'No-one is saying that Bounder's dad is a thief, although for now at least, we must put him on our list of suspects simply because those footprints in the snow were almost certainly his.'

'No way!' protested Jack, shocked.

'Yes, Jack,' replied Lou, looking at him sternly. 'I didn't want to bring it up this evening but since David's mentioned it I will. There are a number of things which don't add up about him. I know that Bounder's your friend, but that doesn't mean his father is any good. After all, I'm your friend and look at my parents. Anyhow, we'll talk about it in the morning. Let's not bicker amongst each other, it *is* Christmas, remember, and we've got what sounds like a delicious meal ahead of us. Let's just enjoy walking through this lovely snowy village of yours and look forward to a huge steaming plateful of beef stew – I mean casserole!'

CHAPTER EIGHT

Lou has an idea

THE four children slept soundly. When Lou eventually woke up, she felt disorientated and unsure where she was at first. Daylight peeped in around the curtains, which meant that it must be at least eight o'clock.

What day was it? Monday! She was going to be late for school! Then it occurred to her that those were not her curtains and this was not her bedroom. In fact, the bed was firmer and more comfortable than her own – small wonder she had slept so well. She was in the spare room at the Johnsons' house and there would be no school that Monday or the one after that. It was the Christmas holidays and she was staying for a whole week of sleepovers with her very best friends!

Lou felt a warm glow inside her as pulled the duvet up and cradled her head deep in the soft feather pillows. She was content to doze for a while until she heard sounds of movement from the others.

After a while, she picked up her book from the bedside table and began to read. It was a detective story, but Lou struggled to focus on it. Her mind kept straying to their own, real-life mystery and what sort of person might be the culprit. She felt extremely suspicious of Mr Bounderton. Certainly, he could not be ruled out simply because he happened to be the father of Jack's best mate at school. Then there was David, who seemed troubled and anxious much of the time. Lou sighed. Other people were always so complicated!

It was half-past nine by the time Jack, David, Emily and Lou had taken their seats round the kitchen table.

Mrs Johnson placed a large pot of tea on the table and some freshly-baked bread. 'Now, Lou, can you manage something of everything? Bacon, sausage, black pudding, mushrooms, fried egg, baked beans?'

'Something of everything sounds great!' she replied. 'I'd be making do with a bowl of cereal at my place, if there was any milk in the fridge, or a piece of toast.'

'Well, it's the start of the holidays and I thought you could all do with a decent breakfast inside you. What are your plans for the day? You could go sledging on the hills by Chumley Towers later – there's been no more snow overnight but there's still plenty on the ground. It's a lovely day, Paul and I have been up for three hours already.'

'Typical grown-ups – get up early, go to bed early – boring!' said Jack. 'Oh mum, is there any tomato ketchup?'

'Hey Jack, wasn't it a row about tomato ketchup that made you storm off in a huff on the first day of your summer holiday at Abersoch – and that's how you ended up bumping into me?' Lou reminded him.

'That's true,' said Jack. 'There was hardly any remaining in the bottle and David pinched the lot – even though he knew I hadn't had any. I was pretty furious with him. On the other hand, if he hadn't been so selfish that day, we'd never have got to meet you, so I have since forgiven him. Talking of pinching things, I'd love to go sledging today but shall we try and keep up our investigation into the thief at Chumley Towers?'

'Actually, mum, Lou and I have a theory that it might have been . . .' began David.

Lou glared at him and interrupted before he had the chance to pin it on Mr Bounderton. 'We have no idea yet, Mrs Johnson. Like all good detectives, we're keeping an open mind and drawing up a list of possible suspects.'

'Well you be careful that the suspects on that list don't

get to find out,' warned Mrs Johnson, as she placed a ceramic dish piled high with bacon, eggs, black pudding and the rest in the centre of the table. 'Remember, this is a close-knit village and people won't take kindly to being wrongly accused of stealing. So have your fun by all means, but keep it to yourselves.'

The children decided that unmasking the thief of Chumley Towers would have to be put on hold for a while, until they had got plenty of sledging done. It was too good an opportunity to miss. They took a rucksack containing a flask of coffee and some of Mrs Johnson's home-made almond and cherry cake to nibble once they had tired themselves out.

They dragged their sledges up onto the slopes near the Towers. Strictly, it was private land belonging to the Somersets, but they had never objected to village young-sters enjoying winter sports when conditions were right. In fact, it was the perfect weather. The previous day's dark clouds had vanished and the soft thick snow spar-kled under a bright sun in a clear sky. The air tasted alpine crisp and invigorating, perfumed with the tang of wood smoke.

The Johnson children could not remember the last time there had been so much heavy snow. The previous winter had seen hardly any. What good luck that it should coincide with the start of their holiday!

They spent a couple of hours wearing the snow smooth until, finally, they gathered at the bottom of the slope, red-faced and panting.

'That was amazing,' said Jack. 'But my legs are going to give way from under me if I drag that sledge back up to the top again. Is there somewhere we can find to sit down and have our winter picnic – and talk through our little investigation?'

'Let's go back into the woods,' said Lou, 'it's not far. I

think we passed a bench yesterday while we were walking. We could sit on that if it's not too damp. Also, the sound of our voices won't carry if we are surrounded by trees.'

They set off and found the bench Lou had mentioned. It was set back from the path beneath a canopy of tree branches so dense that it was bone dry with not a single flake of snow having settled upon it.

Lou took out the flask of coffee and Mrs Johnson's almond and cherry cake.

'This is delicious,' said Jack, wiping the crumbs from round his mouth. 'I didn't think I would be able to eat another thing after the huge breakfast we had but I'm really hungry all of a sudden.'

'That's what fresh air and exercise do to you,' said Lou. 'I've always loved being outdoors – especially since being indoors at my house isn't usually much fun. Now,' she added, glancing at the path along which they tracked the footprints the previous day, 'shall we begin our case conference about the thief of Chumley Towers?'

'What's a case conference?' asked Emily, puzzled.

'It's what police call it when they all get together around a whiteboard and discuss a particular crime,' said David.

'Oh good, I'm glad you're still talking to us, David,' said Lou, smirking from behind a mouthful of cake. 'I think you're right – it's how the cops on TV do it anyway. Now, if you recall, we followed those footprints all the way back to the village and they ended up disappearing down a drive which, by sheer coincidence, belonged to none other than Jack's friend Bounder. Wasn't that a surprise?'

Jack nodded. 'I had no idea that Bounder lived there. I knew he lived somewhere in that direction but I didn't know his house. He's talked in the past about me coming round but it never happened. I couldn't believe it when he came to the door just as we were about to escape!'

'I know, but it was kind of lucky in a way,' said Lou, 'because it has allowed us to find out for sure who made those prints and without a doubt, that person is Mr Bounderton, Bounder's dad. Now the question is, what do we make of that? What do you think, Jack?' Lou looked at him intently. She did not want to be the one to spell out the reasons for making Mr Bounderton a suspect, she would rather that came from Jack.

He looked downcast, and didn't reply.

'Clearly, there's a possibility that Bounder's dad is our thief,' said David, with a hint of glee in his voice.

Lou glanced at him in annoyance. 'If you haven't got anything helpful to say, don't say it. What do you make of it, Jack? No-one's accusing his dad of anything, I just think it's odd, that's all.'

Jack took another bite of cake before replying. 'First of all, how can we be sure that those footprints belonged to Bounder's dad?'

Lou pulled her mobile phone from her pocket. 'Take a look at this. The first picture shows the footprints in the snow. Can you see there is a very clear diamond pattern and some wiggly lines? Well now look at this second picture – it's the underside of one of the boots which appeared on the mat inside the back door at Bounder's house yesterday, after his dad had come in who was, if you remember, just wearing his socks. Also, the boots were damp, as you would expect after a long tramp through snow.'

David and Emily looked intently at the pictures over Jack's shoulder. David opened his mouth to say something but Lou's stern face told him to keep quiet.

'Okay,' sighed Jack. 'I agree they do look to be the same and I suppose there was a good chance the prints belonged to him since we followed them all the way up Bounder's drive. But it doesn't mean that he was up to no good, does it? All it proves is that Mr Bounderton left the grounds of Chumley Towers via a side entrance, and proceeded to walk back to Malpas via the woods. While that isn't the quickest way, it might be that he enjoys going that way more, after all it's off the road and you're not going to meet any traffic.'

'All the lanes around here were impassable due to the snow,' said Lou, quietly. 'Many of them still are, so traffic was not an issue. But I agree, he has a right to walk that way if he so chooses. But what I find especially odd is his behaviour upon returning home. He doesn't go indoors as you might expect. He goes straight down the garden via the garage or side gate and neither his son, nor Gisela the maid had a clue that he was there. Even more bizarre, is that Bounder believed his dad had gone to town for a Christmas shopping trip and when he mentioned it to his dad, Mr Bounderton let him carry on thinking so. Why didn't his dad say, well actually I didn't go shopping, I've been up at Chumley Towers? For some inexplicable reason, Mr Bounderton did not want his comings and goings to be known by his own family yesterday and appears to have lied to them regarding his whereabouts. That suggests that he's up to no good. Isn't there a chance that he brought something bulky back from Chumley Towers that didn't belong to him and which he did not wish others to see, so he headed straight for the garden shed to offload it? There's another thing, did you notice some of the antiques dotted around the Boundertons' home? He clearly has an interest in such things.'

'Fair enough,' said Jack, slowly. 'I agree that his behaviour was strange. But we must make sure that our suspicions don't get back to Bounder – he's my best friend at school and I don't want to risk that.'

David puffed out his cheeks and made a noise that sounded rather like 'pah'.

'What was that, David?' asked Jack. 'For some reason, David isn't very keen on Bounder, I think it's because he's jealous he hasn't got a glamorous friend like him.'

'I think he's a phoney,' said David. 'He pretends to be good mates with Jack but isn't really. There's something a bit odd and fake about him. He has this exuberant, matey image but it's hard to know what he's really like underneath.

Jack glared at David and looked at Lou, hoping she would spring to his friend's defence. She didn't.

'Hmm,' said Lou, deep in thought. 'Well whatever Bounder is, good or bad, doesn't matter. The task we've got is to try and suss out his father. What job does he do, exactly? Might he have been at the Towers yesterday on legitimate business?'

'I think he's in something financial, a stockbroker of some kind,' said Jack, hesitantly, 'but I'm not really sure to be honest.'

'It must be pretty good to be able to afford such a big house – and pay for an extension with gold taps in the bathroom,' said Lou.

'And to employ a maid,' chipped in Emily. 'Actually, I didn't much like the way Bounder spoke to her yesterday, just because she accidentally spilt a drink.'

'I bet she's paid a pittance,' said Lou, in exchange for bed and board and an opportunity to live with a British family and improve her English. Nonetheless, it's something most families can't afford. Certainly at the moment, I have to say, Mr Bounderton tops our list. The point is, our list isn't very long. I think what we ought to do is to pop round to Chumley Towers and see if we can get a chat with the Somersets themselves.'

The Johnson children gasped in unison.

'I don't think we can do that,' said Jack.

'They'd never speak to mere children,' said David, loftily.

'Well you might be a mere child but I'm not,' said Lou getting up from her seat and stretching. 'We'll get to speak to them if we go about it the right way. They may give us a far better insight into what has happened than just reading about it in the newspaper. Bearing in mind the police seem to have done very little to help them, they might be grateful for us lending a hand.'

The others all looked at Lou. A steely determination to get her own way was written across her face and in her sharp, lively eyes which sometimes disappeared behind her fringe of dark hair. They admired her self-assurance and iron will hugely, although they doubted it would be sufficient on this occasion. They would not have dreamt of calling on Lord Henry Somerset, Ninth Marquess of Chumley, any more than knock at the gates of Buckingham Palace seeking an audience with the Queen.

CHAPTER NINE

At Chumley Towers

WITHIN half an hour, the children found themselves walking up the long drive to Chumley Towers, flanked on either side by plane trees, their greyish-yellow trunks rising strikingly from a canvas of pure white. The stately home loomed tall ahead of them, solemn and forbidding.

Lou, a few paces ahead, beckoned them forwards as they halted at the foot of the wide stone steps leading to the main entrance. They followed, hesitantly. She rapped the brass door knocker boldly. For a minute or more, nobody answered, then with what sounded like something of a grunt and a sigh a portly chap in a dark uniform opened the door.

'I'm afraid Chumley Towers is not open to the public today, due to the poor weather,' he said, in a deep, gruff voice. To the children he looked like something out of the Victorian age.

That came as a surprise to Jack, David and Emily, for it usually opened seven days a week, whatever the weather. Were the spate of thefts partly responsible for its closure? In any case, the three of them were relieved to have an excuse not to remain there any further and began to back away, happy to be defeated at that point. Lou, however, stood her ground.

'We are not here as members of the public to look round the building,' she said, in her confident, clear voice. 'We have come to see the Marquess of Somerset, if he is available.'

'I see. I am Mr Wilson, his butler. I was not aware that his lordship was expecting visitors this afternoon. Do you have an appointment?'

Mr Wilson looked in turn at all four of them, noting the nervousness in the faces of Lou's three companions. His eyes blinked disbelievingly at them and his throat puffed out from under his starched collar making him look rather like an old, grand toad.

'We wish to see either Lord or Lady Somerset about the recent thefts,' persisted Lou. 'We believe we may be able to help or at least we wish to try.'

'Indeed,' said Mr Wilson, with what sounded like a throaty chuckle or it might possibly have been a rasping scorn, it was hard to be sure. 'I'm sure Lord and Lady Somerset will be most grateful for your kind offer and I shall duly inform them of it. However, the matter has been placed in the hands of North Mercia Constabulary and we must trust that they will eventually bring those responsible to book. Now, unless you wish to leave a calling card, I will bid you good day.'

As he went to close the door Lou jabbed her foot swiftly across the threshold to stop him. Mr Wilson glared at her.

'You might at least ask if they would be willing to meet us. We've come all the way from the village especially to see them,' she said.

'Really? With sledges under your arms?' said Wilson, with just the hint of a smile. Satisfied with the look of defeat on their faces, he added, in a more benevolent tone: 'Listen, it would be frivolous of me to ask Lord and Lady Somerset whether they would like to call upon the help of children to catch the offenders but undoubtedly they will be appreciative. Now be gone with you and get some more sledging done while it's still light, that would be my advice.'

Lou reluctantly retracted her foot as the butler firmly pushed the door shut. The children walked despondently away.

But as they reached the bottom step, they heard the

heavy door, stiff and swollen due to the cold and wet, judder open again.

'Excuse me, children, can I help you?' called a female voice.

They turned round. An elegant middle-aged woman in a tweed jacket over a purple top smiled down at them.

'I'm sorry about Wilson,' she said, in a pleasant, well-spoken voice, not unlike the Queen's. 'He's very protective, you know, especially at the moment, with all this upsetting business going on. It's so kind of you to call and offer to help, really it is, I'm most touched. I'm not terribly sure there's much you could do, my loves, although it's awfully sweet of you to volunteer yourselves. But you all look dreadfully cold and dejected. Why don't you come in and warm yourselves up a bit and we'll have a chat. You must be awfully cold. We can take tea together, would you like that, or perhaps some nice hot chocolate?'

'Actually, we've got a drop of hot chocolate left in our flask, your ladyship,' said David.

'Oh *David*!' exclaimed Lou, Jack and Emily in unison.

The Marchioness of Chumley gave a tinkling chuckle. 'That's most sweet of you, young man, but perhaps we'll ask the kitchen to send up some fresh! Come along, you can leave your sledges by the door. And don't worry about Wilson, he's not half as fearsome as he looks!'

The children trooped into the Towers after Lady Somerset, taking their damp boots off and leaving them carefully on the mat. They looked around in awe as they stepped into the entrance hall. Lou had never been before, while Jack, David and Emily had visited a couple of times with their parents. Yet to be allowed in, not as members of the public but as guests of the Marchioness somehow made the place seem far grander and more important – a building of real splendour, not merely a tourist attraction.

'Come along my dears, let's go into the library, unlike the public libraries, we allow people to talk in ours.' Lady Somerset laughed her tinkling laugh again. They followed her through heavy oak doors. The library walls were lined with tall glass cabinets filled with leather-bound books with gilt lettering. They looked very old. David yearned to browse through them.

The children sat down round a circular table in the window overlooking the main garden. Before long, Mr Wilson entered with a trolley containing steaming pots of tea, coffee and hot chocolate, a plate of warmed scones and sweet pastries. It was an elevenses fit for royalty, and the Somersets were not much below royalty in the social pecking order, of course.

'Do help yourselves,' said Lady Somerset, 'and then we can talk, although sadly there isn't a great deal I can tell you. I've given a full description of what has been taken to the police. It was Wilson, in fact, who brought the matter to my attention. He spotted that items had gone missing. He is wonderfully particular about there being a place for everything, and everything in its place. Around half a dozen things were taken somewhere between Saturday, November 29th and the following Wednesday, December 3rd including a silver and enamel trinket box, hand-crafted in 1884, with cherubs playing on the lid, which my husband was especially fond of. It was a christening present given to his great-grandfather, Edwin Somerset.

'Numerous other items dating back to his era were also taken, including a solid silver tankard with a christening inscription for Edwin. Several other things disappeared on Friday, December 12th. One of them was a Victorian rosewood music box which was very dear to me. Again, such items may seem small but they are of enormous sentimental value belonging as they have to several generations of Somersets.'

'We saw the newspaper article in the *Whitchurch Herald*,' said Lou. 'Was that broadly accurate, as far as it went?'

'More or less,' said Lady Somerset. 'But they missed out some of the items taken and gave very few details. I have a full inventory of what was taken and on what dates, which I can let you have a copy of. Also, I have photographs of one or two of the missing items which I've included. Here, take mine, I can easily run off another copy, everything's all on computer these days, isn't it?' Lady Somerset handed Lou a stapled two-page list detailing what had gone missing.

'Can you be absolutely sure that the second raid took place on December 12th?' said Lou, taking a sip of excellently-brewed coffee. 'That's quite significant.'

'Yes that's right, my dear, Lou isn't it?' said Lady Somerset. 'It's a pity we can't be sure of the exact date the first time, but let's just say we were more vigilant after that and noticed that evening that items had gone – well Wilson did, anyway.'

'Is it possible to say that it was likely to be a visitor? You clearly don't suspect that anyone actually broke in?' asked Lou.

Lady Somerset looked down at her long, elegant fingers and paused. 'We have to hope that it's a visitor, since the building has not been broken into and one would certainly not wish to suspect any of our staff. We don't have many people working for us – it's not like you see on TV's Downton Abbey, you know, stately homes these days have to make do with a gardener and a butler and a maid or two and not much else. And we've known Wilson, Edwards the gardener, Mrs Clifford the cook and Joan the maid for many years. They're as honest as the day is long, as the saying goes. They're like part of the family. It would be too awful to think that any of them could be responsible.'

Lady Somerset looked distressed.

Lou spoke quickly. 'Of course not, Lady Somerset. Nobody would think for a minute that they would take anything. But nonetheless, have you had any casual staff working for you recently who might not owe you the same loyalty?'

'Not as such, but we have a fairly new gamekeeper, Mr Timothy Hickman, who has taken over from Mr Bellingham, who's now retired. I have to say I can't vouch for his probity. But frankly, I doubt Hickman would have either the intelligence or the desire to steal valuables. He's a slow, dour sort of chap whose only interest in life seems to be the outdoors. Give him a hedge to clip or a pheasant or a rabbit to go after then he's your man. But take him indoors and he's like a fish out of water, poor thing. I can't see him as the culprit, somehow.'

'So, if it isn't the staff or burglars in the middle of the night, then it must be a visitor. What makes you think that the thief is local, how can you be sure?' asked Lou, picking up and munching a stray walnut half which had fallen from her slice of coffee cake.

Lady Somerset sighed and gazed out of the window at the snow lying pristine and flawless across her land. 'Nobody can be sure of anything, that's the problem. It's an intelligent guess. According to the police, if visitors from far afield pinch something from a country house such as ours, they rarely return to the same place for a long while, if ever. They prefer to target another mansion the next time and then another. The thefts have occurred within a short space of time and, bearing in mind the types of objects stolen, the police believe that it's most likely the same person who is probably local. That theory is reinforced by the fact that on the last occasion the weather was truly dreadful – the most terrific high winds and torrential rain. We were open all day but had only a handful of visitors. It would seem unlikely that anyone should have travelled any distance to reach us in such conditions. That's why we decided to close today – it's not worth keeping the place open when the weather is bad.'

Lou nodded. 'But did no-one see anyone acting suspiciously? Did nothing happen which was out of the ordinary?'

'In truth, visitors are at liberty to amble around more or less unsupervised. Perhaps we are too trusting but we simply haven't previously had any reason not to be. A young woman, Julia Oldfield, took money on the door from each visitor but she hasn't long lived round here and wouldn't have known whether people were local or acting out of character. She told me that she didn't see anything untoward. The police have spoken to her but she wasn't able to give them anything useful. We do actually have CCTV footage of people coming and going through the entrance, but the police weren't very interested in that, they said it would take far too long to check.'

'What's CCTV?' asked Emily, timidly.

Lady Somerset smiled. 'It stands for closed-circuit television. It's a form of surveillance – when you put cameras up to film a particular spot. So for instance, we film the entrance to our home on the days we open to the public, so there is a record of everyone who has been in. However, visitors leave the building via the laundry and scullery at the far end, which is not covered, unfortunately.'

Lou's ears had pricked up. 'Even so, it's great news that you have a photographic record of all visitors entering the building. It's odd that the police were not interested in viewing it.'

Lady Somerset nodded. 'I agree. It's a manpower issue, apparently. They do not have the resources with all the spending cuts at the moment to have officers deployed scouring hours of CCTV footage. Detective

Sergeant Simon Walker said there would be no obvious way of drawing up a shortlist of suspects, particularly since we can't be sure on what day the first items were taken. He feels it would be unreasonable to assign an officer to trawling through five days' worth of CCTV footage covering the first raid, plus the footage from December 12th. Mr Walker also felt it would be of little value to question numerous visitors without any specific evidence of wrongdoing.'

The children looked at Lady Somerset in silence. She had an air of resignation about her, as if she felt powerless to stop the thief in his tracks and uncertain what to do next.

'To be perfectly honest,' she continued, with a trace of bitterness, 'I fear they don't see this matter as being of especial importance. It's too difficult and complicated for them to solve, for what in their eyes is hardly the crime of the century. I think they feel that my family is a throwback to the landed gentry of old for whom the loss of a few hundred pounds of valuables is of little importance. They gave me a crime reference number, I think they called it, to pass on to our insurance company so we could claim the value of what's been taken. And they've appealed for information from the public in the local Press and that's about our lot, it would seem.'

'I appreciate that nothing can compensate for the sentimental value of the items lost but are you able to claim for the financial losses incurred?' asked Lou. 'It's just that we've heard rumours that you are not fully covered,' she added.

Lady Somerset's lower lip wobbled. 'No,' she replied, woodenly. 'We can't claim a penny. The building itself is insured but the contents are not covered, save for the most priceless heirlooms. The cost would be phenomenal for a place this size with the number of valuables we possess, especially since we usually open daily to the public. We are rather stuck, I'm afraid. It seems the only way we can protect ourselves is to close our doors but if we do that, then we sacrifice the income we receive from visitors which is crucial to our being able to remain here. You see, whatever some people might think, we are not terribly well off. Certainly, we live in a wonderful building, with breathtaking views in all directions and a long, sweeping drive, but the maintenance costs are huge and if Chumley Towers doesn't pay its way, then we are likely to have to tread the same path as so many other titled families in the past, and be forced to sell off our assets. And to us, this place is not merely a very fine mansion, it is truly our home. My husband, Henry Somerset, was born here. He's lived here all his life.'

The children listened solemnly. Everything was quiet save for the occasional far-off clatter of pans down in the kitchen.

'So yes, I'm afraid we have been talking about selling up and moving to somewhere smaller. Sometime before the thefts took place my husband and I had mooted the idea as something we might one day have to consider. But we would be loathe to since we love the place so, and we know what Chumley Towers means to local people, particularly in Malpas. We Somersets have always had a good relationship with villagers and, I like to think, are thought of with a reasonable degree of affection. But what folk would think of us if we cast aside our ancestral home I shudder to think, particularly if the Towers were to fall into the wrong hands. Indeed, what might our own five children think of us, one day?'

Spontaneously, Emily reached out and clasped Lady Somerset's hand. 'We'll find the thief, or at least, we'll do our very best. Our Christmas holidays have only just started. We've got a whole two weeks off before we go back to school.'

Lady Somerset chuckled. 'You're a sweet child, and

I'm very touched that you all want to help. I don't suppose for one minute you will be able to get anywhere, but at least you are willing to try, and that means a lot.'

'We'll definitely try,' said Lou, glancing around at the quiet elegance of their surroundings. 'History somehow comes alive here, doesn't it? It's as if previous centuries live on inside these walls. It's dreadful that anyone should seek to diminish that by quietly taking treasures away from where they belong – where they've stood the test of time for years.'

Lady Jane Somerset's eyes moistened. 'I quite agree, I couldn't put it any better,' she said, simply.

Lou placed her coffee cup firmly down and looked Lady Somerset in the eye. 'We'll start by watching your camera footage from December 12th if you'll let us,' she said, in that brisk, business-like voice she used when disagreeing with her wasn't an option – even for a peer of the realm. 'It might give us some insight into the person we're looking for. I do think it's terrible the police weren't willing to go through it.'

'You would be most welcome to view it if you wish,' replied Lady Somerset, 'only there is about eight hours' worth. I suppose another reason why the police were reluctant to bother was that they would not have recognised barely a single person since none of the officers assigned to the case are local.'

'But *we* are local,' pointed out Jack. 'We've lived in Malpas nearly all our lives, which in my case is nearly thirteen years. That's a heck of a long time to get to know who's who around here.'

'What's more, it won't take eight hours to view the footage if we speed it up,' chipped in David. 'I can easily set a DVD to play twice as fast or more. In which case eight hours will become four hours or less.'

'Good idea, David,' said Lou, 'I hadn't thought of that.' She had, in fact, but was anxious to get David to feel more confident and cheerful. His face lit up with a rare smile. 'Of course, we will have to stop and start the discs so it will take longer than we might think but that's fine by us, like Emily said, it's just the start of the holidays.'

'Excellent,' said Lady Somerset. 'Then I have a proposition for you. Why don't you watch for an hour or so now, then I'll get the cook to send you up some lunch, and then carry on afterwards? How would a few baskets of scampi and chips suit? Our cook Mrs Clifford makes lovely scampi and her home-made tartare sauce is a delight.'

Lunch at Chumley Towers! The children looked at each other in excitement. They would have a tale and a half to tell when they got back later!

'That would be great,' said Lou, with a grin. 'Oh Lady Somerset, I nearly forgot, I wanted to ask you about a single set of footprints we saw in the snow leading away from a side entrance in the wall around your formal gardens yesterday afternoon. We just thought it rather odd.'

Lady Somerset listened intently. She ran her hands through her shoulder-length, greying blonde hair as Lou explained their little piece of detective work the previous day. She looked with interest at the photos on Lou's mobile phone of the footprints in the snow and the matching boot prints, and antique items in Bounder's house.

'Hmm,' she said, hesitantly, frowning slightly. 'I was not aware of Mr Bounderton visiting the Towers yesterday. 'My guess is that if he left via the door in the side wall, he had been to see one of my staff. Certainly, he was not here as a member of the public. I agree that is slightly strange, but it is not unheard of for our staff to receive visitors in the servants' quarters sometimes. However, none of the antiques you photographed are from here, that I can tell you.

'Oh goodness,' added Lady Somerset, going pale. 'It has just occurred to me that if anything untoward *was* going on yesterday involving this Mr Bounderton, then more items might have been taken. Wilson has not notified me of anything, but he's been out in the yard all morning dealing with workmen who have come to repair our antiquated boiler. I will go and scout around. I'll get Wilson to bring you the DVD containing the relevant CCTV footage. You can watch it on that television set over there.' She pointed to a corner of the library where a small, widescreen television sat discreetly on a bureau desk. Now if you'll excuse me. Oh it really is too dreadful to have to live like this.'

Lady Somerset got to her feet, brushed a couple of crumbs from her skirt and left. Chumley Towers suddenly seemed very quiet, save for the tick-tock of a grandfather clock somewhere.

The children felt very sorry for her. The house was so huge and contained so many treasured possessions, it must be wretched to have to check everything was still where it should be day after day.

Lou glanced up at a huge oil painting in a gilded frame. A haughty, impressive figure in ermine robes looked down upon them amid the endless rows of books. She went across and glanced at the name underneath: Lord Edwin Somerset, Sixth Marquess of Chumley. What, she wondered, would he have made of his family's current predicament?

CHAPTER TEN

The strange gamekeeper

MORE items *had* been taken! The thief or thieves had struck again for a third time. The butler gave the children the news when he brought them the DVD containing the camera footage from December 12th.

This time, a barometer had been taken off the drawing room wall in the west wing; a small oil lamp had disappeared from a bureau desk in the adjoining study along with a glass paperweight, and an Edwardian brass kettle was missing from the hearth in front of the fireplace.

They were all there yesterday morning, I can vouch that for a fact,' said Mr Wilson, looking grave. 'I distinctly remember dusting around them and, indeed, tapping the barometer to see if the prevailing low pressure conditions were likely to persist. Yet they appear suddenly to have vanished into thin air. I am embarrassed to say that on this occasion I failed to spot they were gone this morning, although I have been terribly busy. Her ladyship has just brought the matter to my attention.'

He tutted and shook his head. 'I don't know what the world is coming to, really I don't. It wasn't like this when I was a boy. People had respect in those days. I ask you, the cheek of it, to take such items right from under the Lord and Lady's noses, in their own home! It quite beggars belief.'

Mr Wilson was himself visibly upset, so Lou spoke gently. 'Mr Wilson, could you let Lady Somerset know that we are very sorry to hear what has happened. Would you also, if it's not too much trouble, enquire whether there is CCTV footage available from yesterday that we might view? It might be particularly valuable bearing in mind that there were presumably not too many visitors yesterday, with the snow so bad.'

Mr Wilson scrunched up his leathery nose as if Lou's request was in somewhat poor taste. Then he sighed and said, 'very well, I will see what I can do. It should be the police looking through all this, of course, not a bunch of children – meaning no offence – but since they are far too busy, I suppose it can hardly do any harm for you lot to take a look, especially since you are local.'

Lou wasn't, of course, but she wasn't about to correct him. 'That would be very good of you. Listen, Mr Wilson, we don't want to interfere, all we want to do is to help.'

'I understand,' he said. 'Leave it with me and I will bring the additional disc for you when luncheon is served.'

After he had departed the children looked at each other in excitement. Awful though the news was for Lord and Lady Somerset, it did at least mean that they would be able to compare two sets of footage after all. If the same faces appeared on both the previous day and December 12th, then that would give them a very interesting shortlist of suspects indeed. With extra material to watch, the children had several hours of laborious research ahead of them. Jack texted his mum to tell her that they were 'having lunch at Chumley Towers' and would be assisting the Marchioness throughout the afternoon, and not to expect them back until the evening.

'Well, I can't compete with that, can I?' came the reply. Jack grinned. He couldn't wait to brag about what they had been doing later on.

The children began their task with relish but it proved more time-consuming than they had expected. They played the DVDs at reasonably high speed which worked well for the long periods when no visitors arrived. But each time someone came through the main entrance, they needed to freeze the film to get a good look at each visitor in turn. Lou had her pocket camera with her and pointed it at the TV and took pictures of each of them. It was fortunate that the poor conditions on both days had greatly reduced the number of visitors. Jack, David and Emily were pretty certain that most were local, although they struggled to put names to many of the faces.

'Goodness me, this is slow going,' said Lou at one point. 'But I feel I've got to take snaps of more or less everyone at this stage – we can narrow things down tomorrow on your computer at home. We'll only seek to find out names if the same visitor appears on both occasions. That will make our shortlist.'

It felt as though they were wading through very thick treacle, but then came a breakthrough as they whizzed through the footage from December 12th.

'Bounderton, it's got to be,' yelled Jack, triumphantly, as Lou hit the pause button to freeze the picture.

'I thought you were hoping Bounder's dad would be in the clear,' whispered David.

'I just want to catch the offender,' retorted Jack, although David words had jolted him, he really did not want it to turn out to be his best friend's father.

'Interesting,' said Lou, pointing her camera at the screen. 'I wonder if he will appear on yesterday's tape. That would be a bonus.'

He didn't. Yet they knew perfectly well that Kevin Bounderton had been back at Chumley Towers the previous day, since they had followed his prints all the way home.

In all, the Johnson children recognised around thirty people of whom they were pretty sure that around half a dozen appeared on both occasions. They would be able to verify that when they got home having examined each set of photographs which Lou had taken from the moving footage.

Apart from twenty minutes' break to enjoy the most delicious home-made scampi, chips and tartare sauce they had ever tasted, the children worked steadily. The winter sun was sinking westwards by the time Lady Somerset came into the library to see how they were getting on.

Her eyes looked red and puffy as if she had been crying and her voice, although clear and musical as before, had lost its jollity. 'I'm sorry to have abandoned you all this afternoon,' she said, 'but these thefts have made me very weary and, frankly, a little frightened. You know what people say, one's home is one's castle, well, almost literally in our case – but now it feels as though someone is repeatedly violating the place where one should feel safest in all the world. Anyway, I should not burden you with my troubles. How have you been getting on?'

'It's hard to be sure, Lady Somerset,' said Lou, honestly. 'We'll have a better idea by tomorrow. We've photographed everyone who visited from the CCTV footage we've viewed. What we need to do now is to compare the two lists and work out who turned up on both occasions. If we come across anything interesting, is it okay for us to ring you, or email you, if that is easier?'

'Yes indeed, my dear. You can do either. Allow me to give you a business card with our details on. Where it says *contactus@chumleytowers.co.uk* if you change that to *ladysomerset*, all one word, then it will come through to me directly. Now my loves, do you want to get off for the day, you must be terribly tired after working so hard, or shall I fetch you some more refreshments?'

'No, we'll head off if that's okay, Lady Somerset,' said Lou. 'You must be very tired, too. We've got all we need for now and we promised Jack's mum we'd be back in time for dinner. Thank you so much for your hospitality, the scampi and chips were heavenly and that home-made tartare sauce was amazing.' The others all nodded.

Lady Somerset smiled. 'It is me who should be thanking you. Your efforts have quite cheered me up, even if they should prove fruitless. I'm so pleased you enjoyed your lunch. I shall pass on your compliments to Mrs Clifford, it will make her day, she's very proud of her scampi and chips. Now, our new estate manager and gamekeeper, Mr Hickman, is heading down to the village in a minute or two, would you care to jump into his pick-up truck and he can give you a lift? There'll be plenty of room in the back for your sledges.'

The children gratefully accepted her offer. They felt weary and glazed over from so much time spent staring at grainy images from a security camera. A trudge down cold lanes wasn't too appealing.

Lady Somerset ushered them out, thanking them again for their hard work and promising to let them come again any time they liked. If nothing else, thought Lou, they had done her a good turn – rather as they had with old Mrs Owen of Mynytho. When untoward events happen under your own roof it is deeply unsettling and Lady Somerset had clearly appreciated their support.

The journey back in Mr Hickman's truck was rather strange, however. The sledges had the best of it, sprawled out in the back, which was empty save for a few pheasant feathers and odd tuft of rabbit fur. The four children were squashed into the two passenger seats in the cab.

'Thanks for giving us a lift back,' said Jack, as the truck juddered forwards.

'I do as her ladyship tells me,' grunted Mr Hickman in a thick, rural accent.

'It must be an interesting life being a gamekeeper,' ventured Jack, keen to be a bit bolder in his conversations with grown-ups as Lou was, although on this occasion, she seemed to have nothing to say.

'It pays the bills and that be about all it do,' said Mr Hickman, 'with precious little left over for luxuries. It's all well and good for Mr Bellingham – he gets to live in a tied cottage on the estate free of charge – even though he's retired, will ye believe it! If I'm doing that job of his now, why don't he hand the keys over to me? It's downright unfair. His lordship says as he 'asn't got the heart to throw old Bellingham out after so many years' faithful service and what's more, he'll have the use of that cottage 'til the end of his days. Well that's fine and dandy for him but meanwhiles, I have to fork out a sky-high rent for a tiny terraced cottage in the village from the pittance his lordship pays me – and put food on the table as well so my wife and kids don't go hungry. It's a struggle I'm tellin' you. If it weren't for bringing in a bit of extra cash 'ere and there and living off my wits and my cunning I don't think I'd manage it.'

'All the same,' persevered Jack, breezily, not quite sure what to say after that long outburst, 'it's a decent enough lifestyle, roaming the countryside in the fresh air. I bet you prefer it to city life. And I don't suppose Lord and Lady Somerset have got much cash to spare. Sounds to me like they are struggling to keep going as it is. Any job's got to be better than none at all, I suppose.'

'Oh and you'd know that you would you, aged ten, goin' on forty?' bristled Mr Hickman, sarcastically, turning his weather-beaten face towards Jack, his dark eyes blazing at him. 'Do you think I need lessons in life from a little squit like you?'

Jack's face crumpled and he fell silent. He was mortified beyond words at being dubbed a ten-year-old in front of Lou – the same age as his sister. After all, he was nearly a teenager like Lou.

'Hey, don't speak to Jack like that,' said Lou, leaning forwards and glaring back at Mr Hickman. 'He was only trying to be friendly. I'm sure Lady Somerset would not be happy to hear you talking in that way to guests of hers.'

'I didn't mean to snap,' said Mr Hickman, gruffly, aware that he had offended Jack. 'It's just that you kids don't know how 'arrd it be to earn a living these days. The food on your plate tonight 'as to be paid for and don't ye forget it.'

Jack said nothing more, unwilling to engage the game-keeper further in conversation, but by now, Lou's ears had pricked up.

'No you're quite right, Mr Hickman,' she said. 'Everything has to be paid for and it must be a struggle for you to make ends meet. It's the same for my mum and dad. They've hardly got a penny to rub together most of the time. Sometimes they try and raise a bit of extra cash, you know, by selling stuff they don't want – old vases, bric-a-brac, that sort of thing.'

'Oh aye, that's the way to do it all right,' said Mr Hickman. 'I never overlook an opportunity to put a few extra quid into my back pocket. On occasion I goes a-gleaning through the fields when they're done 'arrvest-ing, it's amazing what you can pick up.'

'What's gleaning?' asked Emily, interrupting.

'Taking what crops are left after harvest,' whispered Lou, putting a finger to her lips. She wanted Mr Hickman to keep talking.

'That's right,' said Mr Hickman. 'It don't do no-one no 'arm, nor does helping yeself to the occasional bit of game or a rabbit or two. I goes a-foraging for firewood as well, to 'elp keep the missus warm. The best things in life are free, as they say,' he added, making himself cough as he chuckled wheezily to himself.

'Have you ever sold any . . .' began Lou, but before she could continue, Mr Hickman cursed and raised his fist at the windscreen. A cyclist had shot out of a side road right in front of him, causing him to brake sharply.

'Bloomin' varmints,' he snarled. 'They didn't ought to be allowed on the road. If I had my way . . .'

'Sorry to interrupt, but it's the next right,' said David, nervously, anxious that Mr Hickman did not miss the turning to their house, although Lou would have happily kept him talking.

Within a few seconds, Mr Hickman's uncomfortable pick-up truck had pulled up outside the Johnsons' drive. The children clambered out, grateful for the chance to stretch their stiff legs. Lou regretted not being able to ask him any more questions, although perhaps it was just as well. Mr Hickman let down the tailgate and tugged the rope attached to their sledges, sliding them out one by one.

'Hey lad, sorry I were a bit harsh on you earlier,' said Mr Hickman to Jack. 'Be obliged to you for not mentioning it to her ladyship, I were only pullin' your leg, like.'

Jack, David, Emily and Lou all muttered their goodbyes and thanked him for the lift before heading quickly indoors. None of them had enjoyed their ride home, nor making Mr Hickman's acquaintance, and were relieved to be back.

Lou puffed out her cheeks and breathed out. 'There's something unsettling about that man. I don't fancy taking any more lifts home with him, do you? What do you lot make of him?'

Jack shrugged and his eyes looked as if they were filling with tears.

Lou read his mind instantly. 'Oh Jack, take no notice of that oaf. You don't look ten years old any more than I do. You look twelve going on thirteen – same as me.'

'I look younger than you, I'm sure I do,' he said, petulantly.

'Girls always look a bit older than boys at our age. You certainly don't look ten – so don't act like it. Sorry Emily, you know what I mean. Now come on, what do we all think of Hickman? Did he appear on our camera footage, can you recall?'

The others couldn't say for sure, although Jack, looking brighter, thought he might have. David shrugged his shoulders and Emily scratched her nose as if thinking hard.

'Never mind. Tomorrow, we'll go through all the photos I took and see what we can piece together,' said Lou. 'Of course, if Hickman does appear on the tapes it doesn't tell us much, since he works at the Towers.'

'Do you think we'll get anywhere with this mystery, Lou?' asked Emily. 'Somehow I can't see how we're going to get to the bottom of this one.'

'Who knows?' said Lou. 'I can't see how we solve it either. We might well not be able to. But we have definite leads to follow up and it's going to be lots of fun trying. At least, it will be after we've had a good night's sleep. Let's just see what tomorrow brings, okay? We're doing our best after all, unlike the police.'

'Aha, look who it is!' said Mr Johnson, as the children walked into the living room. 'It's the four detectives. Now what's this I hear about you lot having lunch at Chumley Towers with the Marchioness herself? Tell me that's a festive fib.'

'You can scoff but it's totally true,' declared Jack, who seemed to have brightened up. 'We've been guests of her ladyship all day: we had coffee and cake with her earlier on followed by a huge banquet for lunch.'

'Not quite,' said Lou, smiling. 'Don't exaggerate, Jack.' Lou explained to Mr Johnson what they had been up to and how she now had numerous mugshots on her camera of possible suspects.

'Goodness me,' he said, looking impressed. 'You can download the lot onto my computer in the study if you like, and print them out. Mrs Johnson and I might be able to help put names to some of the faces. Make a start now, if you wish, tea's not going to be ready for an hour at least.'

'I'd rather not if you don't mind, Mr Johnson. We're all a bit bushed, to be honest. We've been staring at these pictures all day. Do you mind if we start afresh tomorrow?'

'Of course not, best to sleep on it,' he said. 'And I promise not to interfere, but if I can help, just ask.'

Lou grinned at him. Mr Johnson was clearly eager to help. Well he could if he wanted to – after all, he was providing a roof over her head. So long as he realised who was boss!

CHAPTER ELEVEN

Analysing the evidence

THE following day, the children woke fairly early. They had slept well but as they surfaced one by one, their heads began to buzz with thoughts of thieves. Who was pinching valuable and sentimental items from Chumley Towers, right from under the noses – as the butler had put it – of Lord and Lady Somerset themselves?

Jack was the first to open his eyes, at just after five o'clock. He had been dreaming about tracking a man through snowbound woods, a sackful of stolen items slung across his shoulder. It had been disappointing to wake up halfway through before he had a chance to pounce on him. But with the dream over, his thoughts turned to their real-life mystery. Who was the thief, or was there more than one?

Could it really be Bounder's dad? Or what about Mr Hickman, the charmless, hard-up new gamekeeper? And what, if anything, would the CCTV footage throw up when it had been analysed carefully?

His head began to whirl with theories about who and why. So too, did Lou's when her eyes opened around three-quarters of an hour later. David and Emily slowly surfaced from deep sleep at around half-past six, when their minds too began to sift through the information they had gathered.

The four children were dressed and in the kitchen by half-past seven, somewhat to the surprise of their parents. They were eager to examine the photographs Lou had taken the previous day but as soon as the aroma of bacon and eggs filled their nostrils, their stomachs insisted on being satisfied before their curiosity. Lou, in particular, loved these cheery sessions seated around the kitchen table – a proper family gathered together, helping themselves to steaming dishes of home-cooked food. And Mrs Johnson was making spiced pumpkin soup for lunchtime – actually *making* it, not merely yanking a can of Heinz out of the cupboard and cursing until she found the tin opener.

After breakfast, Lou and Emily helped clear away. Then, with Mr Johnson's permission, they took mugs of coffee into the study and booted up his powerful computer. Lou took the memory card from her camera and pushed it into a slot along the side edge.

'Oh,' said Mr Johnson, who had come to watch. 'I didn't know you could do that – I thought you had to attach cables between your hardware devices. Is that the right expression? Honestly, you children can't half teach us old 'uns a thing or two!'

'Right then dad, thanks for the compliment, now leave us in peace,' said Jack, cheekily, who didn't much want his father standing over them.

His dad looked rueful. He really wanted to be part of their gang that morning and help with the detective work – but the children were fast reaching the age when they preferred grown-ups to be seen and not heard – and preferably not even seen.

'Fair enough, I'll be in the garden chopping wood or something. If you need me, give me a shout,' he said, heading for the door.

'Thanks very much, Mr Johnson, if we get stuck we'll call you,' said Lou, grinning. 'Right,' she said, briskly, turning to the others. It'll take a few minutes while all the photos I took yesterday download. I'll store them in a folder on your dad's desktop so they won't get in the way of his stuff.'

It took six minutes for the dozens of pictures to transfer to a folder she titled CCTV images. Once the download was complete, Lou clicked on a couple to see what they looked like on the wide screen of Mr Johnson's computer. They were grainier than they had appeared when viewed on the preview screen on the back of her camera. Also, many contained a black bar across which often happens when you photograph a TV image. But the images were nonetheless distinct enough to make out the features of each visitor captured on film.

Lou knitted her brows as she did when she was concentrating hard. 'I'm just wondering how best to sift through all these pictures. Above all, we need to do side-by-side comparisons when we think we have got the same person on both days.'

'Why don't you create two folders, one for mugshots from December 12th and another for Sunday? Between the three of us, we should be able to spot when the same faces come up,' said Jack.

'Okay, that's a good idea,' said Lou. 'Your dad did say we could print them out so if that's ok, I think we'll do that. Then we could make two rows, like a sort of identity parade. It will then be much easier to spot who turns up on both.'

To save time, printer ink and paper, Lou created a Word document and pasted in photographs of the forty-eight visitors from Friday, December 12th; eight per page. As the six sheets rolled off the printer, Emily carefully cut them out and placed them across the desk in one long row. There had been just thirty-three visitors on Sunday and she did the same with them, forming a single row beneath the other.

'Right,' said Lou, gazing at the dozens of images in front of them. 'A thought has just occurred to me. We must keep in mind the possibility that the thefts just might have been carried out by different people. So, if we see someone who looks suspicious on only the one set of prints, we should include him or her on our shortlist as well. I know that complicates things a bit but it is conceivable that more than one person is responsible. Good detectives don't rule out any possibilities or make assumptions. The others nodded. They were sure Lou was right.

The first photograph in the first row was of an elderly couple in dark mackintoshes, with big, old-fashioned metal buttons. The woman clutched a bulging leather bag. They must have been the first visitors to arrive on December 12th. Their hair looked damp and fly-away as if they had walked to the Towers rather than come by car. That was a good sign that they were local and Jack thought he vaguely recognised them.

It appeared to be a promising start but Lou shook her head. 'They don't look all that well off but that bag of theirs is already full, presumably with flasks of coffee and home-baked cake, so they don't have to fork out for refreshments in the tearoom.'

Jack and Emily chuckled. Lou was remarkably adept at assessing people from their general appearance and demeanour.

'What's more, they don't appear in the second row,' said Emily.

'Fine. So for now at least, we can forget about them,' said Lou.

The children soon found that they had to forget about most of the visitors – or at least, find no reason to attach suspicion to any of them. The vast majority did not appear on both December 12th and December 21st. Since it could not be established when exactly the first batch of items was stolen – somewhere around the start of the month – it was not possible to find out whether they might have been present on that occasion.

Nonetheless, an interesting list of possibilities was building up. Among them was a mean-looking old woman in a trim, tight-fitting woollen coat, carrying a large canvas shopping bag which didn't appear to have much in it. Lou recalled that on the CCTV she had appeared to struggle to find the right money to pay the admission fee and did so grudgingly. She was a distinctive character from December 12th and Lou felt sure she had seen her on the footage from Sunday. Had she been to Chumley on December 21st as well? To their great excitement, the answer to that was Yes! Furthermore, Jack recognised her as definitely local, but could not put a name to her.

Up came photographs of Mr Bounderton which had got their pulses racing at the Towers and – Lou was right – Mr Hickman was also among those she had snapped. Mr Hickman appeared on both days, although that was not too surprising since he worked at the Towers. Mr Bounderton appeared on December 12th but as they had already noted, not on Sunday, December 21st.

'I find that rather intriguing,' commented Lou. 'In some ways, that's a better result than seeing Bounderton show up on both occasions on the CCTV. On Sunday, he chose – for whatever reason – not to use the main entrance upon arriving. Yet we know for a fact that he was at Chumley Towers that day because he slunk discreetly away via an obscure gate in a side wall rather than via the drive leading to the main entrance. I wonder what he was up to. Something, that's for sure!'

There were clear matches between the two rows for tradesmen with an obvious reason to be at the Towers regularly, such as Hans Fleischer the butcher, Audrey Lloyd the cake shop lady and historian Mr Whortlebury who regularly gave talks at Chumley.

'Aha!' said Jack at one point. 'Those two lads look mighty suspicious, don't they Lou? I thought they did yesterday when we were running through the film.'

As Jack was speaking, Lou noticed David seemed to flinch and recoil slightly. 'Are you okay, David? Do you recognise these two?'

He had gone pale and trembling, and begun to fidget. Lou recalled that it was exactly how he had behaved that summer when they had all been sitting outside the pub in Abersoch with Mr and Mrs Johnson and he had caught sight of a smuggler. One or both of those lads meant something to him, something unpleasant.

'David, tell me what's wrong. Have you got something to say about these two lads? Actually they look about your age. Are you at school with them by any chance?' asked Lou.

Without warning, David got up and cleared off. 'I've had enough of this,' he said, as he headed through the study door. 'I'm going for a walk.'

'Why don't you wait for us, and we'll all go,' called Lou after him. It was no good. He had disappeared.

Lou and Jack looked at each other.

'Shall I go after him?' suggested Jack.

She shook her head. 'No, leave him be. If he wants to be alone, then let him. It's odd though. If David knows something about them it's a pity he doesn't tell us. Somehow I don't really feel he's part of this mystery at the moment. Jack, can I ask you something, are you sure David's okay about me being here for Christmas? He's such a complex person that I can't always make him out. You're his brother, you would know how he feels. It's only the twenty-third, there's still time for me to get a train home if it would make him feel happier. I don't want him to be stressed out and ill at ease in his own home.'

'Believe me,' said Jack, running his hands though his light-brown hair, 'I don't always feel I know David all that well, especially not lately. But I do know that it has absolutely nothing to do with you. I asked him and Emily if it was okay to invite you – not just mum and dad – and they were really keen, although David did scoff and say there was "no way that you'd want to". Anyway, when I told him that you were actually coming, you should have seen how his eyes lit up. And they don't light up very often these days.'

'Lou, Jack's right. The three of us were leaping round the house cheering when we knew you were coming and mum and dad were all smiles about it, too,' chipped in Emily, who had looked alarmed when Lou talked of going home.

Lou gave Emily's wrist a squeeze. 'That's good! I'm really enjoying being here too, and I'm determined to get to the bottom of what's bugging David. So that's two mysteries we've got to solve! Hey come on, let's keep going through these pictures. Do those lads appear in the second row? Yes they do, there look! Oh actually, no they don't. They look similar age though and equally dodgy characters.'

Jack squinted at the pictures, glancing from one to the other. 'I'm pretty sure I recognise them,' he said. 'They look like they're from David's year. What's more, I've a good feeling they are all part of the same gang. That's really puzzling, don't you think? They are not the sort to turn up at a stately home and pay money to marvel at the architecture and the prized possessions.'

'That's a good point, you know, thinking back to the CCTV footage, I'm not sure I actually saw any of them hand over money,' said Lou. 'Most likely they gave some excuse that their parents were following behind and would pay for them and the woman on the till just let them through. You're right, it's really odd that pairs of boys of our age would go to look round a stately home on their own. Maybe it's the sort of thing David might do, but not these thuggish types.'

Someone else quickly caught Lou's interest: a young man, late teens or early twenties, with frowning, dark features and a beard. She had not paid him much attention before when viewing the CCTV footage but careful scrutiny of the two rows of mugshots revealed that he had been at Chumley on both December 12th and 21st. Furthermore, he did not appear to fit the profile of the typical visitor either. Apart from his youth, he was casually dressed in a jacket with a T-shirt underneath with some sort of emblem on it. They couldn't name him, but Jack was fairly certain he had seen him before.

There was a youngish woman, thin, mid-thirties, with a furtive, slightly guilty-looking face, whom Lou recalled came clucking in on her own on both occasions, like a wren pecking about in the undergrowth. Lou had captured two clear shots of her on both dates. She wore a dark, shabby coat several sizes too big. The others did not know her name, nor did they think they recognised her. That might be one to run past Mr Johnson, since he was keen to help out.

The hard-up Pippa Swift had also been there on December 12th and 21st, each time wearing a long winter coat and leather or suede gloves – it was hard to be sure from the grainy images. That was very promising!

Frustratingly, however, Malcolm Finchfield, or Mr Creepy as they preferred him to be known, did not appear on either occasion which was a pity, since he would have made an excellent suspect – especially since they already knew that behind his genteel, respectable image was an unscrupulous, ruthless character.

'Don't be too despondent,' said Lou, looking round at three glum faces. The Mr Bigs of the antiques world probably prefer not to get their hands dirty by doing the stealing themselves, they would sooner send their minions to do it. The same holds true for property developers like Reginald Whitehouse. I've just had a thought,' she added, clicking her fingers. 'Isn't it perfectly possible that those two pairs of dodgy lads who visited Chumley on the dates we know about were sent there by the likes of Mr Creepy? And possibly the first raid was carried out by members of the very same gang?'

Jack and Emily nodded. Neither of them understood what minion meant, but they guessed it was some sort of servant or dogsbody.

'So er, what's the next step to take, Lou?' asked Emily, hesitantly.

'We finish ploughing through these pictures, then we draw up a clear list of all our suspects so far,' said Lou, decisively. 'Let's not assume anything. Everyone who is a possibility goes on the list and they stay on it unless they can be eliminated.'

'But how exactly do we go about eliminating people?' queried Emily.

'I'm not totally sure, to be honest,' admitted Lou. 'I haven't been a detective for very long! Listen, we're all groping in the dark. We're children and we've never done anything like this before. When we were on the trail of smugglers at Whistling Sands that was different. In a way it was easier, because we more or less knew who we were after. When Mick came out of the Vaynol pub patting his tummy and walking off up the hill we knew that he was our man – or at least David did, and he followed him and found out where he was going. This time we're chasing shadows. We don't know who the bad guys are, but thanks to our hard work over the last couple of days, we're aware of who they *might* be. We just have to feel our way forwards and play to our strengths. We're not the police; we don't have powers of arrest and a pair of handcuffs to lock round people's wrists, but as children we can be pretty inquisitive without people having a clue what we're up to.'

Lou got up and stretched, turning to Jack and Emily and looking at them both with her piercing emerald eyes. 'We have another advantage, too, over the police – don't we?'

Jack nodded, understanding instantly what she meant. 'We have the determination to get to the bottom of this mystery. Whereas they can't be bothered.'

CHAPTER TWELVE

Who could it be?

LOU, Jack and Emily set about compiling an 'official shortlist of suspects' as Jack rather grandly insisted on calling it, although it wasn't as short as he would have liked.

'I see no reason whatsoever for including tradesmen like butchers and cake shop owners and official guides,' he said. 'They are bound to be going to and fro from Chumley Towers on a daily basis, as Lord and Lady Somerset source much of the refreshments and hot food that they serve in the tearoom locally. We have known these people for years and they're very well thought of. There's no way they would stoop to thieving from Chumley Towers. I find it rather unpleasant to have to put them on our list.'

'Fair enough, so these people are not prime suspects,' said Lou. 'I'm not suggesting for one minute that the likes of your cheery village butcher and baker are anything but remote possibilities. Nonetheless, anyone who was there on both December 12th and 21st automatically merits being on the list for now.'

'It's more of a long list than a shortlist,' objected Jack.

'Also,' said Lou, ignoring him, 'like I said before, I want people included who only appeared once or who didn't appear at all – if there is the slightest reason to suspect them. We have to bear in mind that the thefts might be the work of more than one person.'

'Fair enough,' said Jack. 'But I'm not going to call it a shortlist for now, I shall just call it a list.' He took a pen and crossed through the word 'short'.

'Fine,' said Lou, wearily. 'Call it what you like.

You're beginning to sound rather like David, by the way. Come to think of it, I wonder what's happened to him. I hope he's all right. Do you think we should go after him?'

'He often goes off in a huff,' said Jack. 'There's no need to worry. He just prefers to be on his own sometimes.'

Lou pursed up her lips and pushed her dark fringe out of her eyes. 'Okay, as long as you're sure. Let's sort our shortlist out – or rather our "list", then if he's not back by this afternoon, we should try and find him.'

By the time the list was finished, nearly two hours later, an appetising aroma of spiced pumpkin soup was wafting through the pencil-thin gap beneath the study door.

'Lunch will be in about twenty minutes,' called Mrs Johnson.

'Hey mum!' shouted Jack, through the door. 'Can you come here for a minute, and get dad too if he's around? You might be able to help us with something.'

'You're dad's in the garden moving a load of logs he's had blocking the garage for the last three weeks into the wood store,' called back his mum. 'Hang on, I'll see if I can find him. He was ever so keen to give you a hand with your detective work. Paul, Paul!'

In a couple of minutes, Mr and Mrs Johnson appeared in the study to find the three children poring over their rows of mugshots.

'Before you ask, David's gone for a walk,' said Jack. 'Anyway, can you help us try and identify a few characters from the CCTV footage? These are the photos that Lou took each time we froze the film. We need some help on a couple of them. We think they're local but it would be good if you could confirm that.'

'That young chap with the beard is, er, oh dear, what's his name now?' stuttered Mr Johnson. 'I tell you where he works – in the Bull's Head pub in the high street. He's a barman there. Isn't it maddening, his name's on the tip of my tongue. His nickname's Vlad, but his real name is erm, Colin, that's right, Colin.'

'Oh good,' said Jack. 'What about his surname?'

'Don't his parents run the general stores a few doors further down?' said Mrs Johnson.

'That's right,' said her husband. 'Drayman's – good little place, although a bit overpriced, if you ask me.'

'True but the point is, the children want to know his surname, well then presumably, it's Drayman,' Mrs Johnson pointed out.

'It is! It's come back to me now, you're quite right, Colin Drayman,' said Mr Johnson. 'But as I say, we all known him down the Bull's Head as "Vlad".

'Why?' asked Lou.

'Well, it's a couple of things,' said Mr Johnson. 'Firstly, because he looks a bit like Vladimir Lenin, with his dark, frowning looks and goatee beard, and secondly because he's a revolutionary, too – or would be, given the chance. I don't know if you've come across Lenin in history at school – he was the chap who led the Russian revolution in 1917 and had the royal family overthrown. Very into his politics is Vlad, of the Left-wing variety. He's Malpas's resident communist, you might say.'

'Your dad's been a communist in the past, hasn't he, Lou,' said Emily, in a serious, dead-pan voice, to peals of laughter from her parents.

'No, Emily, he's been a *columnist* on a newspaper – and he wasn't plotting the revolution either,' said Lou, chuckling. 'A communist is someone who believes that all property belongs to the state, rather than to private people or companies, and everyone contributes according to their abilities and needs, is that more or less right, Mr Johnson?'

'Yes,' he replied. 'But there's a bit more to it than that

– communists resent wealthy people for having too large a slice of the cake, as they see it. They want to deprive them of much of their wealth and redistribute it to those who are needier. There's a lot of jealousy involved, if you ask me.'

'So, this Vlad as you call him, is that how he thinks?' asked Lou. 'Does he believe in taking from the rich – say, people like the Somersets, and handing it over to the poor?'

'Something like that,' replied Mr Johnson. 'Yes, come to think of it, that's very much what he believes. We have some fiery old ding-dongs with him sometimes when he's behind the bar of the Bull's Head. We're all Tories you see, in the main, and he doesn't half get it in the neck when he starts blathering on about the privileged upper classes and how the aristocracy don't have a place in twenty-first century Britain.'

'And what does he have to say about the Somersets, specifically, after all they are aristocrats?' asked Lou.

'Yes, quite. Oh hates them, really he does. He says that stately home of theirs should be bulldozed or turned into a hospital or an old people's home or something, and put to good use for the community. He was banging on about it only the other night but the landlord, Steve, told Vlad to calm it down a bit and then he sent him down the cellar to change a beer barrel. By the time Vlad had surfaced we had all moved on to football and whether Chester FC would ever make it back into the football league. Vlad hates sport so he shut up at that point and went off round the pub picking up empty glasses.'

Jack and Emily were staring vacantly out of the window at this point, bored of their father's tales from the pub, but Lou listened intently.

'Mr Johnson, you see that T-shirt Vlad is wearing on the CCTV image. Can you make out what that strange emblem is on the front of it?'

'Yes indeed. It's a hammer and sickle. It's a communist symbol. The old Soviet Union, what we now know simply as Russia, used to have that on its flag.'

'Good,' said Lou. 'That's very interesting. We must find out more about Vlad. While you're both there, what about these other characters whom we saw on the CCTV?'

Mrs Johnson was able to identify the old lady. 'I recognise her. She's a dreadful, mean old thing. Do you know what she does at church each week? Throws two single coppers into the collection plate. Oh yes, drops them in at some height too, so they make a loud chink as they land. Mary Armstrong, her name is. A "Mrs" not a "Miss" apparently, although who she was ever married to is a mystery. I've certainly never seen her with anyone. Probably bumped whoever it was off, I shouldn't wonder.'

'Oh really, mum!' said Emily, shocked, her big blue eyes opening wide. 'You shouldn't say such things. She can't help it if she's poor – what does the Bible say about the small donations from those who can least afford it being the most important.'

'True, true,' said Mrs Johnson. 'At least she does actually go to church which is more than can be said for most people these days. I don't really care what she throws in the collection box, I just wish she'd spend what little she has on soap so she smells a bit fresher.'

'What about her?' asked Lou, trying hard to keep a straight face. She pointed to a picture of the fairly young woman, whom she had likened to a wren clucking about. 'She was there on both occasions. She caught my eye because there's something a bit not right about her. She looks rather startled, as if she'd just seen a ghost and that coat is way too big for her. There's certainly room to stuff a few small items in.'

'Hmm, you're right there, Lou,' said Mr Johnson, 'and

a couple of rabbits too, I'll be bound. It's a lovely old poacher's overcoat she's got on.'

'I do think we're being rather mean to these people,' objected Emily, who was very sensitive to this sort of thing. 'We've just been taught in school that you shouldn't judge people by their appearance, but by their personalities and their character.'

'You're quite right, Emily,' said her mother. 'Only Mary Armstrong doesn't have a nice personality, that's the problem, or if she does she keeps it very well hidden. As for the youngish woman in the over-sized coat, I have no idea. I don't recognise her at all.'

'Nor me,' said Mr Johnson. 'She's probably not from round here.'

'No, she may not be,' said Lou, 'it's just that on these two occasions, the weather was so dreadful we think it unlikely anyone would have travelled from far afield. The roads were blocked with snow on Sunday if you remember. It's a good thing I got here the day before, come to think of it.'

'They're still not great,' said Mrs Johnson. 'And a lot of the minor roads have started to become very icy. I nearly toppled over earlier on when I went to put the bins out. It's another lovely, sunny day but it's freezing cold. I hope David gets back soon, it's not like him to be out for hours in conditions like this.'

'I'll go out and scout around for him,' said Lou. 'Jack, you stay here and finish off our shortlist, okay? And Emily you help him. Here, I scribbled a few notes while your parents were talking. See if you can make sense of it then add it to the Word document I've created.'

Jack's face fell momentarily. He would have liked to accompany Lou. But he sensed that she wished to go alone. It was probably the best option. David could be such a complex person sometimes, it would not do for all three of them to be scouring the village for him.

CHAPTER THIRTEEN

David in trouble

'ARE the roads safe enough for me to cycle on, do you think?' asked Lou, looking up at Mr and Mrs Johnson. 'I was planning to borrow Jack's bike.'

'Yes, you should be okay, just about,' said Mr Johnson. 'The wheels have got rugged outdoor tyres fitted which should grip reasonably well, and most of the village roads are passable now. The gritters have been out and done a good job.'

'Is that okay, Jack? I know you want to come too, but compiling a clear list of suspects will be a brilliant job done. Also, I really want to get to the bottom of what's bugging David and I might have more chance on my own,' said Lou.

Jack nodded. He felt pleased that Lou had entrusted him with the task of drawing up the official list of suspects, and noting down what was known about them and the reason why they were under scrutiny. He felt a growing sense of unease that their prime suspect would turn out to be Kevin Bounderton – his best schoolmate's dad, of all people! But as Lou said, it was important not to assume anything at this stage.

He came outside to wave Lou off as she rode away, her green woollen hat pulled down firmly over her ears and thick suede gloves on her hands. It was another bitterly cold day. The sun hung low in a milky blue sky, its feeble rays brightening the deep snow blanketing gardens and rooftops but offering little warmth.

Tomorrow would be Christmas Eve and Lou hoped that the wintry conditions would endure through Christmas Day and beyond. It was lovely to be surrounded by such a beautiful spectacle and to share that experience with Jack and his family. She was determined, too, to discover what was bugging David and do what she could to cheer him up. It would be a pity if the most perfect Christmas was marred by his sulky gloominess. It wouldn't spoil the occasion for her, but it might for the others. Above all, David himself should enjoy the day. Yet for reasons she could not fully fathom, David seemed to be retreating into himself again.

She overtook a milk float parked at the side of the road and smiled at the milkman as he unloaded a crate of pint bottles. Then she turned into the slushy high street, where great mounds of discoloured snow were building up in the gutters. Lou cycled up and down, peering into shop windows as best she could. David wasn't a great one for shopping trips, of course.

Blow David! Lou would have preferred to spend her time more usefully, buying a few presents for the Johnsons with the twenty-pound note given her by Mrs Owen of Mynytho for her kindness at half-term. Then she could write and tell her how she had spent the money. The old dear would be pleased. But that would have to wait. Finding David was the priority. It could prove a harder task than she had expected. Malpas was only a village but it was far bigger than the hamlets with a scattering of houses and farm buildings that she was used to in mid-Shropshire.

If she was to have any hope of finding him, she had to think as he would. He was feeling fed up. What sort of place would appeal to him in such circumstances? The middle of a busy shopping centre thronging with cheerful folk doing some last-minute Christmas shopping? Probably not. He would doubtless have felt as she did walking through Church Stretton on Saturday – like a miserable outsider. No, David would go somewhere quieter, more reflective, possibly somewhere steeped in history. The church, perhaps, or the churchyard? Or a solitary stroll down some dark lane around the back of it?

She took the steep road leading towards St Oswald's. It rose up in front of her; a fine, gothic structure – seven hundred years old according to Mr Johnson, built from huge blocks of red sandstone. Hideous gargoyles glared down from above the gated, arched entrance porch topped with ornate pinnacles. A Victorian-style street lamp stood nearby, capped picturesquely with a dusting of snow. In the distance lay undulating, snow-bound fields.

Lou could imagine David sauntering mournfully about the churchyard, reading inscriptions on the graves and seeking out the headstone with the oldest date on it. Yet there was no immediate sign of him. She would know soon enough. All she had to do was spot his small footprints in the snow. She leant Jack's bike against a railing and locked it before climbing the steep steps. There were no prints on the path itself but then she noticed a series of meandering indentations matching David's boots across the snow-covered grass, veering off to the rear of St Oswald's. She followed them.

Suddenly, they were joined by numerous others. Behind the church was a large expanse of lawn, dotted with conifers and broadleaved trees. The snow had been disturbed in several places; worn so thin that green slivers showed through. It looked like lumpy parsley sauce. Had there been some sort of scuffle?

Instinctively, Lou pressed her lean frame against the church wall, tucking herself in behind a protruding buttress. She stood poised, on the balls of her feet, as she often did when she sensed danger. She listened intently. A noise, like a low thudding, was coming from further off – seemingly from beneath the tall, solemn yew tree.

She tiptoed silently across, taking cover behind a shrub, then peeked out. A gang of five boys, aged eleven or twelve, were scraping up snow in their bare hands and hurling snowballs towards the base of the tree. Lou could just make out their target: another lad. His face, hair and upper body were caked in white. He looked almost like a comical snowman taking shape. He was shaking and whimpering. Lou guessed it was David. She bounded forward and sprang at one of the boys who had just shaped a huge snowball, packed hard with the intention to hurt.

She leapt on him, taking him completely unawares. He staggered backwards and fell. Lou thumped him hard in the stomach and he doubled over in agony. Lou rushed over to their target and brushed the snow from his face and neck. It was David. His cheeks were mottled pink and blue with the cold. Crimson beads of blood formed a dotted line where a sharp sliver of ice had cut him. His eyes were puffy; his hair sodden wet. She helped him to his feet, then turned to the others, fixing them one by one with a fierce, contemptuous glare.

'What on earth have you done to him?'

'We were just having a friendly snowball fight. It was only a bit of fun. He's our mate, aren't you, Johnson?' said one of them, wearing a black puffer jacket which made him look chunkier than he really was.

'You weren't having a bit of fun, you were attacking him. Look at the state of him!' Lou's eyes flashed with anger. 'You covered him in thick snow and pelted him with snowballs packed so tight they're like solid ice. He could have got hypothermia and frozen to death. I've a good mind to report you lot to the police for assault. You sicken me.'

The lads looked sheepish and uneasy. They had not expected their activities to be interrupted by a girl barely older than themselves but vastly sharper and more intelligent.

'He had it coming,' said another one, smallish build, wearing glasses, with a mean, sly-looking face.

'Why did he have it coming?' asked Lou.

'He's in our class at school, okay, and he's been a right pain all term. He thinks he's posh, yeah, 'cos he lives on Green Lane in a big detached house whereas we all live on the council estate at the bottom of the hill. Anyway, he's been bragging about the stuff he gets up to in the holidays. We've asked him to prove he was telling the truth and if he couldn't, he was going to get a punishment. Well, he's just had his punishment.'

'I was only telling them about our brush with the s-smugglers at Abersoch, Lou, and our hunt for Anglo-Saxon treasure in St-St-Staffordshire,' stammered David, his teeth chattering with cold.

'You should be careful that it doesn't sound like boasting,' said Lou. But that's no excuse for your disgusting bullying,' she added, turning back to the gang. 'And for your information, everything that David told you was completely true. He wasn't making any of it up – he didn't need to.'

'Are you Lou then,' said the chubby lad in the puffer jacket. 'We've heard all about you. We thought he'd made you up as well.'

'Never you mind what my name is,' said Lou. 'Now you better apologise to David for what you've done.'

'If it's true,' said the mean-looking boy in the glasses, 'then what happened to all that treasure you dug up? Finders keepers innit? So David should have a good few gold coins and daggers and stuff like that. If so, how come he's never shown us any?'

'All the treasure that we dug up in Staffordshire was handed over to the authorities,' said Lou, matter of factly. 'An inquest will be held next March to determine its value and what happens to it. It's not finders keepers. We haven't got a single item because we don't have the right to keep anything – that's why David has got nothing to show you.'

'He won't tell us where you dug it up, neither,' said puffer jacket. 'We'd like to know and take a trip down there ourselves, see if we could find a few things. We do a bit of buyin' and sellin' of old stuff, you see,' he added, trying to sound important.

The mean-looking boy chuckled. 'Peter just picks up anything, anywhere he can find it. He's always getting old dears in the village to give him bits and bobs, thinking he's a sweet boy and then off he goes to flog the lot at markets and car boot sales.'

'Really,' said Lou. 'I'm amazed anyone falls for that. Anyway tell them, David. It's quite okay. Let them know. In return, I want you to promise to leave him alone from now on, do you understand?'

David looked hesitantly at her. 'We dug up what has become known as the second Staffordshire Hoard in a field just north of the village of Wall in Staffordshire near to the A5, very close to a pond in a farmer's field,' he said, nervously.

'There you are,' said Lou. 'Now you know. The first Staffordshire Hoard, in case you're interested, was found nearby, just south of the A5, close to the village of Hammerwich. Happy digging. Now do the decent thing and apologise to David. He's far more outgoing and adventurous than any of you lot give him credit for. He's one of my best friends in the whole world and I won't have you treating him like this.'

One by one, the boys said they were sorry, including the beefcake whom Lou had shoved to the ground. They looked at David with a mixture of shame and grudging respect. There was obviously far more to him than they had imagined and clearly, all the tales he had told about his holiday adventures were true.

'Right, now clear off, the lot of you before I make that phone call,' said Lou. The yobs didn't need asking twice.

Lou took David's freezing hands in hers and squeezed

them. 'Your fingers are like icicles,' she said, looking concerned. 'Hang on, I've got a spare pair of gloves somewhere.' She reached into her inside jacket pocket. 'They're only slim leather ones but they're better than nothing.'

He accepted them, a little reluctantly, and pulled them on.

Lou took off her woollen hat. 'Here, put this on too and pull down over your ears. Come on, David, it's not as if it's pink or anything. Now, let's get you well away from these thugs and into somewhere warm.'

She linked her arm with his and they walked back as quickly as David could manage to the front of the church and down the steep steps to the pavement below.

'I'll take you to a café and treat you to a nice cup of something hot and a slice of cake or something,' said Lou. 'And you are going to tell me exactly what's been going on, do you understand?'

David nodded.

'Hang on a second,' said Lou, putting her hand inside her jacket pocket. 'I'll just check I've got that twenty-pound note safe that Mrs Owen gave me. She paused for a moment, screwing up her face.

'Oh no. It's not here! I'm sure I put in my inside pocket, folded up. It's gone! It must have fallen out when I pulled out that pair of gloves. How totally careless of me. Do you mind if we just retrace our steps a short way? I'm sorry, I wanted to get you away from here as quickly as possible.'

'No, it's fine,' he said. 'Come on, twenty pounds is a lot of money, let's go back and look for it, before those lads find it.'

They dashed back up the steps and as they did so, saw a tall, gangling figure coming along the path towards them, wearing a top hat and long dark coat. Lou's first thought was that he must be an undertaker.

'I say, you two,' called the man, waving a piece of paper in his hand. 'I think one of you has dropped some money. I saw this banknote flutter along the path behind you.'

'Oh, is it my twenty pounds?' asked Lou. 'I think I dropped it as I fished out a pair of gloves from my pocket. We were just coming back to look for it.'

'It is indeed a twenty-pound note. I must say I do dislike these shiny new notes with their lurid splodges of purple. In my day, banknotes were things of beauty. Here you are, my dear, and much good will it do you, I hope, although do remember that the best things in life are free.'

'Indeed,' said Lou, putting out her hand gratefully. 'It's, er, Mr Whortlebury isn't it? I bumped into you on Saturday in the high street with my friend Jack.'

'Why, how clever of you to remember me, having only made my acquaintance for a fleeting moment,' said Mr Whortlebury, his florid face lighting up beneath his whiskered cheeks. 'You must apologise to young Jack, if you'll be so good, for my brusque demeanour, I'm afraid I had a rather pressing engagement.'

'Hello Mr Whortlebury,' said David, nervously. He still had the jitters from before and was shivering with cold, and wasn't really in the mood for small talk. 'I'm Jack's younger brother. Well, not much younger, Jack's fourteen months older than me.'

'And I wouldn't have put it a day more!' said Mr Whortlebury, holding out his hand to David and bowing slightly. 'It is so terribly nice to meet you young people and on sacred ground to boot. Have you been looking around the church, it is a most impressive structure, is it not? I simply adore historic buildings such as these and, indeed, Chumley Towers. We are incredibly lucky to have such venerable and imposing edifices in our midst. Why, I could spend all day strolling around them and imagining myself back in a more wholesome, bygone age. Aah, it pains me that you young folk will never know the England of yesteryear, save from old books. Times have changed and I have not, I fear, changed with them.'

'Mr Whortlebury is incredibly knowledgeable about the history of the area,' explained David. 'He's an expert on Chumley Towers and St Oswald's Church and does guided tours of both which are very popular. And his illustrated talks are one of the biggest draws at mum's history society meetings.'

Mr Whortlebury swelled with pride. 'It is kind of you to mention it, young sir, I certainly have much to say on these subjects. I can only hope that Chumley Towers remains in its present form for me to continue to talk about it. It pains me greatly to hear of the difficulties the Somerset family are facing at the moment – we are distantly related you know – and wounds me to learn that they are considering selling up altogether. And then to be targeted by some thieving scoundrel, it really is quite terrible. One can only pray,' he continued, turning reverently and gazing up towards the church steeple, 'that the good Lord will ensure that they resolve their problems and that the majestic Towers, of which they are custodians, will survive long into the future.'

Lou and David nodded. 'Have you any idea, sir, who might be responsible for the thefts?' asked Lou.

'None whatsoever,' he replied, looking troubled. 'Someone with the base motive of lining his own pockets, I don't doubt. Unfortunately, all too many people are willing to help themselves to what isn't theirs, if they think they can get away with it. How many passers-by would have shouted after you that you had dropped such a large sum of money a few moments ago?'

'It was incredibly decent of you to hand it me back,' said Lou. 'It was a gift to me from a dear old lady and I would have been heartbroken to have lost it.'

'Think nothing of it, my dear, it was my pleasure,' said Mr Whortlebury, bowing again and tapping the rim of his top hat with his finger. Turning to David, he added, 'you look after her, young man. Good day to you both. Do drop in sometime for coffee if you're passing my place – the Old Smithy along Bluebell Lane. You can't miss it. I have a fine collection of egg shells and stuffed birds gathered from across the empire which might interest you.'

The children said goodbye to Mr Whortlebury and made their way towards the high street.

'Look after me indeed!' scoffed Lou. 'Other way round, methinks. Honestly, he is of the generation which regards all females as helpless, fragile creatures. He's a good sort though,' she said, patting her pocket to which the twenty-pound note had been safely returned. 'And he's quite right, not everyone would have the honesty to hand it over. I rather like people like him. So what if he's eccentric and a little mad? It makes for a more interesting world, if you ask me.'

'He's a very kind-hearted person. He's always check-ing up on the "old folk" of the village, especially those who live on their own – even though he's fairly old and lives on his own himself,' said David.

'How are you feeling now?' asked Lou, shooting a glance at him.

'I'm fine, honestly. Thanks for everything. It wasn't a very nice experience.'

'No, it wasn't. Anyway, since I still have my twenty-pound note, let's do as planned and get ourselves a nice hot drink and some cake in a café somewhere. And in return, you are going to tell me about those lads and how they've been tormenting you. No wonder you've been so moody these last few days.'

David sighed. 'Okay,' he said.

CHAPTER FOURTEEN

Lou cheers David up

'WHERE would you like to go?' asked David.
'I have no idea, you're the one who lives here,' retorted Lou. 'How about somewhere with the word "Café" over the window?'

David grinned at her good-natured put-down, rather than scowling, as she had expected. That was progress!

'There's the café in the Old Fire Station,' he said. 'Let's go there.'

The pair found a table by the window. It was lively and noisy enough inside for them to talk without being overheard. Lou texted Jack to let him know that she had caught up with David and there was nothing to worry about. She would leave it to David to explain what had actually happened, if he felt able to. Over frothy lattes and generous slices of coffee and walnut cake, David began to tell Lou what had been going on.

'I've never been all that popular at school,' he admitted, slowly stirring his latte round and round with his spoon. 'But I wasn't unpopular, either, I just kept to myself and didn't socialise much. Then, after our adventures in the summer I changed. For the better, I suppose, in that I was more confident and outgoing. Meeting you in the summer and all the amazing things the four of us got up to really boosted me. Anyway, I don't think people were expecting me to suddenly become more extrovert, and made me feel like I was putting on an act. It was as if, I don't know, I wasn't allowed to be anything other than nerdy, moody David. And when I mentioned how we chased after smugglers, they didn't always believe me.'

'But some of that got into the papers,' pointed out Lou. 'They could have read it for themselves. Much of it was provided by my journalist of a father – it's what has kept our family solvent over the last few months. Couldn't you have shown them some of the articles written at the time?

'I did and they sort of believed me in the end, but when I went on to tell them about our hunt for the missing part of the Staffordshire Hoard, that's when I came really unstuck,' said David, taking a bite of cake. 'Of course, it made the papers too and on TV but our role in it wasn't made public. It wasn't felt appropriate, was it, that people should know the identities of the children who found a great pile of Anglo-Saxon treasure and who might one day come into a lot of money arising from its sale.'

'There was good reason for that, David, and it was very unwise of you to brag about what we did,' whispered Lou, glancing round the café to check no-one was eavesdropping. The busy, converted fire station was filled with mainly older women with bags of Christmas shopping pushed under the tables. Lou could hear disjointed snatches of numerous jolly but mundane conversations, largely concerning what the weather would be like on Christmas Day and groans over what chores remained to be done ahead of the big day.

Lou leant over to David and hissed in his ear: 'don't forget that you live just down the road from Malcolm Finchfield who will continue to show an interest in what becomes of the Staffordshire Hoard. He might well turn up for the treasure inquest in March and might even seek to address the inquiry and try to contest our claim to be the rightful finders.'

David stared back at Lou, wide-eyed. 'Surely the old devil wouldn't do such a thing?'

'As you say, he's an old devil. Mmm, this cream bun is yummy, but it's very hard to eat without making a mess,' she added, rubbing her mouth with a serviette. 'Come on, David, don't look over the hedge for trouble. Mr Creepy got a caution from the police for what he did to us – that will take some explaining – and no-one is seriously going to believe that he found that treasure and not us. Having said that, you really must learn to be more discreet about these matters. I'm more worried about these yobs than old Creepy. I haven't mentioned a single word at my school about our involvement in finding the second Hoard and, unlike you, I know how to take care of myself and deal with jealous classmates.

'Because that's what that gang are, David, can't you see that? They're jealous of you for your involvement in it all and they can't stand the thought that the quiet, dorky kid in the corner with his head in his books has suddenly become far more outgoing and adventurous in a few short weeks than they'll ever be. Their lives are mundane by comparison and they don't like it.

'Added to that,' continued Lou, solemnly, 'they can't bear to think that you might come into a lot of money arising from the sale of the treasure. At the very least, they have a greedy desire to get their hands on some of what we found or to go back to the site and dig up some daggers and gold bracelets of their own. I suppose you told them – as I tried to, earlier – that we haven't held on to a single item, but they refused to believe you?'

'I couldn't win,' said David, miserably, staring vacantly through the café window. They mainly thought I was making the whole thing up, hence why I couldn't show them anything from the hoard. But also there was a suspicion that I might have my bedroom drawers stuffed with treasure.

'So, I was either a liar or a mean-spirited Scrooge who wouldn't share the spoils of his adventures with his "mates". They've been telling me for weeks that I would "get it" sometime over the Christmas holidays. I'd been living with it hanging over me for ages. Obviously, this morning I went off for a walk in the churchyard, which I love because it's peaceful and relaxing, and they happened to be out and about and they pounced on me.

'Looking back, I know I should have kept my mouth shut. But in fairness, it sort of slipped out by accident – someone was talking about the Staffordshire Hoard at school and I couldn't resist dropping it into conversation that we had found the second half of it. I know it came across as boasting but I hoped that the more they knew of our adventures, the more they would think of me and, I suppose, want to be friends with me. I was proud of what we had all achieved.'

'Pride comes before a fall, as the saying goes. You were daft, David, there's no other way of putting it. From now on, say nothing about anything, do you understand?' said Lou, her vivid eyes looking hard into his.

'But why then, did you tell them this morning exactly where we had dug up the second hoard and the location of the first one?' asked David, hesitantly. 'I couldn't puzzle that out.'

'To get you off the hook, of course,' retorted Lou. 'I had to tell them something. I needed them to believe you once and for all and hopefully now that they do, they will leave you alone. They know from me that all we found has been handed over. If they want to take their spades along to either of those fields and have a jolly good dig then let them, they won't find anything. Every item has been removed from both sites long ago, which have been scanned with professional archaeological equipment several times over. There were a handful of treasures that we did not recover that were found subsequently by experts. But your classmates won't find so much as a rusty cartwheel now.

'The important thing moving forwards, is that you steer clear of them, do you understand? Look at me,

David,' said Lou, fixing her eyes on him. 'I care a great deal about you, Jack and Emily. I'm a proper friend of yours. These others are scum. They might be bigger, stronger and louder than you but you are worth a dozen of them. Their friendship isn't worth having. Take me, for instance. I prefer to be on my own. I don't have many friends but the few I do have are really important to me and I know would do anything for me – like you three.'

David nodded. 'Lou, can I ask you something? What do you think of Bounder? Jack's blown away by him but I disliked him from the moment I met him.'

'I can't stand him,' whispered Lou. 'He's false and up to no good and the same goes for his dad. Do you know something? It wouldn't surprise me if the pair of them were mixed up in some way with the Chumley thefts – and possibly also that gang who set upon you. In fact, David, I need to ask you this, why did you have a funny turn this morning when we were going through the CCTV footage? You went all pale and nervous at the sight of those two shifty lads. Also, there were two others who looked a similar age who appeared on the CCTV from Sunday, December 21st. Are they part of the gang who attacked you this morning?'

David began to tremble. His coffee cup quivered in his hand. Lou took it from him and put it back on the saucer.

He shook his head but then nodded. 'Peter, the one in the puffer jacket, was on the earlier CCTV footage – I'm not sure about December 21st. I'd need to see the pictures again. But yes, they're all part of the same gang.'

'That's interesting,' said Lou, quietly. 'I wonder.'

'No!' pleaded David. 'We can't go after them. Think what they'll do to me if they find out that we suspect them of being the Chumley Towers thieves.'

'We have to put them on our shortlist,' said Lou. 'Look, unlike you I know how to behave subtly, without arousing suspicion. I wouldn't dream of putting you in any danger from them. But like I said, there must be a chance they are the culprits or at least, involved in some way. Think about it,' said Lou, her eyes gleaming, 'it's like we've said before, if you are someone well known and well respected in the community, such as an antiques boffin like Mr Creepy, or a professional something or other like Mr Bounderton – then you are most likely not going to want to get involved with something grubby and disreputable like stealing from a stately home. So you get a bunch of scallies like your classmates to do the dirty work for you, while you remain at a safe distance.

'So, if anyone is to get caught it will be a bunch of kids and not you, a pillar of the community. You slip them a fiver or two for their efforts which they think is great and then off you go, selling the stolen goods on for a small fortune. Plenty of reward and almost no risk. Isn't that *exactly* the way someone like Malcolm Finchfield would operate?

'Remember, the general public round here don't know him as we do. They just see him as someone suave and sophisticated, an expert in his field. Unlike us they haven't been held prisoner by him in a locked barn. Oh and think back to what that Peter said this morning after I turned up. He said they like to "do a bit of trading in antique stuff". Then that mean-looking boy said that Peter liked to persuade "old dears in the village" to give him things which he would then flog at markets and car boot sales.'

'Yes, the one in the glasses, pale spotty face and a blue fleece with a hood – that would be Harry,' said David. He gazed at Lou in admiration. She was more intelligent if anything than he was and infinitely sharper and more adept at analysing information and solving problems. It had simply not occurred to him that the thefts from Chumley Towers might be the work of a ring of people, with children at the bottom of a chain of command leading up to the likes of Mr Creepy. How satisfying it would be if that unpleasant man could finally be brought to book and put in prison where he belonged!

CHAPTER FIFTEEN

Shortlist takes shape

'YOU'VE been ages,' said Jack, irritably, as Lou and David walked in. 'What took you so long? Hey, David, your face is scratched, what happened?'

'Let's go into the study and we'll tell you all about it,' said Lou. 'How have you got on with your official shortlist?'

'Really well, it's looking good. I've typed it all up on the computer so it's neat and done some print-outs,' said Jack, proudly. 'You'll notice I've put the names of the suspects, where they are known, in bold type. I've also started with the main ones and then finished off with the less likely ones.'

'Good job,' said Lou. 'That looks really clear and well organised. We may have to amend it a bit though. David will tell you why, it's best that he explain. Where are your parents, by the way?'

'They've gone out to the village hall – there's a Christmas tree festival or something taking place,' said Jack. 'Mum says not to expect them back until around 5pm because there's mulled wine and mince pies and they're not coming home until they get them.'

Lou grinned. 'Fair enough,' she said. 'I don't blame them. Okay, let's hold our next case conference, shall we, and take a good look at your shortlist. It's great that you've typed it out on the computer, which means we can easily update it when we need to.'

Jack, David, Emily and Lou went into the study and pulled their chairs round in a circle. Jack handed round print-outs of his shortlist.

'So what happened this morning?' he asked. 'Where

exactly did our annoying brother get to?'

He glanced at David, expecting the familiar scowl, but his brother appeared reasonably relaxed and cheerful. He began to stutter and stumble a bit though, as he talked about how the gang from his school leapt on him out of nowhere in the churchyard, pushed him against a tree and pelted him repeatedly with tightly-packed snowballs.

His voice wavered and Lou could tell he was still upset and emotional underneath. He told the others everything with a bit of prompting and encouraging from Lou. They listened sympathetically.

'Lou was amazing,' he said, a little sheepishly. 'She just turned up and floored Andy Smith with a knock-out blow, then she turned on the others and pulled them apart – not literally, I don't mean, just the way she dealt with them. They were left speechless by her.'

'I felt like pulling them apart literally,' said Lou. 'It was a very unpleasant ordeal that they put David through. I'm just glad I got there when I did. Anyway, the interesting thing was what those boys let slip. No wonder they were so keen to know about our search for the missing part of the Staffordshire Hoard.'

Lou recounted exactly what had been said and David chipped in that two of the gang, including Peter, who had attacked him that morning, had visited Chumley Towers on December 12th, which was what made him tremble and get upset when he saw the picture taken from the CCTV.

'Were any of them there on Sunday?' asked Jack, eagerly. 'Did they show up on the CCTV that we watched, I must admit I can't remember seeing many youngsters of our age.'

'What do you think, David?' said Lou, pointing to the picture in the second row of two boys aged around eleven. 'One of them looks vaguely familiar from this morning, although unfortunately the picture isn't as clear as it could be.'

'Yes,' said David, decisively. 'Him on the left,' he said, pointing. 'That's Harry – he was helping Peter plaster me with snowballs this morning. If you remember, Lou, he was wearing a blue hooded jacket and glasses.'

'Oh yes, mean-looking face, that's right,' said Lou. 'I do recognise him now. And these other two boys – the one who was with Peter on December 12th and the other with Harry on Sunday 21st, what do we know about them?'

David shrugged. 'Nothing, really, except that they are members of the same gang. Matthew Cartwright is with Peter and it's Jason Curtis with Harry on the 21st. They are all in my year but I don't really know Matt and Jason that well. They are all as rough as each other, that's for sure. Certainly not the type to want to spend their free time walking round museums and stately homes.'

'I've just had a thought,' said Emily, quietly. She felt that she really ought to try and contribute something useful to the discussion and hoped this was it. 'December 12th was a Friday, wasn't it? In that case, surely they should all have been at school.'

'No,' said David. 'It was a training day for teachers. We were all given the Friday off. I remember quite distinctly it being a three-day weekend. I'm sure because I recall thinking it was bad that we should lose out on a day's education just a week before we broke up for the Christmas holidays.'

Emily looked disappointed, while Jack and Lou chortled at David's expense.

'Only you would be concerned about such things, David!' said Jack, with a grin.

'Anyway, it was a very good point to make,' said Lou to Emily, keen not to discourage her from taking part. So, everybody, I think we're making good progress.

'I'm sure David is quite right,' continued Lou, 'none of these four characters are the sort whom you would associate with visiting stately homes, unless possibly dragged there by their parents. It's puzzling and intriguing that members of a disreputable gang have turned up, in pairs, to stroll round Chumley Towers. I can't remember exactly from the CCTV footage whether I recall them actually paying.'

'Yes, it's hardly the sort of day out you would expect them to spend their pocket money on,' said Jack. 'So what on earth were they up to, I wonder?'

'Is it possible that members of this gang are targeting Chumley Towers in pairs, taking away whatever they can squeeze into their coat pockets – oh that's a point – they all appear to have their school bags with them,' Lou added, squinting at the photographs. 'Perfect for pushing in a few items as they walk around.'

The others looked hard at the pictures. They were grainy and dark in places but Lou was quite right – in both shots, the four boys could be seen to be carrying bags. On one, Jack could just make out the emblem of Bishop Heber School.

'I suppose,' said Emily in a timid voice, 'that if they were up to no good, then the likes of Mr Creepy, Hickman and Bounderton must be in the clear.'

'Not necessarily,' said Lou. 'These lads might be working for adults like them, in particular a certain individual with a genuine interest and love of history, an expert knowledge of the antiques trade and – that crucial ingredient – a ruthless and dishonest character.'

'Mr Creepy!' chorused the other three.

'But what about Hickman and Bounderton?' asked Jack.

'They may well be involved too,' said Lou. 'Don't you see? Mr Bounderton might be using his shed at the bottom of the garden as a storage facility. Stolen goods are kept safely locked up in there for a few weeks until the initial publicity about their disappearance has subsided. Then, they are quietly released to the likes of Creepy for dispersal in a worldwide antiques market.'

'As for the surly Mr Hickman,' chipped in Jack, 'he has the supreme advantage of being an employee of Chumley Towers, with privileged, round the clock access to the building and its grounds – making him a very useful member of this ring of crooks.'

'Absolutely!' said Lou. 'Good thinking. Hey do you know something, we are really getting somewhere now.'

Jack, David and Emily all looked at Lou in excitement.

'But why would these men need to use a handful of schoolkids to do their dirty work for them?' said Emily, looking puzzled.

'David and I were talking about this in the café earlier: because people like Kevin Bounderton and Malcolm Finchfield are professional individuals with high-status jobs and held in esteem by the local community. They won't want to get their hands dirty and risk the humiliation of being caught and publicly shamed. Much better if a bunch of good-for-nothing kids can be called upon to do that for them.'

'And paid a pittance for their efforts, probably,' said Jack.

'Exactly,' said Lou.

'Fair enough,' said Emily, 'I see what you mean. But if that's the case, then why would Mr Bounderton need to turn up at Chumley Towers himself? He was there on both occasions – why would that be necessary if children are being used to take the items?'

Jack, David and Emily looked intently at Lou.

She sighed and paused as if deep in thought. 'I don't know, Emily. That's a good point. Obviously, you'd expect Mr Hickman to show up at the Towers because that's where he works. Mr Creepy doesn't appear on either occasion but you're right, Mr Bounderton was there both times. Having said that, if you recall, he only showed up on the CCTV footage once – on December 12th – not on Sunday just gone. Yet we know he was there on the Sunday because we followed his footprints back through the snow. It's tricky. Why, as you say, did he turn up at all, if those boys were doing the stealing?'

'I've just thought of something else,' piped up Emily, keen to make a more positive contribution after having uncovered a flaw in Lou's theory.

'Go on,' said Lou.

'I wonder if Mr Bounderton was waiting to meet those boys in the grounds of Chumley Towers as soon as they had left the building, and took the stolen items from them at that point,' said Emily. 'That would then tie with our theory that he was carrying something he didn't want people to know about. So, he goes home via the woods, then straight down his garden rather than entering the house – not with a sack of Christmas presents, but with treasures looted by these schoolboys from Chumley Towers!'

'Fantastic!' said Lou, 'well done, Emily! That would all tie in nicely. Except, of course, that for whatever reason, Mr Bounderton *did* go through the main entrance at Chumley Towers on December 12th. I can't explain why. Perhaps he felt it useful to pose as an ordinary visitor on that occasion or possibly he was looking for specific items he wished the boys to take. Who knows what was going on in his mind? But if our theory is broadly correct, then his garden shed holds the key to this mystery.'

Lou got up from her seat and stretched. 'We need to take a look inside it, and the sooner the better. The question is, how?'

The others gazed at her, recognising that look of in-tense determination. Yet this seemed like another near impossible task. They hadn't a clue how they could possibly manage even to peer through the shed windows, let alone get inside. But if anyone could, it would be Lou!

'It's a shame that my list of suspects isn't much use any more, but never mind,' said Jack, a touch jealous that his ten-year-old sister had shone so brightly in Lou's eyes. Why couldn't he have thought of all that?

'Of course your shortlist is still of use,' said Lou, pacing round the room. 'Just keep updating it. Who knows? We might be completely wrong. There are still numerous possibilities and like we've said before, good detectives never assume anything. But certainly I think there's a chance, a real chance, that we have hit on the trail of the thieves of Chumley Towers!'

The others all looked at her exultantly. Wouldn't that be simply fantastic? They waited patiently for her to continue.

'Okay, how shall we go about it?' demanded Lou. 'Come on you lot, don't make me do all the work. It will most likely be me who ends up inside that shed so it would be useful if you helped decide how we can get in there.'

'Hmm,' said Jack, tapping his forehead repeatedly.

'Great,' said Lou, rolling her eyes.

'I mean, er, why don't we er,' spluttered Jack.

'Why don't we arrange to go back and see Bounder,' said David, suddenly, looking decidedly more animated. 'After all, Jack is a good friend of his, or so he claims. If we can invite ourselves back in again for more tea and biscuits, we might get a chance to nip down to the shed and at least peer through the windows.'

'I doubt we will be allowed to nip anywhere in that garden,' said Lou, thoughtfully. 'Certainly not to go anywhere near that shed. Bounder didn't seem to like the idea of us going out the back at all. I wonder what his father has said or done in the past to make him feel so jumpy. It's quite a long garden, isn't it, is there a way for me to get in from the bottom end? What's the other side? Is there any chance I could sneak in and at least take a look through the shed windows while you lot were indoors, being entertained by Bounder? Ideally we'd need to make sure we called round on a day when his dad wasn't there.'

'Hey, you might be on to something,' said Jack, slowly. 'That row of houses all have long, thin gardens which sort of peter out at the edge of the village playing fields. There's a boundary fence or wall of some kind but it should be possible to climb over. I doubt it's particularly high. I'm not totally sure about ringing him up and asking ourselves round, though, particularly as we just turned up out of the blue only a couple of days ago. It seems a bit pushy to me, I'm not sure Bounder would like it.'

'He seemed to like me,' pointed out Lou, matter of factly. 'So make clear I'll be with you or pass me the phone if you like and I'll talk him into letting us come round. Obviously, I won't actually be with you, but you can make an excuse for why I'm late and then I'll join you once I've either succeeded or failed to get into his dad's shed.'

'But how can you possibly get through a locked door?' asked Emily.

'With a key, the same as everyone else,' retorted Lou. 'Your job, you three, is to find me that key. You'll need to think on your feet a bit. Perhaps tell Bounder you need to go to the toilet. Then nip upstairs, discreetly open a window, look out for me in the garden and when you've spotted me, throw the key as far as you can towards me, preferably not into the middle of a bush or anything. I should easily see it cut a hole in the snow. I might even be able to catch it.

'Ok but there is a downstairs loo in the hall. So that's

the one we would be expected to use,' said Emily.

'Not necessarily,' said Lou, 'you might prefer the privacy of using the upstairs loo, no-one is going to object, are they? Or if you prefer, two of you ask to go to the loo at the same time, whereupon one of you will be directed up the stairs. No-one will go up the stairs until you've come down because they'll be polite and wait. So you'll have time to find a window and throw out the key. They open easily enough, you depress a button and turn the handle. If by any chance they're locked, the tiny stainless steel key sits in the lock on the handle itself.'

'But Lou, how on earth are we going to find the key to the shed, that's impossible,' objected Jack.

'Nothing is impossible,' said Lou, her bright green eyes flickering with impatience. 'There was a set of keys on a hook alongside the back door. Almost certainly they will be the ones. They were the sort of sturdy, old-fashioned mortice-lock keys that you'd have for garages, sheds and outbuildings and that's exactly the sort of place you would hang them. There were others on hooks inside the kitchen, I noticed, but they looked more like car or office keys or something.'

The others marvelled at Lou's powers of observation. None of them had noticed so much as a single set of keys inside Bounder's house, let alone analysed which would be used where.

'If we're going to give it a go,' said Jack, 'we better get on with it. Tomorrow is Christmas Eve, remember. Most likely, Bounder's dad will be at work but then he'll probably be off for a week or more, like our dad.'

'Very true,' said Lou. 'Let's try and get over there this afternoon, or tomorrow morning at the latest.'

Jack swallowed hard and looked nervous. Having suggested they act swiftly to invite themselves back round to Bounder's house, he began to have a severe attack of nerves. Although usually bolder than David, he was nonetheless capable of being shy among strong-willed boys in his class like Bounder. Usually, he would respond to a summons from the likes of Bounder, not be the one to seek out a meeting.

Lou read his thoughts instantly and was worried. Jack needed to hold it together when he called Bounder or he might cause him to become suspicious.

'I tell you what, shall I just text him?' said Jack.

'No!' replied Lou. 'I don't want to hang around waiting for his reply. Now either you ring him or I will.'

Diffidently, and swallowing hard, Jack picked up the house phone and dialled Bounder's number. Gisela the maid answered. She went to get him.

Jack stuttered and stumbled and turned red in the face as he asked, in a trembling voice, whether they could call on him again that afternoon or the following morning. Evidently, Bounder was not exactly leaping at the prospect of seeing them all so soon.

'Oh okay,' said Jack lamely, into the receiver. 'Maybe after Christmas then.'

'Here, pass me the phone,' said Lou. 'Hi Bounder, how are you, it's Lou here. I'm good thanks. Hey listen, we don't mean to impose or anything but we'd all love to come round and catch up again. I enjoyed meeting you the other day and it'd be great to see you again. I suppose you're a bit worried your parents might not want us crowding round, is there any time we could just pop by when they're out, or something?'

Fine,' said Lou, after a pause. She gave the others the thumbs up. Bounder had clearly changed his mind.

'See you tomorrow then. Yeah, looking forward to it,' she concluded, hanging up.

She turned to the others with a grin. 'Bounder seemed to appreciate my suggestion that we call by when his parents aren't there. He says we're to come round at quarter past eleven tomorrow morning. His mum and dad are due round their friends' house at eleven for a coffee. It doesn't sound like they'll be out all that long but hopefully it will be long enough. Gisela is bound to be in the house but I don't expect that will matter.'

THEFTS FROM CHUMLEY TOWERS

INVENTORY OF ITEMS TAKEN, FOLLOWED BY OFFICIAL SHORTLIST OF SUSPECTS

Compiled by Jack Johnson, Tuesday, December 23rd, updated after snowball attack on David:

Please note: The thefts have so far occurred on 3 separate occasions. There is only CCTV footage available from the 2nd and 3rd occasion. (For a full description of the items taken, refer to the inventory provided by Lady Somerset).

1st occasion: Sometime between Nov 29th and Dec 3rd. Items taken:
1) A trinket box
2) A solid silver tankard, with a Christening inscription on it
3) An antique set of drawers
4) A gold-plated carriage clock

2nd occasion: Friday, Dec 12th. Items taken:
1) Letter opening knife
2) Silver teaspoon set
3) A Victorian rosewood music box, which plays six airs including Home Sweet Home, The Last Rose and Auld Lang Syne
4) A silver hip flask
5) Solid silver condiment set on a tray, including salt and pepper pots and a mustard dish

3rd occasion: Sunday, Dec 21st. Items taken:
1) A barometer
2) A small oil lamp for a writing desk
3) A small oil painting of a ship in stormy waters

4) A Victorian glass paperweight
5) An Edwardian brass kettle

THE FOLLOWING INDIVIDUALS ARE SUSPECTS:

Gang of school pupils from David's year:
Two pairs of schoolboys from David's year visited Chumley Towers on December 12th and 21st respectively. All four are members of the same gang which attacked David in the churchyard earlier today (December 23rd). They have been plaguing him with questions over the last term about the Anglo-Saxon treasure we found in Staffordshire and demanding to know its location and what happened to it – and subsequently bullying him and calling him a liar.

On Friday, December 12th, Peter Blacksmith, accompanied by Matt Cartwright, visited Chumley Towers and could be clearly identified from the CCTV by David. On Sunday, December 23rd, Harry Jenkins and Jason Curtis could also be clearly seen going through the main entrance. None appeared to have parents with them. They all had their school bags which could easily have been used to carry stolen items.

Of these four, Peter and Harry took part in the attack on David, along with Andy Smith and another lad whose name David isn't sure of. After Lou floored Andy, as he was about to pelt David with more snowballs, Peter revealed that they liked to "buy and sell old stuff" and Harry mentioned that Peter liked to persuade "old dears in the village" to give him things which he would flog at markets and car boot sales. Bearing in mind that both Peter and Harry visited the castle on the two occasions when there were known to be thefts, these comments seem highly suspicious, making these two and fellow gang members prime suspects. It is also considered possible that they are supplying the antiques trade via unscrupulous grown-ups like Malcolm Finchfield (Mr Creepy).

Kevin Bounderton:

A stockbroker or accountant of some kind. Father of Jack's friend Tony Bounderton (Bounder). Kevin Bounderton was at Chumley on both Dec 12th and Dec 21st. On 12th he entered via main entrance and appeared on CCTV. On Dec 21st he was not picked up by the camera but was definitely there because we followed his fresh tracks through the snow emerging from a side entrance to the Chumley estate back to his home in Malpas via the woods. Furthermore, it is believed that Mr Bounderton did not enter his house directly but via the garage or side gate.

He then proceeded straight to the shed at the bottom of his garden with a bagful of items which he deposited before returning to the house. It was at this point that the four of us (by this time we were with Bounder in the lounge) met Mr Bounderton for the first time. Mr Bounderton himself revealed that he had gone straight to his shed with a bag of what he claimed were Christmas presents. He had earlier told his son that he was going off Christmas shopping in Chester. There is strong reason to believe that this is not true and that he was seeking to conceal the true nature of his activities that day and the items he chose to store in his shed.

Timothy Hickman:

The new gamekeeper and estate manager at Chumley Towers, having recently taken over following the retirement of Alfred Bellingham. He appeared on CCTV on December 12th and 21st although this is not too surprising as he is an employee.

He came across as a surly, bad-tempered and unpleasant man when we were given a lift home by him in his truck after our day spent watching CCTV footage at Chumley. He talked mockingly about the Somerset family and the wages he was paid by them. Seemed bitter about the fact that he didn't have access to a tied cottage like the retired gamekeeper. Talked about the need to make money elsewhere to make ends meet by whatever means he could.

Malcolm Finchfield (Mr Creepy):

Antiques expert and historian who runs an antiques shop, M. Finchfield Antiques Emporium, in Malpas high street. No evidence that he visited Chumley Towers on dates in question. However, he is an unscrupulous character who tracked us down to mid Staffordshire where we were on the trail of missing Anglo-Saxon treasure and held us prisoner in a barn. He is clearly someone capable of resorting to desperate, illegal measures in his quest to make money. Furthermore he is an expert in antiquities and makes his living from buying and selling collectable items. He might well be involved in receiving stolen goods from Chumley and using his connections and expertise to sell them on.

Colin Drayman (often known as Vlad):

Young man, late teens to early 20s, with thick, dark hair and dark goatee beard, dark eyes, pale complexion, visited Towers on both Dec 12th and Dec 21st. Casually dressed, wore a T-shirt with a hammer and sickle design on it on both occasions under a scruffy linen jacket, carrying a hold-all. Works as a full-time barman in the Bull's Head pub in Malpas High Street, where he is often known by his nickname 'Vlad', short for Vladimir Lenin, leader of the 1917 Russian revolution. Colin is known to be a revolutionary communist who hates the aristocracy, including families like the Somersets. He doesn't believe they should still live in a big mansion like Chumley Towers and has been heard holding forth on the subject to regulars in the pub. Believes Chumley and its contents should be sold off and the money go to help the needy.

Bearing in mind his views, it seems very odd that he should wish to visit somewhere he despises within the space of two weeks and on the very days that items go missing.

Mary Armstrong:

Mean-looking old woman in a trim, tight-fitting woollen coat carrying a large, seemingly empty canvas bag. Spotted on CCTV visiting Chumley Towers on both second and third occasions items went missing. Her manner was odd; reluctant to have to pay the admission price. Was she arguing for a discount? Positively identified as Mary Armstrong by Mum, who described her as follows: "a dreadful, mean old thing." Regular church-goer but very stingy when the collection plate comes round.

Woman, mid 30s:

Name unknown. Youngish woman, thin, mid-thirties, round-shouldered, slightly stooping with a furtive, guilty-looking face and startled eyes, appeared on both Dec 12th and 21st. On CCTV she looked almost like a wren pecking about in the undergrowth. Nervous, as if she'd just seen a ghost, wearing a coat way too big for her with deep "poacher's" pockets.

Philippa (known as Pippa) Swift:

Aged around 40. Turned up on CCTV both times. Former newspaper journalist turned regional TV news presenter, before going freelance. Had a lucky break with national TV presenting but work has dried up. Lives on her own and believed to have huge debts including a large mortgage and keen to make more money quickly. Interesting coincidence that she should be at Chumley on the two days when thefts were known to have taken place.

Charles Whortlebury:
Retired university history lecturer and active member of Malpas History Society, aged late 60s / early 70s. Well known for his flamboyant personality and Victorian-style clothing. Regularly works as a volunteer tour guide at Chumley Towers, and often gives talks on Chumley, St Oswald's Church, and other notable aspects of Malpas's heritage about which he is considered an expert. Seen entering Towers on both December 12th and 21st.

Hans Fleischer:
Appeared both times on CCTV. German, originally from Munich, who moved to the village with his English wife Sarah. He has run the village butcher's shop for many years, and regularly delivers meat to Chumley Towers' main kitchen and tearoom. Well known and well liked.

Audrey Lloyd:
Appeared both times on CCTV. Runs the cake shop and patisserie in Malpas high street. Regularly delivers cakes, buns, biscuits etc for serving in Chumley's tearoom.

Julia Oldfield:
Young woman, late teens / early twenties. Works on the till at the entrance to Chumley Towers, responsible for taking payment from members of the public and could be seen dealing with visitors on both December 12th and 21st. Nothing much known of her.

Reginald Whitehouse:
A local property developer known to be keenly interested in getting his hands on vacant land with a view to building housing estates on them. Believed also to wish to acquire large old buildings which have, for whatever reason, fallen out of use and to snap them up at a bargain price, for conversion into flats and bedsits.

CHAPTER SIXTEEN

At Bounder's house

ON Christmas Eve, the following day, Bounder appeared visibly disappointed and a touch irritable when only Jack, David and Emily appeared on his doorstep at precisely 11.15am. Jack quickly reassured him that Lou had been delayed but would be along shortly.

Jack did not, of course, have any real idea how long it would take for Lou to carry out her task, or indeed, if she would be able to. It hinged on them being able to find the right keys to Mr Bounderton's shed and, somehow, to hurl them into the garden for Lou to pick up. Jack was uneasy with that idea but couldn't think of a better one. This operation might not prove as straightforward as it had sounded when Lou explained it. Now, without Lou alongside him, it no longer seemed straightforward at all.

They trooped into the house feeling, once again, like uninvited guests. Gisela's quiet, studious face appeared to take their orders for drinks. That was the easy bit. There then ensued an agonisingly awkward silence after she had departed, as if none of them had a clue what to say. Bounder looked from Jack, to David and then to Emily. Interestingly, a groove had developed in the end of his straight, beak-like nose.

'So,' he said, pushing back his rather foppish, wavy hair. 'This is a surprise. I didn't realise I had become so popular all of a sudden. I'm pretty busy to be honest, so if Lou isn't going to show . . .'

'No, she'll be along in a few minutes, I promise,' said Jack, a touch desperately. His face was sweaty and pale and he looked visibly nervous.

'You don't look that good,' observed Bounder. 'Whatever's up with you?'

'I don't know,' said Jack. 'I could do with a glass of water if that's ok.'

'I'll get Gisela to fetch you one,' said Bounder.

'No need,' said Jack, suddenly and decisively, getting to his feet. Bounder's concern for his health had given him an idea. 'I'll just pop to the kitchen myself if that's ok. I'm feeling a little dizzy, I could do with strolling around for a minute or two. Actually, do you mind if I just let myself out of the back door for a little fresh air?'

Bounder looked uncertain for a moment but clearly felt unable to refuse. Jack really didn't look well. 'I don't see why not, I'll come with you.'

'Actually, I'll go with Jack if you like,' offered David.

Just as Bounder opened his mouth to insist that he would accompany Jack, Emily surprisingly came to the rescue.

'I say Bounder, I plan to drink my hot chocolate while it's still hot. Why don't you stop and talk to me,' she said, 'and let my brothers go and get cold together? I'd love to hear more about, you know, what you were talking about the other day.' This was incredibly bold for Emily and she hoped he hadn't detected a tremble in her voice.

'What I was talking about the other day?' said Bounder, mystified. 'Erm, oh yes, do you mean about all the work my dad's having done to the house, or the new Range Rover we're having?'

'Yes, both,' said Emily. 'You had me and Lou gripped. That's why we wanted to come back. You're nice to talk to.'

Emily's pale complexion flushed bright crimson. Bounder wasn't to know that it was because she felt miserably embarrassed and guilty for telling fibs. He assumed that she found him irresistibly charming. Bounder was a dreadful ladies' man who liked nothing better than to try to impress females of all ages, including his mother's own circle of friends.

'Okay that's fine,' he purred. 'Since my parents are both out it should be okay, but please stay close to the house, Jack. My father does not like strangers wandering down the garden. He's quite particular about his lawn and doesn't take to people walking all over it.'

'No problem,' said Jack. David pulled himself up from the squeaking leather sofa and followed him out. Gisela was in the kitchen clucking about. She poured Jack a large glass of water. He took a couple of sips then put it down on the table. The boys headed through the adjacent lobby room which gave onto the garden. Sure enough, a set of rugged keys were hanging high up next to the back door, almost out of reach of their young arms. David shielded Jack as best he could, in case Gisela were suddenly to appear, while he reached up on tiptoe to whisk them from the hook.

But the back door was stuck fast! It was swollen by the heavy snow lying firmly against it. Eventually, with a huge wrench, it juddered open. Jack and David spilt nervously out onto the patio. By this time Lou should already have scaled the bottom fence. There was no sign of her, however.

It occurred to Jack that if Emily could keep Bounder distracted for a few minutes, he and David might get down to the bottom of the garden and hand the keys to her directly. That would be safest. Gisela might spot them disappearing through the kitchen windows but she was unlikely to attach much significance to that. It just had to be hoped that Bounder, with a female to impress, would be more interested in her than he was in them.

'Come on,' whispered Jack to his brother. 'Let's go and see if we can link up with Lou. Just saunter along, so as not to look suspicious.'

A path led from the vast expanse of lawn towards a

smallish orchard and vegetable patch. Barely visible through the branches was what Bounder had referred to as his dad's shed. As they approached, they realised it was in fact a brick-built outbuilding, far larger than a typical shed.

'I must say, it's done me good to pop out for some fresh air,' said Jack. He spoke loudly on purpose so that Lou would hear him if she was around. 'I was feeling quite ill inside the house.'

'Yes,' agreed David, also speaking loudly. 'You definitely looked quite pale and jumpy.'

Jack and David glanced about them. Where was Lou? They fell silent and listened. A scraping, scratching noise came from behind the wooden compost bin at the end of the garden, next to the rear fence. It was as if some creature was stuck and trying to pull free. It could only be Lou, surely, and it sounded like she was struggling!

Hesitantly, Jack squeezed behind the compost bins. The fence was six feet high! It towered over him. No wonder Lou was having problems.

'Lou, is that you, are you okay?' he whispered through a hole in the wood.

'Yes,' came a hushed reply, 'but I am having a job getting over. I'm not tall enough. I thought you said it wasn't very high, you clot! Is there something you could throw over that I could stand on, like a crate or something?'

'Hang on,' said Jack, looking about him in desperation. He had somehow just assumed that Lou would have been able to scale that fence without a problem. How maddening if their slightly crazy plan were to fail – quite literally – at the last hurdle!

'Ah,' he said, as Lou tutted in exasperation on the other side. 'I can't actually see any crates but there's a sort of stool beneath the big apple tree. It looks old and a bit crumbly but that might do.'

'Well throw it over then,' hissed Lou. 'Come on, if we waste much more time they'll get suspicious.'

David went to help Jack. The rickety three-legged stool was surprisingly heavy as they hoisted it above their heads and over the fence. Lou grabbed at its legs but it slipped from her grip and landed with a thud on her foot. She gasped in agony. But there was no time to nurse the pain. She jumped onto the stool and grabbed the top of the fence with both hands. She was light, strong and agile and – just about – able to propel herself over. Jack and David helped her down the other side.

'Here,' said Jack, handing her the keys. 'Oh crikey, the stool's now the other side of the fence. What can we do?'

'Nothing. I think I've broken it anyway,' said Lou. 'We can't waste time worrying about that. You two clear off back to the house but don't run or anything. I'll join you as quickly as I can.'

Jack and David nodded and headed back past the apple tree and through the trellis gate. Every now and then, Jack clutched at his stomach, as if to indicate that he was really not feeling good for the benefit of anyone who might be watching through the windows.

Bounder *was* watching – and from half-way up the garden. He was coming to meet them, with a puzzled expression on his face, and a very pronounced groove in his nose.

'Wherever had you two got to?' he said. 'I glanced out of the window and couldn't see you anywhere. Why did you go wandering off down the bottom of the garden when I asked you not to?'

'I'm really sorry,' said Jack, looking suitably green with embarrassment. My stomach wasn't right at all and I thought I was going to be violently sick. I felt it best to disappear to a quiet corner somewhere.'

Bounder's lip curled for a minute as if the prospect of coming across a puddle of vomit somewhere in the garden revolted him.

'Anyway, I bent my head down between my legs and after a minute or two I didn't feel nauseous any more,' said Jack. 'I'm fine now.'

'Good,' said Bounder. 'That's a relief. Let's go inside then – so long as you're sure you've recovered.'

Jack and David followed him nervously indoors, hoping that Bounder, visibly rattled, would not notice the now bare hook by the back door. As for Lou, they could only pray that she would be speedy and join them swiftly in the house. She would have to present herself at the front door, which would be no easy task.

'So, where has Lou got to then?' asked Bounder, sprawling back down across the plush leather sofa, as the boys sank into the matching armchairs. His voice sounded casual but slightly strangled, as if he was cross but trying hard not to show it.

'Oh, who knows with Lou,' said Jack, his voice quavering. 'To be honest, Bounder, her timekeeping's never been her strong point.'

This was a colossal fib and Jack could feel his face prickle knowingly in response. Lou's timekeeping was impeccable. It was Jack who would usually run late for appointments as he sought desperately to find his shoes or coat or some such thing.

Another awkward silence. Jack, David and Emily all felt most uncomfortable and Bounder was doing little to put them at their ease. They struggled to think of anything much to say other than trite small talk about Christmas.

Eventually, Emily tried to come to the rescue again. 'Er, Bounder was telling me while you were outside that he and his parents and his brother Lucas are flying off to Tenerife in January. So he'll get an extra couple of weeks' holiday while we're all slaving away in school.'

'Oh really,' said Jack, brightly. 'Hey Bounder, you

lucky thing. Our mum and dad would never let us do that. They think parents who take their children on holiday in term time are damaging their education.'

'Are you saying my mum and dad are bad parents?' said Bounder, frostily, the indentation in his nose deepening again.

'Erm no, not at all,' said Jack, reddening. 'I, er, I didn't mean it like that. I'm just jealous that's all. I've never been to Tenerife, I'm sure it will be great fun.'

Bounder looked at his watch. David gazed out of the window. Emily, unwilling to seek any further attempts at light banter, fixed her eyes firmly on the coal-effect gas fire. All three were wondering how Lou was getting on and hoping desperately that she wouldn't be long.

CHAPTER SEVENTEEN

Lou gets a shock

NO sooner had the boys disappeared than Lou scampered to the large brick outbuilding which Mr Bounderton called his 'shed'. It looked the kind of place where you could easily store belongings securely without risk of them getting damp. That would be ideal if it was being used for the purpose they suspected. She went up to the windows. Immediately, it was apparent that peeking through them was not an option.

They had been covered with a thin reflective film so that it was like looking at a row of mirrors. All she could see was her own face staring back at her. Either that had been done to keep the interior cool and shaded, or possibly to prevent anyone from seeing what was inside.

She flicked quickly through the keys in her hand, glancing at the door lock as she did so. It was a traditional mortice lock as she had anticipated. Only two keys of the five on the ring would be a possible fit. The first, a sturdy dull grey one didn't work! Lou tutted in exasperation. Perhaps that was for the garage. It had better be the next one, or this little operation would end in failure.

Her heart beating, she took the other mortice-lock key, shiny and newer-looking. The outbuilding itself looked fairly new, so maybe that was the one.

'Here goes!' she muttered under her breath.

The key slid into the lock and turned smoothly, the bolt drawing back with a satisfying click. Lou's heart beat faster still. She pulled the handle down and nudged the door open. It did not creak mysteriously as you might expect in some TV thriller – but sleekly and silently. Whatever would she find? Lou could not wait!

The interior was dark with a fruity, musty smell which Lou couldn't quite place. The view through the windows looked tinted and slightly unreal. That would be because of the reflective film stuck to them.

She could dimly make out a light switch on the wall but chose not to flick it on lest it be seen from the house, although that was unlikely. Slowly, her eyes began to adjust. She could make out two large white rectangular boxes in front of her. They emitted a gentle humming sound. Both bore switches glowing orange. Alongside was a long wooden workbench with what looked like a block containing knives.

Lou glanced upwards, and gasped! She staggered back and put her hand to her mouth. A lump came into her throat and she felt like she was going to be sick. Hanging from the rafters were row upon row of dead birds and animals, trussed up with garden twine. This was the last thing she had been expecting. She put out a hand to the wall to steady herself.

She staggered outside and gulped deep breaths of fresh air. How utterly revolting! She had steeled herself to expect any number of things to be in there, from glittering stolen treasures to the mundane clutter so often thrown into garden sheds, including her own family's. But not this!

Then the same calm but stern voice inside her which had once saved her from panic as she patrolled the coastal path overlooking Whistling Sands in darkness, spoke again: 'Get a grip, Lou. Do what you have to do!' Her mission was not to be a squeamish girl but to keep calm and find out exactly what was going on in that shed.

With one final deep gulp of fresh air, Lou went back inside.

Keeping her eyes lowered, she looked around her, into all four corners. It was clear at a glance that there were no precious artefacts being stored, not from Chumley

Towers or anywhere else. Nor was there a stash of Christmas presents which Mr Bounderton claimed he'd put in there. Bounderton had been lying but nonetheless, their theory was wrong. She forced herself to look upwards again at the grisly sight above.

In fact, now that she had overcome her initial shock, the sight wasn't quite as grisly as it had first appeared – not to a country girl, after all. The hanging birds were mainly cock and hen pheasants; Lou recognised their distinctive feathers instantly. Among them were a few wild ducks and wood pigeons and numerous rabbits.

It was becoming clear what was going on. These birds and rabbits were *game* – wild meat destined for dinner plates. Hanging them for a few days improved flavour and tenderness. After that, they would be prepared for cooking on what was evidently a butcher's table, which would explain the block of knives. A Belfast sink with hot and cold taps sat alongside the table. On a shelf above was a pile of labels and black felt tip pens. In one corner was a stainless steel machine with a shiny silver funnel and a couple of black levers and switches. A sausage maker?

The big white boxes must be freezers and Lou could guess their contents. She stepped over and gingerly opened the lid of one. Inside were vacuum-packed bags of what looked like whole plucked birds and various meat joints. She pulled one out. It bore a label in bold black ink stating simply: 'hen pheasant, plucked' followed by the date from a few weeks earlier. Presumably that was when the bird was shot or prepared or something. On another pack was written: '5lb rabbit sausages' with a similar date. Lou opened the other freezer. That looked more or less the same, too – filled with dozens and dozens of meat joints, all labelled with similar descriptions, handwritten in black felt tip.

It was vaguely reminiscent of that time down the man-

ganese mine near Porth Ysgo, when they encountered
row upon row of strange packages. The thought made her
shiver slightly. She closed the freezer lid without seeking
to check out its contents any further, conscious that the
less time she spent in Mr Bounderton's 'shed' the better.

She pulled out her little camera and took a series of
shots. She opened a freezer and photographed the interi-
or. Then on an impulse, cursing herself for taking too
much time, she grabbed a meat packet at random, placed
it on the table with its label uppermost, and got a close-
up shot of it.

Lou allowed herself one final glance around before
leaving the shed and carefully locking it. Her sharp eyes
darted this way and that as she came out, as if she were a
hunted animal. She was exceptionally good at sensing
danger, and something was making her uneasy. She
could see no-one. But then she heard a voice, a booming
male voice and the scrunching of gravel beneath a man's
clumping boots. At a guess, the same boots which they
had followed through the snow the other day!

Lou dashed across to a nearby shrub and hurled herself
behind it. She peeked through its fronds as the man
approached. Yes, it was Mr Bounderton. Drat! Bounder's
parents must be home already. And his dad was sure to
be in a rage if he'd discovered that the keys to his
precious shed were missing! Her heart pulsated in her
chest. She felt vulnerable and exposed behind the flimsy
conifer. She desperately needed to rejoin the others but
whatever could she do? As soon as Bounderton had
checked the lock on his shed, he would be storming
straight back to the house to search high and low for his
keys.

Gingerly, she rose to her feet and peeked over the top
of the conifer. Bounderton was striding through the trellis
gate, stony-faced. He was seconds away from reaching
his precious shed. She stepped away from the conifer so

that she had a clear line of sight to its door, the bunch of keys firmly in her grip.

She would have no second chances to get this right. Lou threw the keys at the door, hoping desperately that her aim was accurate.

Yes! They landed on the paving slab right in front with a clatter, glittering as they were caught by shafts of morning sunshine filtering through the apple tree branches. Now, what would Mr Bounderton make of that, exactly? She would soon find out!

Along he came, muttering and cursing. The sight of his keys lying, as if by magic, right outside his precious shed did not seem to improve his mood very much.

'What the . . . !' he exclaimed. 'I'll be darned if I dropped those keys there! I must be going stark, raving mad. He looked suspiciously all round him, as if considering other possible explanations. Lou ducked her head just in time.

She heard him scoop them up and then peeked out again, observing him select the right one and let himself in. No doubt he would check the place thoroughly for any sign that his butchery empire had been tampered with. Surely she had left the place as she had found it. Hadn't she? Either way, it was too late to worry about that now. She now had a few precious seconds to get herself to safety.

Thank goodness, it occurred to her, that there was barely any snow on the slabs outside the shed due to the apple tree sheltering it. She didn't want him spotting her footprints outside it! Furthermore, she had to be careful of leaving a trail of prints back to the house. She needed a discreet route if possible.

Lou was in luck. A quaint narrow path wound its way beneath an arbour of overhanging laburnum trees. In spring, their drooping yellow blossom would look spectacular. For now they wore a thick white coat.

Whatever shady business Mr Bounderton got up to in his spare time, there was no doubting his ability to create an attractive garden, full of little nooks and crannies.

She scampered along the path, praying he wouldn't see her through the shed windows. Having emerged from the tree-framed tunnel, Lou saw the house looming ahead of her. She came across a little bench tucked into an alcove. She sat down, fished out her mobile and texted Jack: *Just given Bounderton the slip. Need to get in through back door urgently. Is it open and am I safe? If so will go to front door and ring bell.*

Come on Jack, reply, quickly, hissed Lou, staring at the screen of her phone.

A few seconds later, came a welcome beep. *'Back door open as far as I know. We're all in the living room. Bounder's mum doesn't appear to be home. No idea where Gisela is though.'*

It was time to break cover. Lou strolled from the alcove into the garden in full view of the house and made her way to the back door, taking care to mingle her footsteps with others already imprinted in the snow. The door was ajar. In his haste to recover his missing keys, Mr Bounderton hadn't even bothered to shut it. She slipped through the utility room and into the kitchen. To her relief, Gisela wasn't there. The voices of the others could be heard in the living room. She tiptoed swiftly past, towards the hall.

Blow! Gisela appeared from nowhere, with a duster and a tin of furniture polish in her hand. She looked quizzically at Lou as if puzzled that she hadn't seen her earlier on.

'Guten morgen!' said Lou, in German. *'Wie gehts?'* (Good morning, how are you?) Lou smiled at her cheerfully.

Gisela was startled to hear her native language spoken so charmingly and happily forgot her bemusement at

Lou's sudden appearance.

'*Es geht mir gut, danke,*' she replied. (I'm fine, thanks).

Lou, whose knowledge of German did not extend much beyond simple greetings, gave her another cheery grin and headed to the front door. She opened it gently then closed it behind her trying hard to make as little noise as possible.

She now found herself at the front of the Boundertons' house, staring down the long drive. What should she do? Walk away, then come back again? That would look odd if she was seen. Instead she counted slowly from one to thirty and rang the doorbell.

She prayed that it would not be Gisela who opened the door. It wasn't. It was Bounder, who had leapt up the moment he heard the chimes. He looked flustered and red-faced, not unlike his father.

'Where've you been, you took your time,' he said gruffly. 'The others have been here ages. I was getting pretty fed up waiting, to be honest.'

Lou stifled the urge to curl her lip at him. How could he be so unbelievably rude? Did he really think that was the way to make a good impression on a girl?

'I'm sorry,' she said. 'I had a few phone calls to make and some Christmas shopping to do.'

'Hope you've got me something nice!' replied Bounder with a snicker.

Lou smiled weakly.

He stared at her, as if waiting for her to say something.

'Right, well,' he said eventually, after an embarrassing pause, 'now that you're here you'd better come in. The others are all in the living room. I'll get Gisela to make you a drink. What would you like, hot chocolate or something?'

Lou nodded. She might loathe Bounder, but there was nothing wrong with his supplies of hot, foamy chocolate.

A few minutes later, Gisela came in with a steaming mug for her.

'*Guten morgen noch einmal*,' said Gisela to Lou, with a knowing smile.

Lou did not understand the last two words but correctly guessed she was saying something like 'good morning once again'.

'*Ja, guten morgen noch einmal*,' she replied, lifting her mug to her lips and hoping that Bounder would not know enough German to pick up the nuances of Gisela's words.

On the contrary, Bounder seemed positively irritated by Gisela's use of her mother tongue.

'We speak English around here,' he said, coldly, his nose exhibiting its trademark groove.

In case there was any risk of Gisela offering an explanation for choosing to speak German to her, Lou quickly interjected: 'Mmm, I wish I could make hot chocolate like that! How do you do it, Gisela?'

'She opens a tin and measures out three heaped spoonfuls of powder into a mug like everyone else,' noted Bounder, sourly. 'Maybe ours is better quality or something.'

Lou's striking eyes flickered contemptuously.

'Anyway, Lou, I'm really glad you were finally able to get here,' said Bounder, catching her glance. 'So tell me, are you all set for Christmas? I can't believe it's tomorrow. There are going to be some amazing presents waiting for me under the Christmas tree in the morning, costing hundreds of pounds. How about you?'

It had not occurred to Bounder that as Lou was not spending Christmas with her own family, it was not her place to ponder what presents, if any, the Johnsons might have felt able to get her. She was caught off-guard and looked momentarily embarrassed but deflected the question skilfully, pointing out that Christmas was about much more than receiving expensive gifts.

The five of them proceeded to make feeble small talk for another half an hour or so, aware that it would look suspicious if they sought to leave too quickly. Jack, David and Emily chipped in on the festive theme and tried to appear interested as Bounder rambled on about the various electrical items he was expecting.

To Lou's great relief, Jack looked at his watch as the time ticked towards one o'clock and announced that they had better be going as they were expected to be back for lunch, which wasn't strictly true. If they could get away before running into either of Bounder's parents, so much the better.

They politely refused an offer of another round of refreshments but promised to catch up again in Christmas week. Bounder waved them off, looking a trifle mystified as they walked away down the drive.

CHAPTER EIGHTEEN

Unexpected development

THEY scrunched homeward in silence through the snow still lying crisply on the pavement. Lou seemed a little flat. The others resisted the temptation to enquire how she had got on.

Finally she spoke as they turned into Green Lane. 'Isn't Bounder a dreadful specimen? I would have thought you could find yourself a better friend than him, Jack.'

His face dropped and Lou gave his arm a squeeze. 'Sorry, I didn't mean it. Well I did, actually, but I didn't want to offend you. I don't like him at all, I'm afraid, any more than I like his father.'

The others all glanced at her expectantly. That sounded promising. What had Lou found out?

'It's really rather odd,' said Lou, 'not what I was anticipating at all.' She sighed. 'Let's wait till we get back and hold a case conference and we'll try and decide where we go from here.'

The wholesome aroma of roast pumpkin soup and freshly-baked bread filled the house. The children sat down at the kitchen table with Mr and Mrs Johnson and tucked in – their important meeting could wait for a while! Mr Johnson attempted to engage them in conversation about their morning's activities but sensed that the children didn't have much to say. Mrs Johnson suggested that they invite Bounder round for tea sometime but Jack just shrugged.

'Hey, you four, it's Christmas Day tomorrow! I'm surprised you're not bouncing off the walls and being a pain in the neck,' exclaimed Mr Johnson. 'Well, you're probably a little calmer and more dignified, Lou, but our three have usually driven us loopy by this time on Christmas Eve!'

Lou smiled at him. 'Believe me, Mr Johnson, it's pretty easy to feel calm about Christmas Day in our house.'

'Ah yes, I er forgot it's not a great occasion at your place, is it,' he spluttered, rubbing his chin.

'Don't mind him, Lou, he's always putting his foot in it, we'll make sure you have a great Christmas with us,' said Mrs Johnson, beaming warmly at her.

'I'm loving being here with you all,' said Lou. 'I'm having a wonderful time. We're just a bit flat at the moment, Mr and Mrs Johnson, because we thought we were getting somewhere with our little mystery, only it seems like we're back to square one.'

Jack, David and Emily gazed at Lou in dismay. Oh dear! So it *wasn't* good news then. Evidently there weren't any precious artefacts in Mr Bounderton's shed. Jack's mind filled with visions of typically dull shed interiors, brimming with rusty bikes, old toys and half-used paint pots. The three of them were now itching to get down from the table and hold their case conference. This didn't sound good at all!

Frustratingly, Lou seemed in no hurry and instead, gratefully accepted Mrs Johnson's offer of a second helping of soup.

'Don't look at me like that, you three,' said Lou, noting their impatience. 'This soup is lovely and I'm not going to rush it. There *is* something interesting to say about Bounderton's shed, it's just not quite what we were expecting.'

That teasing remark only made the others even more restless. Eventually, Lou scraped her bowl clean and followed them into their father's study.

'So come on, Lou, what on earth did you find in that shed of Mr Bounderton's?' demanded Emily, unable to bear the suspense any longer.

'It was most strange,' said Lou. 'He is up to something, but not what we suspected. Mr Bounderton does not appear to be stealing items from *inside* Chumley Towers but possibly from outside.

'Lou! You're talking in riddles,' groaned David, irritably.

'There isn't a trinket box or a music box or a fancy tankard or a set of silver spoons or anything else whatsoever from Chumley Towers to be seen inside that shed,' said Lou. 'Nor are there any Christmas presents. But you'll never guess what there is: game birds – mainly pheasants, along with a handful of wild ducks and wood pigeons, and a good few rabbits, all hanging from the rafters. I've taken a few photos but perhaps you better not see them, Emily, they might upset you.'

Emily looked green. 'What, they were *dead*? How could anyone be so cruel!' she exclaimed. 'The poor things. We must report him to the RSPCA at once.'

'But why would he do that, Lou, there must be a reason. It can't just be mindless cruelty, surely?' said Jack.

'Oh come on, the three of you,' said Lou, impatiently. 'I thought we were all country folk? I was shocked at first because I wasn't expecting it but it's not particularly horrific. Have you never eaten roast pheasant or rabbit pie, or duck in a tasty orange sauce? These creatures will all have been shot, most likely on the Chumley Towers estate, quite possibly by wealthy friends of the Somersets for sport. Shooting is a common enough pastime, at least it is around where I live.

'Anyhow, Mr Bounderton is clearly acquiring a large quantity and hanging them in that brick outbuilding which he prefers to call a shed. The meat is more tender and flavoursome if it hangs for a few days,' continued Lou, as Emily pulled a face. 'Then he's plucking feathers and butchering on that big trestle table he's got in there, so the meat is ready to be roasted and casseroled. After that, it's all bagged up and placed into two huge chest freezers. Oh and he's got what looks like a sausage machine as well.'

Lou pulled out her camera and showed Jack and David the pictures.

'And then what?' asked Emily, her soft blue eyes opening wide.

'It's over to Bounder's mum to cook everything, at a guess,' said Jack.

'More likely Gisela,' said David.

Lou shook her head. 'Not unless the Boundertons are eating game for breakfast, lunch, tea and supper. Those freezers are packed full. No, he must supplying to pubs and restaurants around here, at a guess, and making a decent bit of additional income for himself.'

'Is that illegal?' asked Emily.

Lou shrugged. 'Not necessarily. It just depends whether he has the Somersets' permission, assuming that all or most of that game comes from their estate, which I'm guessing it does. It's a bit odd though, the labels are all hand-written and very vague. There's just a date and a brief description of the meat: for instance, *Sept 21, hen pheasant, plucked*, or *Oct 17, saddle of rabbit x 2.* There were no reference numbers that I could see or indication of the origin of the meat, or the name of any supplier or processor. You couldn't sell directly to the public with labels like that, so they must be going directly to commercial food outlets and even so, it all seems a bit dodgy to me, as if this supply of wild meat is being carried out on the quiet, with a nod and a wink.'

'In that case, is there a chance that Chumley's new gamekeeper and estate manager is effectively a poacher?' said Jack. 'He takes rabbits and birds from the land without their knowledge and supplies Bounderton, who then uses his facilities at the bottom of the garden to produce oven-ready joints of meat and strings of sausages to sell into the food chain at a nice profit.'

Lou nodded. 'It's quite possible. Remember on my first day how we followed Bounderton's tracks in the snow leading away from Chumley Towers – he might have been carting away game birds then.'

'Also, he disappeared down the garden without even coming into the house,' added David.

'So what do you make of all that then, Lou?' asked Jack. 'It sounds like we've got two mysteries on our hands now.'

'I'm not sure what to make of it,' said Lou. 'If Bounderton is receiving game from the Chumley estate without the knowledge of the Somersets and without them receiving a penny of the proceeds, then that is straightforward theft. It isn't as serious as the thefts from the Towers itself but it's still dishonest and illegal.'

'I bet the Somersets would be interested to hear what he's been up to,' said David. 'And surely, if he is willing to deprive them of game birds and rabbits worth possibly hundreds of pounds, then what else would he be happy to remove from them? Just because we can't yet pin the thefts of precious artefacts on him doesn't mean he isn't responsible. We just don't know where he's keeping them.'

'Hmm,' murmured Lou, deep in thought. 'A lot of country people think it is their right to take a little from the land – it's even mentioned in the Bible. An ear of wheat or a cob of corn or firewood gathered from the forest floor or hedgerows. I've done that myself sometimes. Strictly speaking it doesn't belong to me. So the two don't necessarily follow. Also, we don't have absolute proof that he's done anything wrong with his butchery sideline. We must certainly keep our ears to the ground and our eyes firmly on both Bounderton and Hickman. There's definitely something odd about both of them. But I'm afraid, despite all our hard work today, we really don't seem much further forward and tomorrow is Christmas Day, of course.'

The others looked at her despondently. The mere fact that Lou had suspected Mr Bounderton of thieving from Chumley had been enough to make them more or less sure of it – yet for now at least they had no direct reason to link him. Possibly, he was involved in some sort of criminal activity related to poaching but a collection of dead pheasants and rabbits would hardly have the same significance to the Somersets as the loss of numerous irreplaceable and cherished antiques. They seemed to have hit a brick wall.

'Where do we go from here, Lou?' asked Emily, her cornflower blue eyes beseeching her to come up with a plan of some kind.

'Who knows?' she replied. 'Let's give ourselves tomorrow off, anyway. After all, who wants to work on December 25th? That said, we need to stay alert and on the look-out, using our eyes and ears at all times. It's keen observation and the ability to listen and interpret what we hear that may hold the key. Also, we must keep an open mind. A good detective never assumes anything, and possibly that is exactly what we were doing with Bounderton. We have a list of suspects and must keep evaluating them and working our way through them, adding new names if necessary and taking away others.

'At least we are actually trying to solve this mystery, unlike the police. Come on, don't look so fed up. The worst that has happened is that we appear to have eliminated Mr Bounderton. It still leaves us with plenty of other possibilities involving the schoolboy gang, the gamekeeper and a rogue of an antiques dealer – and others besides. Let me have another look at our official list of suspects. Jack's put a lot of work in on this, it's worth giving it a good read through.'

Lou opened a print-out lying folded in half on the desk and spread it out in front of them. Their eyes scanned down it intently. Would another name pop magically up to relieve their disappointment?

CHAPTER NINETEEN

The next step

'OKAY, for a change, let's read through our suspects from the bottom up, starting with the least
likely first. You never know, it might give us a different
perspective,' said Lou. 'So, we start with Reginald
Whitehouse, the property developer. Is there a chance,
however remote, that he is seeking to undermine the
Somersets and make them feel insecure in their own
home so that they move out? If it can happen in Mynytho, it can happen in Malpas. And what's he currently up
to? How successful is his property empire at the moment?

'Actually, Jack, can you start making notes? Let's get a
few thoughts down about the less likely suspects, just to
see what bubbles up. Okay, so for Reginald Whitehouse,
put that we'll want to log on to his website and check
what he's up to. Has he got any planning applications
lodged with the local council? They all go online these
days as public documents. If he's won planning consent
for another of his sprawling housing estates and his firm
is about to embark on a huge building project, he's
unlikely to be interested in converting large buildings
into flats. My guess is he would far rather build from
scratch, as it's sure to bring in more money. But let's just
run our eye over him.'

Jack nodded and grabbed a pen and paper.

'Who's next?' continued Lou, when Jack was ready.
'Right, let's see.' She ran her finger upwards from the
back page of Jack's list. 'We have a handful of local
tradesmen who deliver regularly to Chumley and who
passed through the entrance on the two days when we

know thefts took place. It's such a pity that Lord and Lady Somerset can't pin down the first occasion more precisely, that would really narrow things down, but never mind.'

Lou smoothed out Jack's crumpled sheets of A4 bound together with a paper clip. Right, we've got Julia Oldfield, the young woman working on the till at the entrance to Chumley Towers. Is there anything meaningful we can say about her?'

The others all shook their heads.

'There *was* one thing, Lou,' said Emily, suddenly. 'I seem to recall that about halfway through the day, the CCTV film showed her getting up from her seat and disappearing and she was replaced by someone else – another woman, I think. I suppose Julia was taking a lunch break or something but nonetheless, that might have given her an opportunity to sidle off, stroll around and pinch a few things and then return to the front desk without arousing suspicion.'

'Yes,' said Lou. 'Also, I wonder who the woman was who stood in for her while she was on lunch break? Lady Somerset would know. It's a pity we didn't think to query that when we talked to her. Okay, well let's make a note of that. We want to know a little more about this Julia Oldfield – oh and didn't Lady Somerset say that she was new to the area? That's worthy of noting that under her entry in our Official Suspects, Jack, because if she's new she won't necessarily have the same feelings of loyalty to the area or to the Somersets – exactly like Mr Hickman. Also, she's young and may be keen to rake in some extra cash for a deposit on a house or something. She can't earn very much working on the tills at Chumley.'

'Sorry, looks like I slipped up a bit with Julia Oldfield,' said Jack, crestfallen. 'I suppose I just never thought of her as a serious possibility.'

'She may not be,' said Lou. 'But think about it, if you were keen on committing a crime – in fact a series of crimes, wouldn't you do your best to appear above suspicion so that no-one thought to point their finger at you? Now, who's next? Oh yes, Audrey Lloyd, the owner of the cake shop and Hans Fleischer, village butcher. Any comments?'

'Both are longstanding, well-respected tradesmen,' said David. 'Audrey grew up in the village and Hans, although he's originally from Munich in Germany, has been here for years. I would bet my hat that they don't have a thing to do with these thefts. They're much loved and respected.'

'No, David, that's not the way a detective would approach this,' said Lou, reprovingly. 'It's perfectly possible to be much loved – and indeed, to be worthy of that love – save for the flaw in your personality which leads you to commit crime. None of us is perfect, after all.'

This time it was David's turn to look deflated.

'Lou's right, David. We can't allow our judgement to be swayed by how much we like or dislike someone. I hated the idea that the father of my best friend at school might be responsible, but in the end, I accepted that that wasn't a good reason for not considering him,' said Jack, perking up.

'Anyway, let's move on,' said Lou, glancing at her watch. 'We've got three or four useful hours left of Christmas Eve to work hard on achieving some sort of breakthrough and then Christmas will be upon us. Next up is Charles Whortlebury, whom David and I bumped into this morning and you and I did, Jack, on my first day here. Now, he's another one – just like the butcher, charming, affable and everyone likes him. But might he be our thief? What skeletons might be lurking in his closet?'

David, believing that Lou no longer saw him as capable of being a detective, was now in full-blown 'sulk' mode. He refused to say anything. This pleased Jack, who was now determined to tease out guilt wherever it might lie.

'Well, he was there on both days, of course,' said Jack, enthusiastically. 'Obviously you would expect him to be at Chumley quite frequently as he helps out as a guide but let's just say he would have plenty of opportunity to take things if he wished. Also, as I put in my write-up, he's an expert on the history of Chumley Towers and its contents so he would be well placed to know what was really valuable and therefore worth taking.'

'Yes, and as you also wrote, he's a retired history lecturer in his late sixties to early seventies and a flamboyant personality who does a great deal in the community and in particular the history society that your mum is chairman of,' said Lou. 'He loves the past far more than the present, seemingly. I wonder if he takes a keen interest in the acquisition and sale of antiques. By the way, is he on his own or a family man?'

'From what I know, he lives on his own. I don't think he's ever married,' said Jack.

'So, no family to support and probably his mortgage already paid off. Therefore, no obvious financial problems to speak of?' asked Lou.

'No, not that I'm aware of. He lives in a grand old house up the hill, towards Chumley Towers,' said Jack.

'He invited Lou and me to go round and look at his collection of birds' eggs when we met him in the churchyard earlier,' chipped in David, whose wish to upstage Jack got the better of his bad mood.

'And he also gave me back my twenty pounds that I'd dropped,' noted Lou. 'That points away from him being either poor or dishonest. Nonetheless, he is of definite interest to us because Chumley Towers is of huge interest to him. In fact, didn't he say something rather interesting, namely that he was distantly related to the Somersets or something?'

David nodded. 'Yes he did, come to think of it.'

'Write that down, Jack, to look into why Mr Whortle-bury might have an especial fascination for the place and what, exactly, is the nature of his family connection to the Somersets. Let's drop his name into conversation with your mum about him next time we get a chance.'

'We next come to Philippa Swift, known as Pippa, aged around forty and a journalist who seems to have fallen on hard times,' said Lou. 'Interesting that she should turn up twice at Chumley Towers on both days when thefts definitely took place. She lives on her own with an expensive house and car to pay for and doesn't have much work. Why, I wonder, should she seek to spend precious time strolling around Chumley rather than contacting media organisations for work opportunities?'

'She sometimes volunteers at Chumley,' said David, suddenly. 'I know because mum told me that she goes along and helps out with guide work there and other history society activities. She and Mr Whortlebury have become quite good friends since her father died suddenly last year. Mr Whortlebury is a similar age and has become something of a father figure to her. From what I gather from mum, he's rather taken her under his wing.'

'Right,' said Lou, glancing at Jack who seemed cross that he was not able to impart that information. 'Well Pippa is of definite interest to our investigation as well. She has what the likes of Mr Whortlebury, and shop-keepers like Hans Fleischer and Audrey Lloyd lack and that is a clear motive. She's hard up – and that's a good starting point for anyone willing to take what doesn't belong to them. I'd like us to keep our ears to the ground with Pippa and find out exactly how she's filling her days and by what means, if any, she is bringing money in.'

'Next up, Lou, is the woman aged around mid-thirties whose name we're not sure of,' continued David, pointing to the entry just above Pippa's. It amused Lou how he could switch suddenly from sulking to being as bright as a button. 'Do you remember, she looked decidedly shifty on the photos. Actually, you know what would have been a good idea with our Official List of Suspects? If we had included everyone's photo captured on CCTV alongside their entry.'

'Hmm, yes, that *would* have been a good idea,' said Lou, mischievously, stealing a glance at Jack who was now glaring at his younger brother. 'Maybe that's something which can be incorporated in the second edition. But it's still a fantastic job, Jack,' she added, clasping his paperclip-bound sheaves of paper in her hand and giving them a little shake. 'This is our blueprint for catching the thief or thieves of Chumley Towers. Your profiles are top-notch, aren't they, David?'

'Yes, they're fine,' muttered David, looking a touch deflated as Jack cheered up.

'Good,' said Lou. 'Now this youngish woman then, as we've noted, appeared to have a strange manner on both occasions when she entered Chumley. Have you got her photo there, Emily, that you cut out?'

Emily found it and Lou stared hard at it. 'Yes, there was something indefinable about her, that didn't seem right somehow. Why was she so fidgety and furtive? And it is certainly a very strange, unfashionable overcoat she's wearing – more of an old man's or, as your dad said, a poacher's coat! And your parents clearly didn't know anything of her or recognise her at all, from what they said.'

'No,' said Jack. 'Sorry, I should have noted that on her entry. It's odd in a way because my parents, particularly my mum, know most people around here, even if it's just by sight rather than by name.'

'Which strongly suggests she isn't local yet she was there on both occasions for which we have CCTV footage and on both those dates, the weather was poor,' said Lou. 'If you remember, Lady Somerset said that there had been "terrific high winds and torrential rain" on the occasion of December 12th, and we know ourselves that the place was almost cut off by snow on Sunday, December 21st. Furthermore, she doesn't appear the type to have travelled far. She intrigues me. Let's keep our eyes peeled for her, okay? If any of us see her hanging around, let's do a little discreet surveillance, and find out what she's up to.'

The others all nodded solemnly. Surveillance! That sounded exciting!

'And the same applies to the equally strange Mrs Mary Armstrong,' noted Lou, looking at the next profile. 'At least she's known to your family and, according to your mum, she's a pretty disreputable character.'

'Very much so,' said Emily, eager to add her contribution. 'She turns up at village social events sometimes and she's always on the take – wanting free tea and coffee and cakes but is never willing to put her hand in her pocket and pay for anything. She'll go to bring-and-buy sales and she might bring, but she'll never buy.'

The others all hooted with laughter at that and Emily looked pleased. 'Well, that's what mum says, anyway.'

'Sounds like an ideal suspect to me!' said Lou. 'You see how we're discovering potential in several on our shortlist – not just the more obvious ones. And now we come to another curious figure, Colin Drayman, often known as Vlad.'

Lou paused as she read Jack's lengthy description of him carefully. Jack looked on with pride. He had done a particularly good job on Colin, based mainly on his father's comments. The others said nothing, waiting for Lou to complete her analysis.

'Your parents mentioned that he was the son of the Draymans who run the corner shop, from memory?' said Lou.

'Yes, that's right,' said Jack, kicking himself for not having included that in the write-up.

'It strikes me as strange that a man who is the son of shopkeepers, having grown up right here in this village and who now occupies himself pulling pints in the village pub should have acquired such a seething hatred of his own upbringing, almost,' said Lou. 'Yet, despite loathing a place like Chumley Towers, he visits it – not once but twice within a short space of time, possibly more than that, for all we know. And while gripping a bulky hold-all which admittedly already looks like it's got something in it from the photo,' added Lou as she reached for the cut-out images of Colin.

'Do you think, Lou, that Colin might have been carrying something dangerous in that hold-all?' asked Emily, timidly, her eyes widening.

'I don't know,' said Lou. 'He's an enigma, this Colin. A strange guy with strange views turns up at a stately home which he hates, owned by people he hates and carrying a hold-all – not just once but at least twice in the space of a fortnight. What's his game? What's in that hold-all and was it substantially fuller and heavier when he left Chumley Towers than when he went in? I'd very much like to find out more about this man. If he's up to the same sort of tricks as the evil Idwal of Mynytho then we need to rumble him, and quickly. Is there any chance while I'm here your parents might take us to the Bull's Head, like they took us to the pub in Abersoch?'

Jack, David and Emily all grinned. When Lou was on a mission, there was no stopping her!

'Dad enjoys a lunchtime pint after church on Christmas Day,' said Jack. 'It's a ritual of his. As we're all a bit older now, you never know, we might be allowed to join him. It's a very family-friendly pub.'

'Oh and there's a new beer on sale there which he raves on about,' joked Emily. 'Of course, it'll be Coke and a packet of crisps for us at a guess.'

'That will do fine,' said Lou, smiling. 'Well look, the point is, we have to take our chances when and where they come up. Like I said before, the offender may not be our obvious choice – he or she will certainly hope not to be.'

'I can't help but feel we're getting nowhere fast,' said David, looking despondent again.

'You have to put up with getting nowhere, until you get somewhere,' said Lou, earnestly. 'That day we went to the Vaynol in Abersoch for an evening meal with your parents, we were all feeling a bit downhearted, if you remember, because our efforts at tracking down the smugglers at Whistling Sands had come to nothing. But look what happened later on – a breakthrough when we were least expecting it and thanks to you, David. Sometimes you have to rely on luck but hopefully we're the sort of people who make their own luck.

'The other thing I notice, looking at the list of items taken on the front page of your print-out, Jack, is that they don't seem especially valuable. Oh I know if you add them all together it comes to a thousand pounds or so but surely there would be more precious items – still small enough to fit into a bag or a pocket – which you could make off with? You don't have to be an antiques expert to understand that a handful of diamond necklaces and earrings from Lady Somerset's dressing table would be worth more than all this lot put together. Does anyone else find the type of items stolen odd?'

'My feeling is that the thief simply grabbed what he could,' said Jack. 'Possibly it points to a more disorganised, less calculating mind, that you take what's easy rather than more valuable stuff which would take a great deal longer to sniff out.'

'Maybe,' said Lou. 'Nonetheless can you note down as well, Jack: to look into whether there is some sort of common thread linking these items and if they might hold some sort of significance to a thief.'

Lou, glanced at her watch. 'Right, we better stop talking and get something done this afternoon while we still can. We've worked our way backwards through the list of suspects to the ones we were already very interested in, namely the schoolboy gang; Mr Bounderton, who no longer seems quite so promising; Mr Hickman the gamekeeper and estate manager; and Mr Creepy. It's nearly three o'clock – it'll be Christmas Day in nine hours' time. Can we achieve anything in the meantime? For now, I feel, we've got to go after the big fish while keeping everyone else on Jack's list under scrutiny.

'Our best bet at this stage, I believe, is to check out two types of suspect: those most likely to have taken the artefacts from Chumley and those most likely to have been the immediate recipients. So that means, investigating the schoolboys as the actual thieves and the people to whom they might turn for disposal of their ill-gotten goods: such as our old friend Mr Creepy. Do you agree?'

'Definitely,' said Jack. 'He's the perfect fit: an expert in antiques and trading them, but at the same time, unscrupulous enough not to ask too many questions about where his stock has come from.'

'Yet intelligent and shrewd enough not to want to be involved directly in any wrongdoing,' added David. 'Especially after his very close brush with the law in Staffordshire a few months back. He won't want to attract police attention again in a hurry.'

'Exactly,' agreed Lou. 'Therefore, we need now to flush him out if at all possible. Of course, he won't have stolen goods openly for sale in his shop but they may be stored under the counter, you might say, to be discreetly offered to the right client. Possibly, he will use the internet to open up a wider market. Now, I suggest we phone his shop posing as a potential customer and ask the vaguest of questions loosely related to the missing items from Chumley. Calling round in person would be ideal but he'd recognise us, of course.'

'Yes but his sidekick Duncan usually minds the shop and from what we learnt in the summer, he's every bit as crooked. The point is, he won't have a clue what you look like, Lou, although he might possibly recognise the three of us,' said Jack.

'Okay, good point,' said Lou. 'I'll nip out and go round then. I could easily be looking for a last-minute Christmas present, after all. This is a good instance where a child can ferret out information without causing suspicion – whereas a police officer would be spotted a mile off.'

'In the meantime, what can the rest of us do?' said Jack, looking at Lou earnestly. He was determined to do what he could to get them back on track.

'Is there any way of discreetly contacting a member of the schoolboy gang? Do we have an email address for one of them or a telephone number? We could then ask them if they had certain items from that list,' said Lou. 'It's a longshot but worth a try. What about car boot sales, or village bring-and-buy sales? Who organises them? Can we find out if any have taken place recently and when the next ones will be, and what sort of things are sold? Your mum might be able to help with this.

'Oh and there's your village gossip, Emma Bennett, who you could speak to. Actually, let's not bother with her unless we're desperate – remember she's as capable of gossiping about what we're up to as about anyone else. Let me think, let me think. Auction houses: they would be worth phoning up,' continued Lou, scratching her nose. 'The big one round here is Hall's, they've got offices in Shrewsbury and Ellesmere just down the road from you. Find out if they've got anything resembling the stolen items from Chumley coming up for a sale in an auction. Be vague at first and if it sounds promising, be a bit more specific. They might well have items listed in online catalogues. Go on the internet and look them up.

'Also, do a search on Google for a few of the missing items – see if they just happen to pop up in some online directory somewhere. Try eBay – the online auction site. Loads of people sell antique and collectable items there. It's too much to hope that the likes of Creepy would be daft enough to sell them directly under his own name but you never know. Give it a try. Remember, we're after a lucky break.'

The others nodded, while Jack feverishly scribbled down all Lou's instructions.

She watched him with amusement. 'Look, you won't have time to do half of all that. Just do some of it. Bear in mind that eliminating suspects is as useful as finding the right one. Well, not quite, but you know what I mean. Right, wish me luck,' added Lou, with a grin and a wink. 'I'll leave you with Lady Somerset's full inventory of items stolen. I can remember most of them in my head and I daren't walk around Creepy's shop with it in my hand anyway! I'll also keep my eyes open for our other suspects, and I might drop in at the parish rooms – see if anyone by the name of Reginald Whitehouse has been lodging any interesting planning applications recently. See you in a bit.'

They had barely time to say good-bye before Lou was gone.

CHAPTER TWENTY

Amazing breakthrough

THE others looked at each other, somewhat dazed. Lou was such a whirlwind when she got the bit between her teeth.

'Right,' said Jack, rubbing his hands together as Lou sometimes did in what he hoped was an authoritative way. 'So, er where shall we start, do you think? Ah, David, I can tell your brain is ticking!'

'I think I've got a telephone number for one of those schoolboys,' he said, slowly. 'Harry Jenkins, the one who accompanied Peter Blacksmith to Chumley on December 12th. He was on a school camping trip that I went on last Easter. Well, all the home numbers of every pupil were written down in a sort of tree, so that if there was a problem, each parent on the list had about another two parents to ring and so on, so that everyone could be told easily and quickly. I'm pretty sure I've still got those details in my personal and social development folder.'

'I'm sure you have, you hoard everything,' said Jack. 'Okay that sounds good. I think I better ring though, don't you, because we don't want to risk Harry recognising your voice.'

David nodded. 'I was hoping you'd say that.'

'Now, Emily, do you want to pick mum's brains about car boot sales, bring-and-buy sales, bric-a-brac fairs, that sort of thing,' said Jack, desperately hoping he sounded as decisive as Lou. 'I'll go online and check out Hall's auction site and give them a call while David finds Peter's number.'

David and Emily scampered off and Jack turned on his dad's computer, logged onto Google and searched for

Halls as Lou had suggested. It came up instantly. Jack picked up the cordless phone from its cradle on the desk and nervously dialled the number. He hoped he didn't sound too young and green to the nice, well-spoken lady who answered. She regretfully told him that they didn't have items of the kind he sought coming up in any current auction. She could, however, recommend he try a couple of local antique dealers – one of whom was Mr Creepy. She also suggested he try eBay, as Lou had done.

As he hung up, David walked in with the number for Harry Jenkins. Jack swallowed hard, then rang it, feeling more anxious than ever. Harry's mother answered, and he tentatively asked if her son was available.

''Ang on, he's out the back yard throwin' stones at the pigeons, would ya believe,' said his mother. ''Arry, someone on the phone for ya!'

Harry eventually came to the phone but was no help whatsoever. He sounded surly and suspicious and wanted to know how 'Simon' as Jack called himself, had got hold of his number.

'Simon who?' he asked suspiciously.

Jack hadn't thought to equip himself with a false surname as well. 'Erm, er, er,' he stammered. 'This-tlethwaite,' he blurted out. He had no idea why he came out with such a tongue-twister rather than merely replying 'Smith' or 'Jones' or something.

'Simon Thistlethwaite?' replied Harry, disbelievingly.

'Yeah,' said 'Simon'. 'I er, we er were wondering if Peter had any antiques for sale at the moment, like er, you know, a barometer or an oil lamp or something.'

No, Peter didn't have 'nuffin fancy' like that, just some copper piping, a couple of old television sets and some scrap metal. And no, 'Simon' couldn't have his number – he would have to leave his. Jack didn't fancy doing that. He ended the call quickly, turning round to David white-faced. He sighed. That had been a terrible performance.

Lou would not have been impressed.

'Thistlethwaite?' repeated David, grinning. 'Where on earth . . .'

'I've no idea why I said that. I made a right hash of that phone call,' admitted Jack.

'Well never mind,' said David, sympathetically, aware that he would have been no better at that sort of thing. 'Remember what Lou said, we have to make our own luck. Let's try eBay, we just might find something there.'

It would be wonderful to make some sort of progress in Lou's absence, but Jack didn't hold out much hope. He placed his Official List of Suspects on the desk and alongside, the inventory of items missing from Chumley, a handful of which had pictures which Lady Somerset had included. Languidly, he typed 'eBay' into Google, as a yawn spread across his face.

The study door opened. Emily had returned empty-handed. Their mum had come up with several names of people who organised or served on the committees of bring-and-buy sales, church fairs, and car-boot sales. The girl had plucked up courage to ring, using her mum's mobile as Jack was on the landline. But the consensus was that valuable antiques simply were not sold at these sort of venues – frankly it was mainly cheap tat snapped up by folk wanting a bargain.

Into the search box Jack typed in one of the stolen items for which there was a photograph, since it would be much easier to identify than one without: an early Victorian solid silver condiment set. Up came several dozen listings. Jack scrolled down the pictures and descriptions of elegant old salt and pepper pots. Two or three looked very similar, at least.

'Even if they are a perfect match, it doesn't necessarily mean that those being sold were from Chumley. Whoever made them, may have crafted other, identical items,' pointed out David. 'Oh and look, Jack, on the listing it tells you where the item is located. That seller lives in Dorchester, in Dorset. So it isn't going to be him, is it, unless our thief has already sold it to him and he's selling it on again.'

To the children's frustration, they could not match any of the condiment sets for sale on eBay to the one missing from Chumley Towers. They painstakingly trawled the website for the five other stolen items for which there were accompanying pictures. If they tried to be too specific, some searches would return zero results, while vaguer key words yielded dozens, even hundreds of possibilities. They quickly realised that they faced hours laboriously going through listings one by one. Many items were sloppily described by sellers, which didn't help. The children were left with the need to scrutinise the photographs on each listing carefully to have any hope of finding a perfect match.

'We're not getting anywhere,' said Jack, looking despairingly at the grandfather clock, which actually *had* belonged to his grandfather, ticking solemnly in the corner. For instance, there's a small oil lamp, the right height and design, which might conceivably be from Chumley but the item location is given as Hong Kong.'

'I've just thought of something,' said David, snapping his fingers, which was another Lou mannerism. 'Is there a way to search for sellers in a specific area, rather than the items they sell?'

Jack combed through the various complex search fields eBay provided. 'Yes,' he said, 'actually there is. You can look for sellers within a certain geographical area, down to a radius of just ten miles.'

'What does radius mean, exactly?' asked Emily. 'Is it like in maths where you draw a straight line to the edge of a circle?'

'That's right,' said David, who was keen on maths. 'A radius of ten miles from Malpas would mean that every seller within those ten miles, in whatever direction you go would be included, but no-one else. So it should allow us to narrow down the results just to people living locally.'

'This could be really useful. Well done, David!' said Jack, sounding very like Lou. 'I say, look! There are only twenty-two listings coming up now.'

'A couple of them belong to Mr Creepy!' exclaimed Emily, who had pulled her chair up on one side of Jack, while David stood looking over his shoulder. 'Can you see his user name – M. Finchfield Online Antiques.'

Jack clicked on one of his listings, for an antique cuckoo clock. Sure enough, the item was located in Malpas. There were another five days to run on the auction, which had already received a couple of bids.

'Yes,' he said. 'It certainly is Malcolm Finchfield. It's worth knowing that he is actively selling his wares on eBay. Let's click on where it says "see other items from this seller".'

Up came a number of interesting and unusual artefacts, including a couple enticingly similar to stolen goods from Chumley. Frustratingly, however, none matched.

But Mr Creepy was not the only local person selling antique and collectable items on eBay. The children came across another interesting name from the village: Pippas-pots.

'Pippa Spots?' said David. 'What on earth does that mean – a woman called Pippa selling ointment to treat acne or something?'

Jack and Emily chuckled. David grinned.

'I think at a guess, she means "Pippa's *pots*" said Jack. 'That is the name of this person's eBay shop.'

'Is it Pippa Swift?' asked Emily, 'our resident celebrity journalist?'

'Pah! *Thinks* she's a celebrity, more like,' snorted David.

'Well let's have a look,' said Jack, calling up a listing for a ceramic jug she was selling. 'It could well be her – look, do you see, under the postage costs, it says "Item location: Malpas, United Kingdom."'

'Oh, what's that at the bottom,' said Emily, pointing. 'It says "Business seller information".

A single click of the mouse revealed the following: Philippa Jennifer Swift, of 31 Haybarn Avenue, Malpas, Cheshire, SY14 8DS, tel: 0770 732315.

'Well, well, well. So much for Pippa being a big name – here she is on eBay, selling her wares, with her full name, address and telephone number on public display,' exclaimed Jack.

Jack, David and Emily all gazed intently at the screen. On sale from 'Pippa's Pots' was a long, miscellaneous list of items, new and old. Among them, to Emily's amusement, was a pair of fancy suede Ugg boots.

'Oh just look at those boots she's selling,' she chortled. 'Isn't that typical of someone image-conscious like her that she'd want to own a pair like that with those preten-tious diamond-shaped gold studs down the side and all that white, fluffy woollen lining? They're totally imprac-tical for anything other than swanking around in.'

'Hang on, Emily, aren't they Ugg boots you're wear-ing right now?' said Jack, an amused twinkle in his eye.

Emily blushed. 'Well, yes but I don't swank around in them – and they're not half as fluffy and girly as those that she's selling. Anyway, they were a birthday present if you recall from Auntie Margaret. I don't actually like them much.'

'Maybe she doesn't like hers either, which is why she's selling them,' quipped Jack, scrolling down the list of items for sale. 'Anyway, never mind about her taste in boots – what about that Victorian copper kettle she's selling? That sounds familiar to me.'

David pored over the inventory of missing items from

Chumley Towers, running a finger down the page.

'Drat! It's not the one,' he announced, his finger coming to a halt next to an antique *brass* kettle from the Edwardian era.

Jack continued to scroll down through the various items which Pippa had advertised.

'A nineteenth century silver and enamel trinket box,' read out Emily.

'Aha, now something similar was definitely on the list of items stolen from Chumley Towers,' said Jack, flattening down Lady Somerset's now crumpled and well-thumbed inventory.

'It won't be the same one, of course,' said David, always willing to err on the side of being cautiously gloomy.

'Let's find out,' said Jack, clicking on the listing.

The photograph of the trinket box could now be seen much more clearly. By hovering the mouse over the image, he could zoom in really close. He glanced at Lady Somerset's description of the stolen trinket box: silver and enamel, hand-crafted in 1884. The photograph alongside it was frustratingly indistinct. It had not reproduced well on ordinary A4 paper.

'They look so alike but it's hard to tell for absolutely sure,' said Jack. 'We would need to see the original photograph, which we don't have, of course.'

'We've got Lady Somerset's email address, haven't we? Why don't we contact her and ask her to email the image as an attachment,' said Emily. 'We've been learning how to do that in Design & Technology at school.'

'Yes, we could, so long as the photos she's included on her list of missing items are in digital format,' said Jack.

'They've been incorporated into a Word document, so they will be,' said David, knowledgeably. 'It's got to be worth a go – at least we can tell Lou when she gets back that we've tried our best. I remember her email address from memory, it wasn't difficult at all: *ladysomerset@chumleytowers.co.uk*

'While you two are doing that, I'll go and make us all some hot chocolate and cut some Christmas cake,' said Emily, trying to keep from sounding too jubilant about her great idea. What a pity Lou hadn't been there to hear it!

Lady Somerset went one better. To the children's delight, an email from her popped into Jack's inbox within twenty minutes as the three children sat around the desk, nursing steaming mugs and nibbling biscuits.

It was cosy in Mr Johnson's small, book-lined study which was easily warmed by a tiny radiator. Outside, a swirling flurry of white flakes tumbled down but then ceased. The deep snow upon the ground glowed under the faltering tangerine rays of late-afternoon sun. It looked wretchedly cold. Emily hoped Lou had remembered to wrap up well.

The three children were enjoying themselves immensely. Even if their investigation came to nothing, Lou was sure to be impressed with their efforts when she returned.

They called up Lady Somerset's email eagerly. In it, she explained that she was chained to her computer for the afternoon, desperately trying to attend to administrative matters before Christmas, so they had timed their request perfectly. There had been no more thefts, she was pleased to note, although she and her husband had chosen to keep the Towers shut until the New Year just in case. She couldn't bear the possibility that more items might be taken over Christmas and spoil the occasion for her family.

She was very touched that they were putting in so much effort and enclosed two high-resolution pictures of the trinket box plus shots of four other items stolen. That was all she could find for the present.

The email ended: *'Thank you once again, my dears, do have the most wonderful Christmas and do let me know how you get on, you're all terribly kind. We're both very touched. With kindest regards, Jane and Henry Somerset.'*

'What a lovely email,' breathed Emily, spellbound. 'And look how she signs off with their actual names, rather than "Lord and Lady". We must show Lou as soon as she gets in. I feel so enthused now. Come on, let's open these pictures on the screen and see what they're like.'

Instead of just one fuzzy picture of the missing trinket box, the children now had two, vivid and pin-sharp, taken from different angles as it sat on top of a dark, richly-polished dressing table.

They opened the first. On first glance, it looked the same as the one in Pippa's listing – an oval-shaped silver container with an enamel lid decorated with cherubs playing daintily beneath tree branches.

Jack fiddled about until he got Lady Somerset's photo directly lined up with Pippa's so they could make a side-by-side comparison. The three of them looked repeatedly from one image to the other, then back again, like spectators at a tennis match. There was not a sound to be heard in that study, unless it was the beating of three hearts pumping a little faster than usual. Both pictures were top quality. The trinket boxes appeared identical. But were they? Jack zoomed in on Lady Somerset's. On its side was a small panel in the form of a scroll, surrounded by foliate, in which the interwoven letters ES had been engraved.

'Look at that!' he exclaimed, in excitement. 'Those letters hold the key to this. They would have been engraved by the purchaser, not by the craftsman who made it. If those letters appear on the photograph posted on Pippa's eBay listing then I'm pretty sure that can mean only one thing – these trinket boxes are one and the same!'

Helpfully, Pippa had uploaded several shots, taken from various angles. Jack selected one showing the playful cherubs on the lid facing the same way as in Lady Somerset's. From this perspective, the engraved panel on the side of the missing box appeared directly below the outstretched hands of the cherubs.

He hovered with the mouse over Pippa's photograph so it zoomed in close on the elegant lid. He carefully headed lower, tracing a line down from that outstretched hand, to the scroll framed with swirling leaves. Inside it were the letters ES!

There was no mistake. Not only did the letters match but the Gothic font used was also identical.

'They're the same, exactly the same, aren't they, Jack?' bellowed David into his ear, making his brother wince.

'Completely and totally, one hundred per cent the same,' announced Jack, after a long pause. 'And what's more, there's the tiniest hairline scratch running just beneath the "S" on Pippa's picture and there it is too on Lady Somerset's.' He pointed. 'There's absolutely no doubt. My goodness, isn't this amazing. I can't wait for Lou to get back to show her.'

'Then this can mean only thing, can't it, Jack?' exclaimed Emily, clutching her brother's shoulder, her blue eyes shining bright. 'This trinket box was stolen from Chumley Towers. It is now in the hands of Pippa Swift who is attempting to get rid of it on eBay. Therefore, she is the thief! She must be!'

Jack rose to his feet, went to the window, gazed out at the snow, then turned to face the others as if addressing a large meeting. 'Yes. Absolutely. What's more, *we* have nailed her, not the police! And we have done so just in time for Christmas, isn't that simply brilliant!'

Then his face clouded slightly. 'Oh but what a pity Lou isn't here to share this moment. She's the one who's led us to this.'

The door opened. It was Lou, her hair tousled and cheeks scarlet from the bitingly-cold air. 'Nothing much to report, I'm afraid,' she said, breezily.

CHAPTER TWENTY-ONE

What to do next?

'GOSH, it's cold out there,' gasped Lou, her teeth chattering. 'I went along to the Antiques Emporium and you were right, Jack, it was Mr Creepy's sidekick, Duncan, behind the counter, so I felt safe to go in. He clearly had no idea who I was. I had a good browse. It was your typical antiques shop – earthenware pots, old ceramic and glass bottles, horse brasses, dainty china figurines, copper companion sets for fireplaces, Victorian pocket watches, dark grey pewter tankards, some oil lamps and a couple of trinket boxes.

'But nothing matched our stolen items. I discreetly asked Duncan whether they had more stuff in the storeroom at the back, mentioning certain things off the list, music boxes and barometers and such like.

'He just grimaced – a bit like Creepy – scratched his stubbly chin and said he did have a few bits and bobs that weren't on display but nothing came close to the items taken from Chumley. He did say, though, that if the current weather keeps up they should have some fresh stock coming in from house clearances. I think that might have been an unpleasant joke about old people being more likely to perish in the freezing cold. I suppose he expected a teenager to laugh at that. Needless to say, I didn't.

'Anyway, I got the impression that the shop simply didn't have any of the stolen goods from Chumley. Of course, he might not have trusted me, but I doubt he would have been suspicious of someone my age. I didn't like him much but he was reasonably helpful. He didn't appear to be concealing anything.'

Jack opened his mouth to speak but Lou hadn't finished.

'Anyway, I thanked him for his help and as I was coming out of the shop, guess who I saw? That funny-looking, youngish, stooping woman with the round shoulders and the startled eyes. She had her great, over-sized coat on again and was slinking along the high street, looking this way and that so I followed her from a distance. She went into a clothes store and started rummaging through a rack of tops and a store detective suddenly appeared from nowhere and started watching her. She spotted him pretty quickly and hopped out. She carried on down the high street, turned left and then, would you believe it, halted outside the gates of one of those really posh houses with long drives. The owners must have a walnut tree in the back garden because they had got a big crate of walnuts alongside their gate with a sign attached saying "help yourself, 50p a dozen."

'This woman bent down and started scooping up the nuts and pushing them into her deep coat pockets. Then, if you please, instead of paying, she actually helped herself to a handful of coins left by others in the honesty box alongside it. After that, she shuffled off without even a glance over her shoulder and turned into the estate at the bottom and disappeared into a terraced house about half-way along. I took a note of the address. Now I can't prove this means she was up to no good on her visits to Chumley Towers but our hunch was evidently right – she's perfectly happy to take what isn't hers. Anyway, enough about me, how have you lot been getting on?'

Lou looked round at the three of them, who were nodding politely as she spoke, yet without displaying any great interest in the walnut raid. Jack was standing against the window ledge and the others were still seated in front of the computer. Instantly, she saw the exhilaration in their faces, tinged with awkwardness, as they patiently listened to her account.

'You've found something out, haven't you?' she exclaimed. 'I can tell. Well come on then, blurt it out!'

'Lou, you're not going to believe this,' said Jack, slowly, savouring every word as it was the most exquisitely tasty food, 'but we have cracked the mystery. We know the identity of the thief of Chumley Towers!'

'Never!' exclaimed Lou. 'Who is he?'

'Not a he but a she,' continued Jack.

'I'm gonna shake you in a minute, Jack Johnson, who is *she* then?'

'None other than our resident self-styled celebrity journalist, Pippa Swift,' said Jack breathlessly. David and Emily looked on, intently.

'No! Really? How amazing! Well come on, please tell me absolutely everything, I'm dying to know.'

'We're really sorry you weren't here at the moment we made the discovery,' said Jack.

'Don't be, I don't mind at all. I'm over the moon, it's brilliant. So come on, spill the beans, please!'

'We followed several lines of enquiry first,' said Jack, grandly, 'as you had suggested, before beginning to search eBay for the missing items. We couldn't find anything until David had the good idea simply to search for all items being sold within ten miles of Malpas. That brought up all local sellers and amongst them was Pippa. Half-way down her list was a trinket box which proved to be an exact match for the missing one from Chumley – right down to the engraved letters ES on the side and the hairline scratch underneath.'

Lou grabbed the stapled inventory of missing items and found the trinket box with its accompanying photograph. 'But this image isn't distinct enough to see any engraved letters, or the hairline scratch,' she said, puzzled.

'That's when Emily had a real brainwave,' said Jack.

'She suggested we email Lady Somerset directly and ask her to send over the original high-resolution image, which she did very promptly. And there it is, look.' Jack pointed to the screen. On the left is Lady Somerset's picture and on the right is the one uploaded by Pippa to eBay. The clincher was the engraved initials ES and the hairline scratch.'

Lou squinted at the screen, manoeuvring the mouse carefully over the panel surrounded with swirling leaves.

She turned to the others. 'You're right. It's a perfect match. Those trinket boxes are identical. The initials ES must refer to Edwin Somerset. Do you remember, Lady Somerset told us this trinket box was one of his christening presents in 1884. And he went on to become Sixth Marquess of Chumley, of course, it was his portrait staring down at us that I noticed in the library.

'So, without any doubt, Pippa Swift is selling stolen goods,' continued Lou. 'This is an absolutely fantastic discovery. And what a stroke of genius thinking to email Lady Somerset and asking her for the original picture. That was a cracking idea, Emily. I only hope I would have thought of that. Well done all of you.'

'It was you who got us on the right track, Lou,' said Jack, modestly. 'We couldn't have done it without you. In fact, we couldn't have done it without David and Emily either. I was fairly expendable though, as it turned out.'

'It's a team effort, Jack, that's what important,' said Lou. 'We can't all be brilliant all of the time. I'm so thrilled about this.'

Lou read carefully through Lady Somerset's email, then switched the printer on and proceeded to copy Pippa's eBay listing. 'It's worth having a print-out as proof, just in case her listing disappears, although it's still got four days to run and has already reached a respectable seventy pounds. Oh and er by the way, what about the other items she's selling?' She scrolled down the list. 'Are there more from Chumley Towers, or just the trinket box?'

'Just the trinket box at the moment, it would appear,' said Jack. 'But Lady Somerset has also sent us high-resolution pictures of a few other items so we can look out for them when Pippa lists them.'

'Great,' said Lou. She joined Jack at the window. 'I got back just in time. Look, everyone. It's started to snow properly again. Isn't that a simply marvellous sight!'

The others, whose eyes had been glued to the computer screen, now turned their attention to the wintry scene outdoors. The sky was charcoal grey and darkening. From it came a tumbling multitude of feathery flakes, some of which landed on the window pane and skidded down it.

'Doesn't that awesome sight just cap it all,' enthused Lou, her face aglow. 'I am *so* looking forward to Christmas Day this year, and I have never once been able to say that before. And to think we've snared the culprit on Christmas Eve. It doesn't get much better, does it?'

She span round and looked intently at them all. 'The question now, is what do we do about it?'

'Should we just go to the police at this stage?' asked Emily.

'Would they listen?' asked David.

Jack shrugged. 'I'm not convinced.'

'Nor me,' said Lou, after a pause. 'Especially not to a bunch of kids. It would be too much like hard work for them in any case to have to stare hard at two photographs of the same object and work out that it was identical. And what is a late-nineteenth century trinket box to them? From their point of view, it's hardly the crime of the century. It does raise the question, of course, how is Pippa disposing of the rest of the stuff? Where is it? It looks like she might be putting items up for sale one by one, buried underneath all her Ugg boots and general bric-a-brac. She probably feels that's safest. She might, of course, already have sold some items.'

That was a worrying thought. Pippa should not be allowed to get away with her crimes. They felt an urge to go round her house straightaway and tell her what they thought of her.

'Perhaps we should inform the Somersets and leave it to them to call the police,' suggested David.

'I'm not keen to make any move just hours before Christmas,' said Lou, firmly. 'I don't see the need. Chumley Towers is currently closed and even the worst kind of criminal is likely to give themselves Christmas Day off. We're not going to lose anything by putting things on hold for twenty-four hours and anyway, I think we need a little more time to assemble a case against her.'

The others looked disappointed.

'I'm sorry but although it's great news that we've sussed that Pippa Swift is the thief – or rather, you three have – the fact is we can only link her with one item from Chumley Towers. We will have a far stronger case and much more credibility with the police if we can hand over evidence of her having stolen the remaining dozen or so items, which is our next challenge.'

'How do we do that, Lou?' asked Emily.

'I have no idea,' she replied honestly. 'But we'll find a way, or if we can't, then we give up and alert Lord and Lady Somerset to what we know. With any luck, Pippa will post up another incriminating listing over the next day or so.'

Jack nodded. 'The important point is that we have solved the mystery. We know who the thief is. But real detectives wouldn't necessarily wade in and make an arrest straightaway. They would bide their time, gather more evidence and amass an invincible case before making their move. Is that more or less right, Lou?'

'More or less,' replied Lou. 'Anyway, fellow detectives, you've done absolutely brilliantly – much better than me. And your reward is to down tools, give yourselves a break and enjoy Christmas!'

CHAPTER TWENTY-TWO

A white Christmas

JACK burst into David's room at just gone 6am with an important announcement.

'A white Christmas, I can't believe it!' he cried, snapping his light on and flinging back his brother's curtains. 'I can't remember ever seeing snow on Christmas Day!'

In truth, in early morning darkness the fresh fall of Yuletide snow shimmered a luminescent blue, austere and unwelcoming, rather than a dazzling white.

But later, when the sun finally struggled up at eight o'clock it would undoubtedly make a memorable sight. With temperatures below freezing for a third day, the children were guaranteed their first proper white Christmas.

'Isn't it simply magical,' said Jack, his eyes shining.

'Clear off, Jack,' grumbled David. 'It's not nearly time to get up yet. You've just woken me up and spoilt the dream I was having. Leave me alone. Go and pester the girls if you like, I'm staying in bed.'

'Oh and a Merry Christmas to you too, brother,' said Jack, wondering whether to leap on David's bed and start bouncing up and down. He thought better of it. Seasonal goodwill just might be in short supply if he did that.

'Okay, I'll leave you to sleep but don't be too long, I want to go downstairs and open my presents.'

Jack bumped into their mum on the landing. Mrs Johnson, yawning in a dressing gown, had risen early to put the goose in the oven.

Lou, who always woke early, heard voices outside her door and decided to get up too. This was a particularly special day for her and she wanted to make the most of it.

Mr Johnson, David and Emily, meanwhile, remained cocooned underneath their duvets.

But by nine o'clock the whole family was up and a furious unwrapping session was in full swing. Lou was gratified to discover that there were presents waiting for her under the Christmas tree, too. She in turn, had sourced small gifts for the Johnsons from what remained of the twenty-pound note from old Mrs Owen.

Mrs Johnson refused Jack's earnest requests for a full English breakfast, pointing out that it would spoil their appetite for Christmas dinner.

'You can have a bowl of cornflakes and some toast to stop your tummy rumbling in church and that's your lot for now,' she told him.

'Oh mum, do we have to go to church?' moaned David. 'I love this adventure book you've got me. Can't I stay here and read it while the rest of you go?'

'Certainly not!' said Mr Johnson, intervening. 'Christmas Day is not just about getting presents and stuffing ourselves with food in case you had forgotten, it's about marking the birth of Jesus and also – for a mere hour or so – taking time out to reflect on the important things in life and to give thanks for all that we have got. Now that doesn't hurt anyone, don't you agree, Lou?'

'You're quite right, Mr Johnson. I'd certainly like to come,' she replied. 'Put David alongside me in the pew if you like, I'll make sure he behaves himself.'

Jack looked a bit put out at that. Lou spotted his face instantly. 'It's okay, Jack, you can sit the other side of me if you like.'

'Perfect. A rose between two thorns,' said Mr Johnson, grinning.

'And if I sit between you and mum there will be another rose between two thorns,' Emily told her father, pouting babyishly.

'Absolutely. Good, we're all going then, that's what I

like to hear,' said their dad, pouring himself another mug of now stewed tea from the pot.

Lou did not often go to church, largely because her parents could not be bothered to take her. But as she followed the others up the steep steps into the hushed, timeless surroundings of St Oswald's parish church she felt pleased to be there on Christmas Day; and pleased briefly to escape the hustle, bustle and mayhem of Christmas morning at the Johnsons.

Louise Elliott simply wasn't used to such a frenzied and chaotic scene, with wrapping paper strewn across the floor and freshly uncovered books, games, electrical items and boxes of chocolate piling up and competing for attention like new-born babies. She found Jack, David and Emily's rapacious delight in noisily tearing open one gift after another overwhelming. An hour or so of calm and a chance to reflect, as Mr Johnson had said, on the true meaning of Christmas was welcome.

Looking sleek in a dark turquoise dress, Lou slid along the pew next to a stone pillar. David followed and Jack, to his annoyance, found himself sandwiched between his brother and sister. Emily had her golden hair tied back in French plaits. The boys looked smarter than Lou had ever seen them in shirts and ties, with their tousled hair properly brushed.

Lou shot Jack a rueful grin. She could tell he was cross not to be able to sit by her. Good old Jack. He might think of Bounder as his best friend but without a doubt *she* was, and he knew it. And he was her best friend too, even though they could only meet in holidays.

Lou glanced around her. The church was filling up. Two rows ahead an unmistakeable figure took his seat – Charles Whortlebury, resplendent in top hat and full-length tan-coloured covert coat with dark collars. He looked pure nineteenth century. A youngish woman with shoulder-length dark hair, willowy in a smart navy-blue dress beneath a matching jacket, took a seat alongside him. Lou thought she vaguely recognised her.

'David,' she whispered. 'Who is that woman sitting by Mr Whortlebury? Would that be Pippa Swift by any chance?'

David nodded.

Lou eyed Pippa with interest. So, here's our thief, just a few feet away from us and a similar distance behind Lord and Lady Somerset in the front row. What a cheek she had, turning up to church!

Whether it was the burden of guilt and remorse weighing on Pippa's mind Lou couldn't be sure, but something troubled her. Beneath her stylish jacket, her shoulders were shaking. A couple of times she sniffed and reached a hand to a snuffly nose.

'Here, take my handkerchief,' she heard Mr Whortlebury whisper. He extracted it from his pocket with a theatrical flourish. Unsurprisingly, it was very much a dandy Victorian gentleman's hankie, silk with frilled edges and a purple squiggle in the corner.

What was bugging Pippa? Lou glanced at the others to see if they had noticed. None had. Emily stood on tiptoes, eager to watch the choir's procession down the aisle. She hoped to catch a glimpse of her friend Sally and elder sister Charlotte who were both members. Jack was staring up at the diamond-shaped hatchments above the nave arches, bearing the coats of arms of the wealthy families of the parish – the Somersets, the Brewertons, Tarlestones and the Dodburys. David was flicking disinterestedly through the service sheet.

Pippa whispered in Mr Whortlebury's ear and he listened sympathetically. He was considerably taller and looked down at her with great tenderness. Lou strained to hear their conversation. What was she twittering on about? Was she confessing all to the gentle, kindly Mr

Whortlebury? Perhaps being in church on Christmas Day had jolted her into facing the fact that stealing was sinful. Possibly that was why she had come. But Lou could no longer catch their words. The organ had struck up amid a general low-level chatter as worshippers quickly swapped gossip before the service began.

The vicar, the Rev Frank Lawrence, strode to the front. He beamed at the congregation and wished everyone a Merry Christmas. Pippa seemed to have recovered her composure and looked intently at him, hanging onto his every word. She seemed oblivious to everyone else in church save Mr Whortlebury.

After hymns had been sung and passages from the Bible read, the vicar began his sermon. He cautioned against the greedy amassing of material possessions which, he said, would never bring fulfilment or happiness.

'We should all of us strive to live decent, honest lives in which we look out for one another and do right by each other,' said the vicar. 'We are most fortunate to live in a safe, close-knit and law-abiding community here in Malpas. Many of you will be aware that there have recently been a spate of thefts from Chumley Towers, to the great distress of Lord and Lady Somerset, who are with us today. It is worrying and upsetting that the police believe the culprits to be local.

'Now while one can hopefully rest assured that none of us gathered here today is responsible, nonetheless it is incumbent on us all to keep our eyes and ears open. Yet also, we must be prepared to show Christian charity to whoever is to blame. Often, otherwise good people are tempted to steal as an act of desperation, having fallen on hard times or because something is causing them pain. They too, deserve to be in our thoughts and prayers at this special time of year.'

Pippa appeared to pull nervously at her lower lip. Lou

kept her eyes fixed on her. Jack's eyes were now on her too. Pippa listened impassively to the sermon, then lifted Mr Whortlebury's handkerchief to her eyes and dabbed them. Lou and Jack exchanged glances.

But as the offertory hymn began, Lou's attention was caught by a shabby, bent old woman in a tight, ill-fitting woollen coat half-way along the pew directly in front. She was seemingly making heavy weather of checking her pockets for change to put into the collection plate. She had been on the CCTV footage too, she was sure of it. Wasn't it mean old Mary Armstrong, the woman Mrs Johnson had subsequently identified? Short on both cash and soap?

Fortunately, Lou's nose was just out of range, but her sharp green eyes were well placed to take in what happened next – although she had trouble believing them. The verger extended the collection plate towards the elderly woman. Mrs Armstrong clattered a couple of coins down into the tray then, to Lou's astonishment, dipped her fingers in and plucked out what looked to be a ten-pound note which she pushed into her pocket. The verger looked surprised and puzzled as if unsure quite what he had just witnessed. Mrs Armstrong raised her hymn book aloft and continued to sing loudly and tunelessly. Meanwhile an outstretched hand next to her quivered with a banknote of some kind so the verger moved on to collect it. What else could he do?

The wily madam! Lou had never seen anything so audacious in her life. It was one thing for the needy only to drop in a couple of coppers but to brazenly pilfer from the collection plate as it was being taken round! Unbelievable. If Pippa wasn't already in the frame for the thefts from Chumley Towers, then wicked, shambling old Mrs Armstrong with her canvas bag would fit the bill perfectly. Could it be, as Lou had once suspected, that more than one person was responsible? If Mary Armstrong was willing to take money from a church collection plate, then what wasn't she capable of? Lou stared at her angrily. Why should such people, however hard-up, think they had the right to behave in that way?

As they filed out of church, the Reverend Mr Lawrence stood by the door, shaking everyone by the hand and smiling broadly.

'It was wonderful to see you, young lady,' he said to Lou. 'I confess I don't recall making your acquaintance before. Are you new to the parish?'

'I'm just staying for a few days visiting friends,' said Lou. 'It was a lovely service. I feel really Christmassy now. Oh by the way, vicar, I think I saw an elderly woman steal a banknote from the collection plate. Ten pounds I think. I just thought you should know, that's all.'

He looked grave and pursed his lips. 'I think I know who you mean. Not for the first time either, I'll be bound. Thank you for the tip-off. She is of limited means and rather limited up-top, if you get my drift,' he said, pointing to his forehead. 'We must pray for her. Ah, I see you are in exalted company – you're a friend of the Johnsons.' The vicar had noticed who was standing alongside Lou. 'Well I hope you all have a lovely Christmas – Mrs Johnson is an excellent cook, so I'm told!'

'She certainly is. I have high hopes for our roast goose!' joked Lou.

'Lovely to meet you,' said the vicar, patting her shoulder. 'I hope we see you again.'

'You had rather a chat with Frank, our vicar,' said Jack, curiously, on the steps outside.

'Yes, I was just telling him about that old bat Mary Armstrong, stealing a tenner from the collection plate,' said Lou.

'Oh she didn't! Really?' exclaimed Jack. 'You wait till I tell mum, she will be appalled.'

'She appeared on the CCTV on both occasions of course,' remarked Lou. 'Hey you don't suppose there's any chance that she might also be . . .' Lou's voice trailed off, leaving her sentence in mid-air. Mrs Armstrong, having enthusiastically shaken the vicar's hand and congratulated him on a thought-provoking sermon, was now making her way out through the main doors.

'But Lou, surely you don't think there's someone else involved?' whispered Jack, looking rather dismayed.

'Probably not,' said Lou, in a low voice, 'but nonetheless, I like to keep an open mind. Anyway, we've given ourselves today off so let's forget about mystery solving for now. I'm just enjoying myself being with you all on a day like this – isn't it simply magical that everywhere is carpeted in fresh snow?'

'That's exactly what I was trying to say to David this morning,' said Jack, 'but he was too lazy to get out of bed.'

'It was only six o'clock and I was fast asleep. I couldn't drift off again afterwards – no wonder I yawned through the vicar's sermon.'

'You always yawn through the vicar's sermon, David, even the more interesting ones,' said his dad. 'Right chaps, the roast goose needs to rest a while before your mum carves it so I was planning to drop by the Bull's Head for a quick festive drink before lunch. I won't be long.'

Lou looked at Jack and he caught her glance. 'Dad, I don't suppose we could join you, could we? It is Christmas Day after all, and Lou's a teenager now and I am nearly and it's a very family-friendly pub and . . .'

'All right,' said Mr Johnson, putting his hands up. 'It is Christmas as you say and going to the pub is a fine English tradition after all. You can join me as a one-off treat, I suppose.'

'Oh really, Paul, do you have to teach them your bad habits when they're still at such a tender age?' said Mrs Johnson with a look of amused annoyance. 'Well you'll do as you please, as always. I shall have to go back and finish off preparing lunch or it won't be ready by the time you roll out of the pub.'

'I hardly think I shall be rolling, my dear, I shall confine myself to one pint of their excellent bitter – they've got a new one on tap, brewed in their very own microbrewery at the back of the pub – and the children can have a Coca-Cola and a packet of crisps or something.'

'Very well, but I want you all back by one o'clock sharp,' said his wife.

Lou grinned. Quite apart from the chance for more detective work, she quite liked the idea of going to the Bull's Head. After all, her own parents would be down the pub for sure, having their turkey dinner and feeling smug that they wouldn't have any cooking or washing up to do.

Her parents . . . Lou had spoken to them only once since arriving and not at all on Christmas morning. They really should have rung her but on the other hand, she could have rung them. She switched her phone back on, having turned it off for church. Within a few seconds it beeped. It was her dad*: 'Very Merry Christmas Lulu, with all our love. Hope you have a wonderful time. Dad and mum xxx'*

It was good that they had remembered – he had anyway. As they tramped their way along Malpas's gently curving, mediaeval streets through the fresh, powdery overnight snow, Lou texted back a similar greeting and told him she was loving every minute of her stay. She added that she was missing them both which, every now and then, was true. Despite their shortcomings as parents, they were still her mum and dad, after all.

CHAPTER TWENTY-THREE

Lou is suspicious

THE pungent aroma of beer and wood smoke wafted into the street from the open door of the Bull's Head. The children followed Mr Johnson inside. It was a jolly place packed with villagers enjoying a festive get-together before Christmas lunch.

They reminded Lou of folk round her way – rosy-cheeked, cheerful men in lumberjack shirts and daft jumpers and stylish but rugged women in sturdy shoes and warm clothes. The children felt a little shy entering a pub but on Christmas Day old and young alike were all welcome. Warned to be on their best behaviour, Jack, David, Emily and Lou dutifully sat quietly on bar stools around a table in the corner while Mr Johnson went to get some drinks and crisps.

'Hey this is great,' said Lou. 'It brings back memories of our meal together at the Vaynol in Abersoch last August. Of course on that occasion, we were sitting outside on a lovely summer's evening. This is our second pub outing together – hey, aren't we getting grown up! I'm a teenager already, of course and you will be soon, won't you, Jack?'

'And in a year's time, I'll *nearly* be a teenager,' pointed out David.

'I hope we can all meet up again at Abersoch next year,' said Jack.

'Of course we can, why shouldn't we?' said Lou. 'We can be back together at Easter holidays, during the summer holidays and at half terms with any luck – if our schools are off at the same time. We might even get to go camping by ourselves like we did late last summer. Also, don't forget that there's the treasure inquest in March, into the second Staffordshire Hoard. We should get to meet up then, with any luck. Wouldn't that be brilliant?'

Mr Johnson returned with four drinks perched on a metal tray with a couple of packets of crisps to share. He pulled up a stool and squeezed in alongside them. 'Cheers everyone! Merry Christmas!' he said, raising his pint glass to his lips.

'Cheers! Merry Christmas!' they all chorused, chinking their cola glasses together.

'Mmm, I love Walkers crisps,' said Jack, ripping open a packet. They're the best, aren't they?'

'A lot of people used to eat Golden Wonder when I was your age, wonder what happened to them?' said Mr Johnson. 'I agree though, Walkers are tops, especially their smoky bacon.'

'Golden Wonder do still exist,' said David, rocking back on his bar stool. 'But they were struggling against fierce competition and nearly went under. Then a firm in Northern Ireland took them over. You can still order the crisps online if you can't get them in the shops.'

'How on earth do you know things like that, David? Fairly useless info, but impressive all the same,' said Lou.

'Dad, I didn't realise crisps had been invented when you were still a boy,' said Jack impishly.

'Ha, ha, very funny,' replied his father. 'Now, are you four okay while I go and say hello to a few people, there's a couple of chaps in here I haven't seen for ages.'

They all nodded.

'Isn't it amazing to think we've unmasked the thief of Chumley Towers?' said Emily, in a low voice, after her father had disappeared. 'I still can't quite believe it. I know we said we wouldn't talk about it on Christmas Day but I'm really keen to work out how we could tackle her over it. I wonder if that was why she was getting all tearful in church this morning. Have you had any more thoughts, Lou?'

Wisely, Emily did not mention Pippa's name. It would be easy to be overheard and your comments repeated in a close-knit community pub like the Bull's Head.

'No,' said Lou, taking a sip of cola. 'I haven't. But bearing in mind the blatant dishonesty I saw in church today there's got to be a possibility that other people might also be responsible.'

Jack, David and Emily exchanged despondent glances.

'If that's the case, and it probably isn't, it doesn't for one minute make your achievement yesterday any less,' Lou assured them. 'The fact is, we can so far only pin one item on you-know-who.'

'As for our collection-plate thief, to behave like that on Christmas Day, in a church of all places, suggests that it's reasonable to suspect her of being willing to take just about anything from Chumley Towers small enough to fit into that frayed canvas bag with its black rubber handles which she takes about with her.

'Let's not discuss these matters here though, unless we want the whole village to know what we're thinking,' added Lou. 'This is the sort of place where a good detective will do more listening and less talking. We must stay open-minded right to the end and not jump to conclusions. For instance, have you noticed that there are a couple of others who made it to our shortlist actually in this pub?'

The others looked at each other and back at Lou and shook their heads.

'Well, there's our revolutionary friend Colin Drayman behind the bar and also, none other than Bounder's dad and Mr Hickman, the surly gamekeeper, chatting away together in the far corner. Don't all turn round and stare, though. It's well worth eyeing these people up, listening into their conversations, observing how they behave. Do they seem happy with their lot, or are they down on their luck? Do they possibly bear a grudge of some kind against others? Are they plotting something? A while ago, I read of a murder case being solved because a barmaid overheard a conversation between two men in a pub which provided police with a crucial lead,' said Lou, finishing off the last of the crisps. 'Take a look over at the bar now, what do you see? Colin – or Vlad as your dad calls him – is holding forth about something – let's have a listen.'

The others had forgotten all about 'Vlad'. But Lou was right – there he was, in his red T-shirt emblazoned with a bright yellow hammer and sickle. They weren't sure quite what the real Vladimir Lenin had looked like, but felt sure he would have looked something like Colin, with his dark moustache and goatee beard.

'But we have, of course, nailed the culprit, Lou,' said David, slowly.

'Absolutely but humour me, please, just in case others are involved, let's grab this opportunity to hear Colin in full flow.'

So the children fell silent and eavesdropped on Colin's loud, boorish conversation with an old chap who was propping up the bar and slurping steadily from his pint glass. In any case, Jack, David and Emily couldn't help but feel a trifle subdued. They had been so proud of tracking a stolen item definitively to Pippa Swift, thereby exposing her guilt. But to hear Lou you'd think that the hunt was still wide open.

'They are an irrelevance, an anachronism, a waste of time and money,' said Colin earnestly in a well-spoken, slightly nasal voice. 'I don't feel sorry for them, not one bit. If the poor take just a little from those with more money than they know what to do with, then good luck to them. What does the Bible say? The meek shall inherit the Earth.'

'Didn't see you in church this morning, Colin,' sniggered a portly chap at the other end of the bar, who was also listening in. 'Not like you to get all spiritual on us. I thought religion was the "opium of the people" in your way of thinking?'

'Who's he talking about?' whispered Emily. 'Does he mean the Somersets?'

Lou nodded. 'Almost certainly.'

Colin ignored the quotation from Karl Marx, one of the founders of the Communist philosophy he believed in. 'All I'm saying is that the country can't afford great swanking stately homes like Chumley Towers any more, nor to bankroll the folk that live there. They don't belong in the twenty-first century. Think how many affordable houses you could build if you flattened the Towers and concreted over its gardens. I tell you this, if those thefts rattle the Somersets so much that they decide to sell up then good riddance to them.'

The elderly man continued to sup his beer steadily and did not reply.

'Pah,' interjected the portly chap. 'I hear what you say, Vlad, but Malpas wouldn't be Malpas without Chumley Towers and its aristocratic family. It might be a throwback to a different age but it adds a little touch of magic and charm to the area. This country could spend every penny it had on affordable housing and the National Health Service and the like but we'd be a duller place without a bit of, I dunno, ostentation in life if that's the right word. As for Chumley Towers, I'm guessing that you've never stepped foot in the place, so you're criticising what you don't actually know.'

'Ah that's where you're wrong,' retorted Colin, his dark eyes gleaming. 'I've been a few times to Chumley Towers recently. I know exactly what they've got in there. And I look forward to the day when all their worldly goods will be made available to ordinary working men and women – and make the toffs go out and toil in the fields and factories all day long to make ends meet. I'm a passionate believer in equal opportunities.'

Lou stared at Colin and shook her head. 'What twaddle,' she said, under her breath. 'All that would achieve is creating a new elite and a new under-class, not a society of equals at all. As for the Somersets being wealthy, well we know better, don't we?'

Colin's mouth opened again to resume his political analysis but the landlord, rolling his eyes, cut him short, pointing out that there were empty glasses on tables which needed collecting.

'Vlad let slip something interesting just then, didn't he?' said Lou, turning to the others.

They all nodded earnestly.

'Erm, what exactly,' said Jack.

'Oh really, you lot,' said Lou, exasperated. 'The bit about how he had been to Chumley several times recently and how he knew "exactly what they've got in there". Doesn't that strike you as an odd thing to say? After all why visit at all if he hates the place so much, unless he's up to no good? Is he a sort of political version of Idwal and trying to force the Somersets to sell up, like Idwal attempted to with old Mrs Owen in Mynytho? For very different motives, of course.'

On an impulse, Lou strode over to the bar when she saw that Colin was free. 'Hey Vlad,' she said, cheekily, I'll bet you don't come away from Chumley Towers with empty pockets, do you? Packet of cheese and onion, please.'

Colin 'Vlad' Drayman looked affronted and distinctly annoyed. 'I have no idea what you're talking about,' he said. 'I hope you're not accusing me of anything. Now run along please, children are not allowed to order food or drink from the bar. You'll have to ask an adult to buy the crisps for you. I take it you are here with an adult?'

'Yes, Paul Johnson, over there in the corner. One of your regulars,' said Lou. 'Sorry, I didn't mean to offend you, I was just really interested in your views of the world. It struck a chord with me, you know, the fat cats of this world living the easy life while the rest of us have to scratch around to make ends meet. It doesn't seem fair, does it?'

'Colin's dark eyes scrutinised Lou carefully.

'So er, I was wondering, have you got a website or anything where I could get more information? There's so much I want to find out.'

He paused for a second or two and tugged his beard. 'Hmm, okay, no offence taken. Here, I'll write it down for you. We're the Revolutionary Workers Movement. We've got a website, a Twitter account, and a Facebook page, take a look. You might like to join our youth wing.'

'Yeah, might well do. Hey, now that we're getting on, I don't suppose I could have that packet of crisps?'

The others looked on in admiration. Lou wasn't the sort to take any bluster from the likes of Colin.

Satisfied that she was a potential fellow revolutionary, Colin passed her a card with various contact details on it along with her crisps. 'On the house,' he said, with a wink.

'Oh cheers,' said Lou, somewhat embarrassed, and returned to the others.

'Hey, free crisps and his mobile number, you're doing well there, Lou,' said Jack, enviously, turning as red as Vlad's T-shirt.

'Don't be foolish. That clot had no right to let me off paying for those crisps – it's not his pub so it won't be coming out of his profits. I'll pay the landlord for them when we go, or get your dad to. Interesting though, that he was willing to give me something for free having initially told me that youngsters weren't allowed to buy refreshments from the bar. That shows a possibly corruptible mind and one with no respect for authority. Also, he seemed to flush somewhat and look a bit agitated when I said that I bet he never came away from Chumley Towers with empty pockets.'

'I'm not surprised, that was a bit rude of you, Lou,' said Emily, meekly.

'I wanted to gauge his reaction and I'm glad I did because he reacted curiously. Oh I say, enough about Lenin,' said Lou, glancing towards the door, 'look who's just walked in!'

Mrs Armstrong, almost doubled over, hobbled up to the bar, slapped a ten-pound note down on the counter and demanded a double whisky.

'That will be the same tenner the vile old creature pinched from the church collection plate at a guess,' exclaimed Lou. 'So that's another one in here from our shortlist.

At that point, Mr Bounderton and Mr Hickman drained their glasses and ambled past, heading for the door. Neither noticed the children.

'Actually, spotting those pair in here has given me an idea,' said Lou. 'Do you see the Specials board propped up on the hearth? It claims that the game pie, roast pheasant and rabbit are "locally sourced". I wonder if it all comes from the grounds of Chumley Towers, and if so, do the Somersets know about it?'

'Hmm, how might we find that out?' said Jack, racking his brains.

'We find out like this.' Lou rose from her stool and strode back to the bar.

CHAPTER TWENTY-FOUR

Rabbit out of a hat

'HEY, Vlad. The rabbit and pheasant you've got on the menu – is it really locally sourced?' Lou asked Colin. 'It's just that I'm very into green issues and the environment and I hate to think my food has travelled hundreds of miles to reach my plate.'

'Quite right too, that's how I feel. All our game supplies are certainly very local, walking distance in fact, or should I say, squawking distance,' he replied, as he put a row of clean glasses back on the shelf.

'From where, exactly?' asked Lou, ignoring his weak joke. She resisted the temptation to ask him directly if he meant the Chumley estate.

'The fields around and about,' said Colin, vaguely, with an airy wave of his hand.

'Hey, it's a while since I've eaten rabbit or pheasant. I don't suppose I could buy some off you, could I? It would make a nice present for the family I'm staying with.'

Colin frowned disconcertingly at her, his untidy thatches of eyebrow almost meeting in the middle. 'This isn't a shop, we don't sell raw joints of meat to customers. They're for use by our chefs to turn into the meals you see on our menu or on the Specials board.'

Lou couldn't think of any way to undermine that reasonably sensible observation, so she resorted merely to looking crestfallen and defeated. She turned slowly away.

'Oh look, I tell you what,' said Colin, loftily sucking in his cheeks like some well-heeled duck, 'I daresay I can sort something out for you. I'll find you a nice couple of saddles of frozen rabbit, how about that? On the house too. Shush, don't tell anyone!' he added, theatrically raising his finger to his lips. 'All I ask is that you visit our website and read our manifesto and try and get along to our next meeting in Malpas village hall next week. It would be great if you could come.'

'I'll do my best,' fibbed Lou.

Colin disappeared through a door marked 'staff only' then reappeared about a minute later with a vacuum-packed bag which he handed her.

'Thanks, Colin. That's great. But do let me pay you something for it,' said Lou, reaching inside her jacket pocket.

'No, I wouldn't hear of it,' said Colin, jutting his goatee chin out nonchalantly. 'Hope you enjoy it and do let me know your thoughts on our website. There are a couple of articles from our chairman which you might like to look at and I've written one or two things myself. I'm hoping to become a reporter on the *Morning Star* one day, when I've finished college.'

Lou smiled politely, thanked him again and sat back down with the others.

'What on earth have you got there, Lou?' asked David, in amazement.

'Colin the court jester has just pulled a rabbit out of a hat for me – well, out of the freezer, to be precise. On the house too, just like the crisps. Isn't he generous, giving away what doesn't belong to him?'

'But whatever do you plan to do with a frozen rabbit?' asked Jack, looking at the frosted package Lou had returned with.

'Well, eat it for a start. It's perfectly good food, I'm sure your mum could put it in a casserole or something,' said Lou. 'But I'm particularly interested in the label on the vacuum pack it's sitting in.'

Lou pulled out her camera and flicked through the pictures. 'I thought as much!' She put the camera down and held up the vacuum pack of frozen rabbit. 'You see the label stuck to it is handwritten in black felt-tip pen, and says only: "2 saddles of rabbit, November 17?" Now compare it to this photo I took of a package from Mr Bounderton's freezer. It says "hen pheasant, plucked, November 14". The handwriting is the same on both labels which look identical and the same felt-tip pen has been used. So clearly, the frozen rabbit on sale in this pub – and the pheasant and game pie too, no doubt, have come from the freezers in Bounderton's garden shed. What's frustrating me is that I can't be sure where the meat was originally sourced from. I can guess but the label does not make it clear.'

The others stared at Lou's photo in fascination.

'May I have a look at the frozen rabbit?' asked Emily. She scraped the frost off a section of the vacuum pack, then examined it closely, turning it over and holding it up to the light.

'It's from Chumley Towers,' she said, calmly. 'If you look carefully, you can see the Chumley coat of arms embossed several times across the plastic.'

'Hey, you're right,' said Lou. 'Well done! That's very interesting.'

She pulled out her camera again and selected the photo of Mr Bounderton's frozen hen pheasant. She zoomed in and then scrolled down from the label to the clear, blueish film beneath. Sure enough, there was the coat of arms – exactly the same as on the packed rabbit in front of them.

'That's definitely the Chumley coat of arms?' said Lou.

'Definitely,' said Emily, looking excited. Jack and David nodded.

'We've lived round here all our lives, remember,' said Jack.

'Excellent,' said Lou. 'I'm cross with myself for not

noticing it on my photo but then, unless you zoom in you wouldn't do. So, this is the scenario as I see it: we now know that the rabbit and pheasant being sold in this pub is from the Chumley Estate. Wild meat, still in its feathers and fur, is handed over by the dodgy gamekeeper and estate manager Tim Hickman to his pal Kevin Bounderton, along with a few dozen useful vacuum packs from the stock cupboard at Chumley.

'Mr Bounderton hangs the game for a few days from the rafters of his shed at the bottom of the garden. Then the meat is prepared, placed in vacuum packs with one of his handwritten labels stuck on, then popped into the freezer awaiting delivery to the Bull's Head and similar food outlets. They get their locally-sourced meat and Bounderton and Hickman get a useful extra income.'

'But if Chumley vacuum packs bearing their crest are being used, does it mean that this little enterprise has the blessing of the Somersets?' asked Jack.

'I doubt it,' said Lou, taking a gulp of cola. 'But we'll ask them exactly that question very soon.'

'I doubt it too,' said Emily, boldly. She was delighted at having had a second brainwave in the space of two days and was becoming noticeably more confident. 'I've walked round the Chumley farm shop where they sell produce from the estate – all the packaging displays the insignia of Chumley Towers on professionally-printed labels. The Somersets wouldn't dream of using a felt-tip pen.'

'So, haven't we got some interesting information for Lord and Lady Somerset,' said Jack, with relish.

'Very. But we won't trouble them with it today of all days,' said Lou. 'Let them enjoy Christmas as we should too. Now, help me eat these cheese and onion crisps you lot, I don't want to wreck my appetite for your mum's roast goose. I'm looking forward to that.'

CHAPTER TWENTY-FIVE

Lou thinks things through

DESPITE the extra crisps, Lou and the others found their appetites were on good form by the time they had persuaded Mr Johnson that he really should stop chatting to his friends in the pub and go back for Christmas lunch.

The Johnsons' house was filled with the heady aroma of roast goose, chestnut stuffing, bread sauce, gravy, potatoes roasted in goose fat, roast parsnips in a honey glaze, cheesy leeks, and – David's least favourite – Brussels sprouts.

'Apparently, people who don't like sprouts are believed to have a more discerning palate,' announced David, when his mother waved the bowl at him.

'Oh come on, David, have at least a couple,' said his dad. 'They're very good for you. Would you like me to pretend they're aeroplanes or something and fly them into your mouth?'

'No thank you,' said David, haughtily. 'They have a sulphurous tang and it's because I have such sensitive tastebuds that I notice and judge them not to be worth eating.'

'What's the Welsh for sprouts, David?' asked Lou, suddenly. 'It bugs me when I don't know words for common vegetables like that.'

'Erm, er, I'm not sure,' said David, looking cross with himself. 'Hang on, I'll go and get my Welsh dictionary.'

'You'll do no such thing,' said his mother, sternly.

'Well, I for one would love a few sprouts. In fact, I'd like a little of everything if that's ok, Mrs Johnson. It's an absolute feast,' enthused Lou. 'It's just such an amazing treat for me to sit down to a proper family Christmas dinner. I love meals round the table like this.'

'We'll have to cook that rabbit you brought back from the pub while you're here, Lou,' chipped in Mr Johnson. 'We've got a couple of tasty recipes for rabbit. Vlad obviously took quite a shine to you – don't let him brainwash you, mind, he's got some strange political ideas. We just find him rather amusing, he's our pet revolutionary. Every village should have one. So long as they're all talk and don't get up to any actual harm.'

Lou chuckled. 'I'm not really that into politics, Mr Johnson. If I was, I don't think Vlad's view of the world would quite match up with mine. He's an interesting guy, however, and I found my little chat with him very revealing, you might say. As for the rabbit, I could help you prepare it, Mrs Johnson, if you'd like.'

'That would be kind, Lou. On Boxing Day, tomorrow, we mostly just eat cold meats and pickles but perhaps we could have rabbit casserole the day after, on the twenty-seventh? It will make a nice meal, won't it, Paul?'

'Certainly will,' mumbled Mr Johnson, his mouth full of goose. 'Anyway Merry Christmas!' he said, raising his glass. 'Thank you all for coming!'

They chuckled at that. For a while the conversation dipped as everyone concentrated on tucking into their overflowing plates. Crackers were pulled and party hats placed on heads. David, a keen photographer, suddenly got up at one point to fetch his camera and take a picture of everyone.

'So it sounds as if you've enjoyed being here, Lou,' said Mrs Johnson. 'We've certainly enjoyed having you – I've never known our three so animated. We'll have to put you on the guest list for next Christmas, if you're available.'

'It's been wonderful, Mrs Johnson. I've loved every minute of it,' said Lou. 'You don't know what it means to me to have a proper Christmas in a warm, friendly house. I shan't want to go back at this rate!'

'Could Lou come and . . .' began Jack.

'No, Jack,' said his mother, with an amused smile, anticipating what he was about to say. 'Lou can't come and live with us, I think her parents might object. But she can come and stay whenever you all want her to.'

'Hurrah!' shouted Jack, David, Emily and Lou in unison.

'Now, has anyone got room for pudding?' asked Mrs Johnson, after they had all scraped their plates clean. 'The answer had better be yes, because in addition to my home-made Christmas pud, I have also made a hazelnut meringue topped with strawberries.'

'Hurrah!' yelled the children for a second time.

They had barely finished dessert when Mr Johnson looked at the clock – it was nearly 3pm.

'I'm going to go and see what Liz has to say, if I can be excused for a few minutes,' said Mr Johnson, rising to his feet. 'Not my wife,' he added, grinning at Lou's puzzled face. 'The other Liz.'

'Oh I do wish you'd be a little more respectful,' said Mrs Johnson, clearing away the dishes.

Lou and the others joined Mr Johnson in front of the television in the living room for the Queen's Christmas message to the Commonwealth. Lou glanced around at them all, and felt a fleeting regret that in a couple of days' time she would have to say goodbye and catch a train back to Church Stretton. She really didn't feel like returning home just yet.

As the Johnson household fell silent to watch the Queen, it suddenly struck her why the trouble at Chumley Towers was so painful for the residents of Malpas. The Somersets were a sort of local version of the Royal Family to whom most villagers felt loyalty and affection. It pleased them to have the Ninth Marquess of Chumley and his family living in their midst and occasionally dropping in on village events, adding their touch of glamour. It worried them that the Somersets were struggling with the upkeep of the much-loved Towers and then for some thief – a nearby resident too, in all probability – to repeatedly make off with their treasured possessions, was distressing for them all. Well, apart from Colin, of course.

Colin. He really was an enigma. Lou had not finished with him, not by a long chalk.

'Would you mind if we used your computer in the study for a few minutes, Mr Johnson?' asked Lou. 'We just want to go on the internet for a bit.'

'Of course, feel free,' he said, settling himself down in the armchair. 'I can't imagine I shall want to use it for the next hour or two.'

'He'll be snoring in a minute, Lou. He's had too much wine over lunch, not to mention that beer in the pub,' scolded Mrs Johnson.

She was right. Mr Johnson, full to bursting with festive food and drink, was soon fast asleep.

Lou grinned. 'Hey you three, I know we said we'd give ourselves the day off, but I thought we might do a bit of research into our friendly barman at the Bull's Head. I've got all his details here,' she said, waving the card Colin had given her.

Jack yawned. 'I'd love to, Lou, but I'm rather keen to catch that Harry Potter movie on ITV this afternoon. In any case, I don't quite see the point, bearing in mind we've already nailed the offender.'

'I agree. I'm not really that interested in Colin, and I wouldn't mind having a skim through all the books I was bought as presents,' said David, apologetically. 'Also, Lou, I feel we should focus on building a case against Pippa, like you said yourself yesterday. But not right now, because these books really need my attention.'

Emily, meanwhile, had already disappeared to her room with her collection of presents.

Lou sighed and drew a deep breath. 'Fair enough, I just think we need to put in a little more thinking time that's all. I'm still left wondering if there's more to all this than just Pippa. It concerns me that we can so far only link her with one item. Personally I think Colin needs checking out – preferably by MI5 but it looks like it'll just have to be me for now. Anyway, can one of you boys bring me a cup of tea through in a bit, if I'm to do all the work?'

'I will,' said Jack and David simultaneously.

'Take it in turns if you like,' said Lou, smiling.

A few minutes later, Lou sipped the steaming mug of tea made for her by Jack (with the promise of another from David in half an hour) as she waited for the web address Colin had given her to load. Up came an amateurish page titled Revolutionary Workers' Movement. It was topped with a clumsy cartoon of a yellow clenched fist on a red background.

There were numerous stories denouncing the capitalist way of life and flagging up the plight of various vulnerable groups in society, complete with photos of grim-faced people marching and waving placards. She found an article written by Colin himself denouncing the "toffs" and demanding the bulldozing of Britain's remaining stately homes or their conversion into affordable flats for workers.

Lou called up Colin's Twitter account and his own personal Facebook page. She combed through the exchanges he had engaged in with various people online. In the end she turned away in exasperation. It was all rather childish bravado and synthetic anger from Colin and other young middle class drips like him.

No doubt he had not one jot of sympathy for the Somersets, but she could find nothing linking him to the thefts from Chumley Towers nor to any active desire to target the place or others like it. Of course that didn't necessarily mean that he wasn't responsible, assuming Pippa Swift was not the sole thief. Lou could prove nothing either way, she could only ask herself whether she thought it likely.

And she didn't. Colin Drayman was probably only some five years older than her – not yet out of his teens. He was still a child in many ways, eager to talk the talk and thump the table but without the maturity and determination to actually do much.

As for the poached game from the Chumley estate – that was a matter for the landlord of the Bull's Head and other food outlets. They were clearly willing to take supplies of cheap meat identified with vague, hand-written labels, without asking too many questions. Colin had no role in that, save for thinking, no doubt, that it was perfectly fine to deprive the 'fat cats' of produce which was rightfully theirs.

Lou fished out the inventory of items stolen from Chumley Towers and read through them carefully. So far, they had managed to positively identify one, the trinket box, as being in the possession of Pippa Swift and duly offered for sale by her. To Jack, David and Emily it was more or less 'case closed'. The mystery was essentially solved. They weren't keen on seeking out other culprits, particularly as they were so proud of having nailed Pippa on their own.

But *had* they solved the mystery? Lou took another swig of tea as she pondered that question. She didn't feel entirely convinced. She logged on to eBay and called up Pippa's antique silver and enamel trinket box. It had already attracted seven bids and its price had now reached seventy-four pounds. There were another three days to run before the auction closed.

She clicked on the button taking her to other goods Pippa was selling. Possibly, she had put further stolen items up for sale by now. Lou scrolled through the long list which consisted mainly of clothing and shoes and a few ceramic jugs and vases. There were still no takers for her expensive Ugg boots. More significantly, there was absolutely nothing else listed for sale from Chumley, not a thing.

Lou tapped a few of the missing items into the eBay search box just in case they might pop up from some other quarter. It was not easy because, as before, searches often revealed several potential matches which could only be eliminated by calling up each in turn and checking it.

All she could say with any certainty was that, apart from the trinket box, there was no evidence of any artefact from Chumley being sold on eBay or anywhere else online.

What had happened to the remainder of Lord and Lady Somerset's treasures? Were they sitting in a cupboard under the stairs at Pippa's house, waiting to be dispersed quietly, one by one, on eBay or at a car boot sale or something? Or were they not in her keeping at all?

There was a strong case for believing that Pippa Swift was not the only one with wandering hands. Smelly old Mrs Armstrong might quite possibly have filched a few items. Her blatant display of dishonesty in church proved that. The schoolboy gang which set upon David might also be tied up in it, as indeed might Malpas's pocket revolutionary, even though he seemed all talk and no action. Appearances could be deceptive.

Yet assuming any of them really had the confidence and means to convert valuable antiques into hard cash, why put up just one item for sale? It didn't make sense.

The study door opened. It was David.

'I've brought you another cup of tea,' he said. 'And a couple of biscuits to go with it – a Rich Tea and a chocolate digestive.'

Lou grinned. It amused her the way David and Jack competed with each other to impress her. 'Thanks, the tea will be great. I might pass on the biscuits though because I'm still rather full from lunch, but thanks anyway.'

'Oh,' said David, his face falling a bit. 'Okay well, how are you getting on?'

'Not very well,' admitted Lou. 'I'm still trying to puzzle it all out. There's a missing link somewhere, but I'm struggling to put my finger on exactly what it is. I cannot understand why nothing, save for the trinket box, appears to be on sale. When you think of Bounderton's meat-processing enterprise – there's a clear path: bagged-up birds and rabbits taken by him to his great big brick shed, plucked, jointed up, frozen, then supplied to local pubs and restaurants for commercial gain. But with the items taken from Chumley, there doesn't seem to be a chain, with one exception.'

A long pause ensued before David said, suddenly: 'Maybe Pippa doesn't seek any commercial gain for the remaining items and wishes to hold on to them for her own pleasure.'

'Hmm, yes – because they are meaningful to her. That's an interesting point,' said Lou.

'But if you ask me, Pippa simply hasn't got round to listing the others on eBay yet. It is the festive season, after all,' pointed out David. 'In Pippa's case that probably involves drinking too much and lounging around. Give it to the New Year and she might well have several other things for sale. Or maybe she's being subtle and posting the stolen goods up slowly, one by one, so as not to attract attention.'

'Maybe,' said Lou, distractedly. 'That had occurred to me, too. Anyway, thanks again for the tea and biscuits.'

'That's okay,' said David. 'Give me a shout if you want anything else. I'll only be in the living room reading one of my new books.'

'Fine, see you in a bit,' replied Lou.

Doesn't seek any commercial gain . . . they are mean-ingful to her. Lou chewed those fragments of her conversation with David over and over. Suddenly, a point she had raised before with the others came to her: the stolen items were worth a fair bit but were far from being priceless heirlooms. So could it be that they were taken because they were of *sentimental* value to the thief? Many dated from the late nineteenth to early twentieth centuries – the era of Edwin Somerset, Sixth Marquess of Chumley. Was that relevant?

Not to Pippa Swift, at any rate, busily auctioning the trinket box bearing his initials. She had every intention of turning it into hard cash. But why was she not also flogging everything else? Despite her tears in church, she was pretty hard-faced, Lou surmised. She would waste little time gazing fondly at her ill-gotten goods. She would want to dispose of the lot, quickly and for a good profit. Her attempts at selling clothing and footwear of all kinds illustrated her need to bring in the pennies from whatever direction. Clearly her income as a freelance journalist was insufficient. As the daughter of a writer herself, Lou could understand that.

If those items were taken from Chumley Towers without the desire to make money entering into it, then Pippa was not the thief. In which case, how come she had possession of the trinket box? Could it have been sold to her? That wouldn't make sense either. If the thief loved the artefacts he had taken, then why sell any? Could it be that he simply gave it to her?

But surely you would not give away something you loved, that was precious to you. Unless the giving of that trinket box was an act of love. If the thief *loved* the recipient, he might be willing to part with it, no doubt not anticipating that she would coolly seek to sell it. On that basis, she evidently did not feel the same way about him.

Who, therefore, loved Chumley Towers and everything about it and everything inside it? Who had an emotional tie to all that belonged to the past but in particular to Chumley because of a family connection? And who, thought Lou, her heart beating, *loved Pippa* – enough to give her that cherished trinket box?

Lou smiled, picked up the digestive biscuit and dunked it firmly in her tea. Yesss!

CHAPTER TWENTY-SIX

A job to do

LIKE father, like son, Jack had fallen asleep on the sofa – the excitement of his movie not quite able to compete with the need to digest a huge Christmas dinner. The top of David's tousled head was just visible from inside a book on Anglo-Saxon treasure. It had been a subject of great interest to him after the events of the summer. Emily appeared still to be in her room.

'Oi, wakey wakey,' said Lou to Jack, giving his shoulders a shake. 'Christmas Day only comes once a year, let's not spend half of it fast asleep.'

'Leave me alone, mum, I just want another ten minutes.'

'It's Lou, you silly thing, come on get up, we're off on a little assignment.'

Jack blinked his eyes open and looked around. 'Oh blast, I've missed half of Harry Potter.'

'Never mind about Harry Potter, how about our real-life adventure,' said Lou. 'I know I said we'd forget about being detectives today but it's not working out that way, now come on, we're all going on a walk. If you don't wake up right now, David, Emily and I will just have to go without you.'

That did it. Jack had no intention of being left out. He sat up and rubbed his face with his hands. 'Actually, a walk would probably do us all good. I wish I hadn't eaten so much now.'

'Exactly, so let's go and get some fresh air and exercise,' said Lou. 'And you, David.'

David grumbled a little but put his book down on the coffee table. He went upstairs to find Emily. 'We're going for a walk,' he said, leaning his head round her bedroom door. 'Lou thinks it will do us all good and she's up to something as well, although I'm not sure what.'

'Okay,' said Emily, who was lying on her bed reading an adventure book. She yawned and stretched. 'Isn't it funny how eating lots of food makes you sleepy? Come on then, we better tell mum and dad.'

Mr and Mrs Johnson were however, both asleep – one on the sofa and the other in bed, so the children left them a note instead.

'Actually I rather like going for walks on Christmas Day because there is rarely ever any traffic about,' announced David as they headed up the street. It was a fresh, sunny day with no snow falling but plenty still crunching crisply underfoot. Great dirty clods of ice were now building up in the gutters.

'Oh come off it, David, you hardly ever go walking on Christmas Day, you always complain that it's too cold,' objected Jack.

'David's not like that any more, are you?' said Lou. 'Anyhow, this isn't just any old walk, we're going to pay someone a visit. I think I know the way.'

They headed towards Chumley Towers, turning into Bluebell Lane. On their right, they came upon a sturdy cast-iron gate set in a high sandstone wall overhung with laurel leaves. Lou pushed it open and beckoned the others to follow her.

'This is Mr Whortlebury's place,' said David as they walked along the drive. 'Oh yes, I remember now, he did invite us to call round and see him sometime when we bumped into him in the churchyard. He said he had a fine collection of eggshells to show me. I must say, this is a nice idea, Lou. He's a lonely old chap and I'm sure he'll be delighted to receive visitors on Christmas Day.'

'You're very kind-hearted, Lou,' praised Emily. 'It's

decent and thoughtful of you.'

'Yes it is,' said Jack, who nonetheless felt surprised at her wish to drop in on him like this.

Mr Whortlebury lived in a grand, three-storey house, at least a couple of centuries old, with big sash windows topped with heavy stone lintels. An impressive flight of stone steps led to a black front door. Lou pulled on the old-fashioned bell pull hanging alongside. A distant chime rang out.

It was a couple of minutes before the door slowly opened. Mr Whortlebury peered out, not looking quite so well-groomed as he had earlier in church.

'Good day to you all,' he said, smoothing down his silver hair. 'Are you carol singers? If so, perhaps we might start with Good King Wenceslas. I'll pay you half a crown or so extra – or whatever the modern equivalent is.'

They smiled. There really was only one Mr Whortlebury.

'Actually, Mr Whortlebury, we haven't come to sing carols, although we could if you wished,' said Lou. 'I just thought it would be nice to drop by and see you – if you remember you invited David and myself to call round that day we met you in the churchyard when you kindly gave me back the twenty-pound note I had dropped.'

'Ah yes, I do recall!' said Mr Whortlebury, with a clap of his hands. 'Indeed I do. Well I never, I'm most grateful to you, on Christmas afternoon as well. I haven't long got back from enjoying luncheon and the gracious company of Philippa Swift, our village celebrity, of course. She was most hospitable. Anyway, don't stand freezing on the doorstep, come in, do. Make yourselves at home. Let's go through to the drawing room, shall we, and get ourselves a cup of hot cocoa or something.'

The children followed him past the hat stand in the mosaic-tiled hall and into the drawing room. They were ushered to sit down on a plush green velvet sofa with elaborately embroidered antimacassars over the backs of the cushions. A yellow canary chirruped sweetly in a tall birdcage shaped like a half-sausage. On top of a crammed antique bookcase a stuffed thrush perched on a branch inside a wooden-framed glass box, its shiny black eyes staring expectantly at them.

'Make yourselves comfortable while I fetch us some refreshments,' said Mr Whortlebury, heading towards the kitchen.

Lou's sharp eyes darted in all directions. She rose instantly from her seat and went over to the bookcase, examining the assorted ornaments on top of it alongside the beady-eyed thrush. She moved around the room, inspecting the polished marble hearth in front of a heartily-burning coal fire; the mantelpiece; the coffee table; the baby grand piano in the corner; the colourful Persian rugs strewn across dark oak floorboards; the ornate ceiling rose above.

Her gaze came to rest for a few seconds on a glass display case containing wild birds' eggs inside an alcove set into a wall. They would be illegal to possess if they weren't very old – but they *were* very old, of course, like almost everything else in the room.

The others watched her, baffled. What was she up to? Something, that was for sure! Yet whatever she was searching for, she didn't appear to have found it.

Mr Whortlebury returned with cups of cocoa on a large silver tray and a plateful of tasty-looking macaroons. By this time, Lou had moved over to the window overlooking the back garden and was gazing curiously at an elegant two-storey summer house in the style of a Swiss chalet. She sat back down and sipped her cocoa. It was thick, slightly salty and not particularly sweet. The macaroon, topped with sliced almonds, was delicious.

Lou felt a flicker of remorse at what was coming next

and slightly unnerved that her sweep of the drawing room had revealed nothing. But it had to be done.

'Ouch, I think I've somehow flicked a macaroon crumb into my eye,' said the girl, blinking rapidly and sinking back into her seat. 'I don't suppose you could lend me a handkerchief could you, Mr Whortlebury?' She desperately hoped Jack or David wouldn't obligingly flourish hankies of their own in front of her first.

'Of course, my dear, I would be honoured to lend you a handkerchief,' said Mr Whortlebury, enraptured by her request. 'I always keep two on my person at all times – one for my own use and a second in a pristine state should it be so required by another. All I would ask is that you do not omit to give it me back for these 'kerchiefs are of immense sentimental value.'

Mr Whortlebury whipped a hankie from the breast pocket of his shirt and handed it to Lou. She recognised it as the same style as the one proffered to Pippa earlier in church. As she raised it to her eyes, her fingers traced over the monogrammed squiggle in the corner.

'You're very kind, Mr Whortlebury. The macaroons are divine and this cocoa is excellent,' said Lou.

The others nodded in agreement, although Emily had needed to slip a couple of sugar lumps into hers. The four of them chatted for a while with Mr Whortlebury and exchanged various seasonal pleasantries. After Lou had finished her drink she got up and went again to the window, taking the chance to discreetly examine the handkerchief more closely as she did so.

'Your little summer house looks charming,' said Lou. 'It looks just like a Swiss chalet. You must be very proud of it. It's a wonderful asset to your lovely garden.'

Mr Whortlebury flushed with pride. 'Oh do you think so, do you really? That's most sweet of you. It's not merely ornamental, mind. It is in essence a Swiss chalet proper, if on a rather small scale. And when the weather is clement, it functions as my study. Inside, I sit at my desk and write. Had I told you I was a writer? I pen mainly works of local history, mostly pertaining to Chumley Towers and St Oswald's Church. That's where it all happens, in my Swiss chalet. In there, I find myself at peace in my own little world.'

'It must be a delightful place to sit and write and think,' said Lou, who very much valued her own dens at Abersoch. 'Might it be possible to go outside and take a look?'

Mr Whortlebury looked momentarily taken aback and flustered. 'Hmm, I'm not sure I could agree to that, my dear. You see, it's very much my retreat, my domain. I rarely permit others to enter it. It's my private castle, you might say.'

Any of the others would have backed down at this point, but not Lou. 'I quite understand, Mr Whortlebury, but tell me, what gave you the inspiration for a summer house of that style? It very much resembles the one that Charles Dickens had in his back garden.'

'My goodness!' said Mr Whortlebury, clapping his hands together again and making Emily jump. 'Well I never. I appear to have been well and truly rumbled by another Dickens scholar! It is *indeed* based on that which belonged to the great man. It is almost an exact replica! I have long been a huge admirer of Dickens and when I discovered that he had a Swiss chalet in his back garden – why, I simply felt I had to follow suit, imitation being the greatest form of flattery, of course.

'Were you aware that he wrote some of his finest works inside his chalet during the summer months, including Great Expectations?' he continued. 'Further-more, I have installed a Victorian writing desk inside mine, almost a carbon copy of that upon which he wrote. Alongside is a bookcase containing his complete works, dating back to the 1850s – printed while he was still alive! What do you say to that!' Mr Whortlebury beamed round at them.

'Please Mr Whortlebury, do let us have a peek inside your chalet. I would absolutely love to see your old desk and your antique Dickens novels,' said Lou, her striking green eyes delving deep into his. 'To think that your very own copies ran off the presses during his lifetime. It makes him come alive somehow, doesn't it? They must be very special to you. My all-time favourite, by the way, is Great Expectations and I think there's a touch of Estella in me, if I'm honest. I can be rather haughty and headstrong at times.'

'Really? Well let's hope, like Estella, you meet a Pip to settle down with one day – a fine chap who learnt what's important in life and what is not. It was a voyage of discovery. Ah, Pip,' he repeated reverently.

'Pip – does that name mean a lot to you, Mr Whortlebury?' asked Lou.

'What, eh? No matter. Now what were we saying? Oh yes, my Dickens collection. Well I tell you what, as we are clearly of like minds, why don't we all go and take a brief look inside my chalet? Only this once, mind.'

The children followed Mr Whortlebury through the French doors and across the lawn to his two-storey summer house – or Swiss chalet as he preferred to call it. The upstairs was reached by an outside staircase leading from the side around to a balcony at the front. The ornate, gabled roof hung over the structure, forming a canopy above the balcony and protecting it from rain. It was beyond charming.

'Okay, children, this way,' said Mr Whortlebury, with a flourish of his hand. His reticence at showing them his summer house now seemed to have been overtaken by pride and pleasure at their attentiveness and interest. He unlocked the door and they went inside. He opened the shutters and the children looked around, fascinated. Lou, in particular, swivelled round in a circle, instantly absorbing her surroundings.

Upon the antique writing bureau was a black cast-iron Remington typewriter, with a sheaf of papers alongside it bundled together with a bull-dog clip, filled with elegant copperplate handwriting from the nib of a fountain pen.

'I'm currently working on a piece for the next edition of the Malpas History Society's newsletter about Chumley Towers and my family connection with it,' said Mr Whortlebury. 'I am a descendant of the Somerset family, you know, going back a couple of generations.'

'Yes, I recall you saying that you were related to them, when we met you in the churchyard,' said Lou. 'No wonder the place means so much to you. It must have been tremendously painful for you when you heard talk of the Somersets possibly selling their ancestral home and the place being closed.'

Lou watched intently as Mr Whortlebury's face contorted, as if from a sudden spasm of pain. He tugged at the silk scarf around his neck in an agitated fashion. Then the moment seemed to pass.

'Now, over here in this corner, you will see my prized collection of the complete works of Charles Dickens. Aren't they simply grand?'

They gathered round to look.

'I'm sorry, Mr Whortlebury, I haven't given you your handkerchief back,' said Lou, passing it to him.

'Oh that's quite all right, my dear, I hope your eye is no longer causing you pain.'

'It's fine, thank you. By the way, I noticed the hankie bore the letters ES embossed in a corner. Are those initials significant to you?'

Mr Whortlebury paused for a moment before replying. 'Er yes, yes indeed. They are the initials of a forebear, an ancestor of mine. These were his very own original monogrammed handkerchiefs which is why they are so precious to me.'

'I'm sure. And I notice the same letters on the side of that silver tankard at the back of your desk.'

'Indeed, indeed so. You are an observant young lady. Now, shall we take a quick squint at one of these old Dickens volumes? They need handling with the utmost care.'

'And the letters ES were engraved on the trinket box you gave to Pippa Swift, weren't they, Mr Whortlebury?' said Lou, a hard edge to her voice.

'Aah, um, I say,' he stuttered, as if not quite sure what to say. 'Oh, so you know about that small gift of mine, do you? Well dash it all, that was supposed to be our little secret. I am somewhat vexed to learn that she has blurted it out to you. Mind you, she was very taken with it and I suppose she simply felt the need to tell everyone about it. She's been very down on her luck recently, poor girl, and it's clearly bucked her up no end. One should feel rather flattered.'

Jack, David and Emily gasped and stared hard at Mr Whortlebury. So did Lou.

'You all look rather stern,' said Mr Whortlebury, a slight tremor to his voice.

'That hand-made silver and enamel trinket box dating from 1884, decorated with cherubs playing beneath a tree, was not yours to give, was it, Mr Whortlebury?' said Lou. 'It was a treasured possession of great sentimental value to Lord Henry Somerset in particular because it had once belonged to his great-grandfather, Edwin Somerset, Sixth Marquess of Chumley. Lord Somerset was extremely upset to discover that it had been stolen from under his nose.'

'*Stolen?*' Mr Whortlebury spat the word out as if he had just bitten into something inedible. He opened his mouth to speak but then closed it again. Lou felt certain that he had been about to justify taking the trinket box but thought better of it. She said nothing, waiting for him to continue.

'There must be some mistake, it must be a different trinket box which I gave to Pippa,' said Mr Whortlebury, eventually, sinking into a creaking mahogany chair while holding on to his knee to try and stop it from wobbling.

'No, Mr Whortlebury, you took it when you had no right to do so. Just as you had no right to that antique set of drawers on that table over there, or the rosewood music box placed on top of it which plays numerous little ditties including The Last Rose, Auld Land Syne and Home Sweet Home. Except that home sweet home should be Chumley Towers of course, not your summer house. And you had no right to that barometer hanging on that wall,' continued Lou, pointing, 'or the carriage clock on the window sill.'

Mr Whortlebury shook his bowed head, his eyes now fixed on the floor.

'Here.' Lou fished inside a pocket. 'Take a look at this list of items stolen from Chumley given to me by Lady Somerset. 'I've spotted at least half a dozen in this room. No doubt you are fully aware of where the rest are. You have created a little Victorian paradise for yourself in your back garden, lining your nest with things that don't belong to you, haven't you?'

'But they *ought* to belong to me!' he said, suddenly, tears welling in his eyes. 'I too am the great-grandson of Edwin Somerset, Sixth Marquess of Chumley. And it should have been *me* who inherited the Towers, not Henry, the current Marquess.'

'What do you mean, why should you have inherited Chumley Towers?' asked Lou, disbelievingly.

Mr Whortlebury sighed and shook his head. 'Edwin Somerset was born in 1884. He fathered his first child in 1903. That child was my grandfather, Montague. By rights, he should have one day become the Seventh

Marquess and been handed the keys to the castle, so to speak. However,' Mr Whortlebury paused before continuing, 'Montague was born out of wedlock. Edwin was not married to Montague's mother – my grandmother – Susan Whortlebury, and nor would such a union be permitted.

'Susan held but a lowly position at the Towers, employed as a mere scullery maid. It was, frankly, a scandal to be hushed up and swept under the carpet. Thus it was that Montague took the surname of his humble mother, and did not become a Somerset. Montague grew up, got married and bore a son Frederic, my father, who might so easily have become the Eighth Marquess. I in turn, would have been the Ninth Marquess of Chumley in which case you four ought to be calling me Your Lordship.'

'Instead,' said Lou, unsympathetically, 'we're calling you a villain. You cannot rewrite history, however much you might wish to. You may be an aristocrat – or nearly one – but you're also a thief, plain and simple, and if we were police officers you would now be under arrest.'

Charles Whortlebury looked up at Lou, startled and haunted, then his head sank again almost into his lap. It was a rather pathetic sight. 'I'm going to be arrested and put in prison,' he sobbed. 'Has it come to this? Oh, what would my dear mother say?'

'Get a grip,' said Lou, in a firm but softer tone. 'I'm not going to report you to the police, they haven't been much use in any case, but I *shall* be phoning Lady Somerset to tell her where their belongings have ended up. Or would you like to? It would be better coming from you. Perhaps if you apologise profusely and promise faithfully to return what you've taken, she might find it in her heart to treat you more leniently.'

'Certainly I will, most certainly. Thank you, my dear, for not getting the local constabulary involved, I could not bear the public humiliation. I can only hope that Lord and Lady Somerset will show similar mercy. I will certainly ensure that everything is returned forthwith. I cannot believe how dreadfully stupid I've been. Oh but my goodness, possibly their most treasured item was that little trinket box. I didn't realise how much it meant to them until I'd taken it but I can't return it because, as you know, I've already given it to Pippa. I can hardly ask my dear friend to return a gift – especially not today of all days.'

'You won't need to,' said Lou. 'I'm sorry to tell you this, Mr Whortlebury, but Pippa is currently auctioning that trinket box on eBay. It's got another three days to run. The last time I looked it had reached seventy-four pounds. You better take part in the auction and make sure you're the highest bidder.'

Mr Whortlebury's face clouded and his throat gulped under his silver beard. 'Oh dear, selling it? Really? Well yes, most definitely I will bid for it and reclaim it, however much money it takes. Oh dear, oh dear. I only gave it to her but a fortnight ago, for her fortieth birthday.'

'Why did you do it, why did you take these things?' asked Emily, timidly, feeling almost sorry for Mr Whortlebury.

He sighed again and looked at her from beneath hooded, melancholy eyes. 'I knew they weren't mine in any legal sense although these possessions could so easily have been had fate taken a different course. It was never my wish to spirit them away from Chumley Towers but I simply couldn't bear the thought of them being lost for good were the place to be sold and I had overheard distinct mutterings from his lordship himself, that it might come to that. I realised that upon its closure, my days of being able to visit regularly and view items which I regard as part of my family heritage would be over. I couldn't bear that. So I felt it incumbent upon me to remove just a few things, a mere few, directly connected to Edwin Somerset's lineage, that I might thereby retain my ancestral ties with the place. And, I suppose, this little chalet has become in my mind, a miniature Chumley Towers.'

'Did you not realise that by acting in this way you were making its closure more likely? Were you planning to take more precious items from Lord and Lady Somerset?' asked Jack.

Mr Whortlebury shook his head. 'I hoped that they wouldn't miss but a small handful, when they have so much. I had taken all I wanted – mere mementoes really, symbols of what might have been.' He fell silent. His lined face looked grey and careworn. Lou guessed that her revelation about what Pippa was doing with the trinket box had punctured his soul more surely than anything else.

'We'll leave you now,' said Lou, gently, realising that he was very distressed. 'Do make that phone call soon, please. I will be phoning Lady Somerset in one hour's time and I expect to be told that you have already spoken to her.'

He nodded. 'Quite so, my dear. Leave it with me. Thank you again for your clemency. Would you still like to look . . . no, no, another time, another time.'

Lou glanced at the others. 'Come on,' she said. 'Let's go.'

CHAPTER TWENTY-SEVEN

Boxing Day banquet

T HE children all filed solemnly out through the door of Mr Whortlebury's Swiss chalet, along the balcony and down the staircase. They slipped away through a side gate. Mr Whortlebury would no doubt remain a while in his private world reflecting on what he had done before, hopefully, calling the Somersets and confessing. He would have a lot of explaining to do.

'You really are amazing, Lou,' enthused Jack as they walked away down Mr Whortlebury's long drive and back towards their home. 'How on earth did you get from Pippa being the thief to Mr Whortlebury?'

'Somehow it just clicked earlier,' said Lou, modestly. 'In fact, David said something which helped me get on the right track.'

'Absolutely,' said David. 'I'm glad what I said helped.'

'David, you have no idea what you said to Lou that was a help, so stop bluffing,' said Jack, impatiently.

Lou chuckled. 'David suggested that the thefts might not have been for commercial gain. That was where we had been coming unstuck all along. Once I pursued that thought, I was on the right lines save for the fact that Pippa *was* pursuing commercial gain but seemingly only for a single item and not the rest.

'And the rest, of course, were not in her possession. Mr Whortlebury was hoarding them and no doubt would have done so to the end of his days. He gave away one of his precious ill-gotten goods to a woman whom he's grown very fond of – too fond, probably. Unfortunately, Pippa's need for hard cash was greater than her affection for that trinket box, or indeed, for Mr Whortlebury himself.'

'I still think you're a genius,' said Jack, admiringly.

'Listen, it was you three who unearthed Pippa's connection to all this, which was the stepping stone I needed to get to Mr Whortlebury, pointed out Lou, fairly.

'Ouch,' Jack yelled, before he had a chance to respond. He put his hand to his cheek, which smarted with pain.

'Oh Jack, you're bleeding,' exclaimed Emily.

'It's nothing, honestly,' said Jack.

'Here, dab it with my hankie,' said Lou. 'It's only a graze, fortunately. But whoever did that is a prat,' she added, looking around.

There was no-one to be seen but at Jack's feet was a snowball packed so tight that it remained intact. It was, essentially, a ball of ice, similar to those with which David had been pelted two days earlier.

'Got you!' came a familiar voice. Bounder leapt out from behind a bush. 'What a shot! Sorry Jack, I wasn't aiming for you in particular, I just wanted to hit either you or David, I didn't mind which.'

'That really hurt, you fool. Why did you pack the snow so hard like that?' protested Jack.

'Oh come off it, it was only a bit of fun,' said Bounder. 'And don't call me a fool.'

His voice had taken on that slightly strangled quality it did when he appeared to be trying hard to stay calm when underneath he was boiling with temper. And his nose had again developed its tell-tale groove.

'Listen, I've got a bone to pick with the pair of you,' he continued. 'I'd like to know what happened to that antique stool that was sitting under our apple tree. It happened to disappear on the very day that you two came round and went for a wander down to the bottom of our garden. Seems a bit of a coincidence, don't you think?

And they looked to be your footprints all around it.'

His voice had now lost its strangled quality but was as sharp and ice-cold as the snowball he had hurled at Jack.

'I'm really sorry, Bounder, I didn't mean to call you a fool,' muttered Jack, looking flustered. 'As for the er stool, erm . . .'

Lou interrupted him. She felt emotionally drained after her humbling of Mr Whortlebury earlier and was in no mood for a smart aleck like Bounder. 'How dare you accuse my friends of stealing your stupid, rickety old stool.' She locked him in one of her withering glares.

'Sorry Lou, I wasn't accusing anyone,' said Bounder, his voice gurgling again as he tried desperately to sound casual and light-hearted. 'It's just that it went missing on the very day you all came round.'

'Well none of us pinched it, Bounder,' replied Lou. 'We're not that sort of people. You shouldn't judge us by your own family's standards. If you really want your stool back, I suggest you take a look over the fence at the bottom of your garden. You might find it lying in the long grass on the other side.'

'Oh, how strange. I can't help but wonder how it got there – did the pixies come in the middle of the night and throw it over, or something?' he said, his voice and the groove in his nose indicating that he was still seething beneath his weedy attempt at humour.

'Quite possibly, why don't you go and ask them,' said Lou, coldly. 'Now clear off, Bounder, and leave Jack and David alone.'

Bounder gasped, speechless. His mouth opened and shut without anything coming out. He looked crestfallen that Lou, whom he assumed found him amusing and rather charming, appeared to hold him in utter contempt.

Lou, Jack, David and Emily all trailed past him without another word.

When Bounder was out of earshot, Lou turned to Jack.

'I'm sorry for being so rude to your friend, but to be honest, I can't stand him and that encounter was the final straw. That wasn't a ball of snow, it was a ball of ice – like the sort those yobs were throwing at David the other day. He could have really hurt you. And then to effectively accuse you both of stealing that stool. I didn't mean to mess up your friendship with him, Jack, but there's just something not very pleasant about him.'

'I know,' said Jack, nursing his sore cheek. 'If I'm honest he's never really been a good friend to me – he just uses me as a sort of useful dogsbody at school to fetch and carry for him. For instance, he would never have invited us round to his house if we hadn't invited ourselves. And he only really put up with us because he sort of took a shine to you.'

'Well don't put up with him, or those other yobs,' said Lou, earnestly. 'When you go back to school next term – and you, David – you need to stand up for yourselves and not allow the bullies to push you around. People like that are not friends, it's people like us who are friends.'

When they got back home, Mr and Mrs Johnson were up and about and the kettle was boiling in the kitchen.

'You're just in time for a cup of tea and a slice of cake, if you can manage it,' said Mrs Johnson. 'We saw your note. I must say you put us both to shame, going for a long walk in the fresh air. Even David went with you, I see. You all look very rosy-cheeked, I must say. Oh Jack, is that a smear of blood on your face?'

'It's nothing, mum, really. I just got hit by a rather painful snowball chucked by a classmate who we happened to bump into. Anyway, we've got some important news!'

'Let Lou tell the story, Jack,' cut in David.

'We'd love a cuppa, if that's okay, Mrs Johnson,' said Lou, refusing to be rushed into saying anything. 'Hey could I ask a favour? Would you mind if I used your telephone for a couple of minutes?'

'Not at all, I expected you'd want to ring home.'

'Well I do, but not straightway. I actually want to contact Lady Somerset. It's a bit of a long story but I need to speak to her quite urgently.'

'Really? What about? Do tell!'

'We've nabbed the thief of Chumley Towers – and in fact another one whom I don't think she even knew about,' said Lou, grinning.

'Goodness me!' exclaimed Mrs Johnson. 'Well yes, by all means.'

Lou had kept Lady Somerset's number safe in her diary. She took it out and rang it, although she had not given Mr Whortlebury quite the full hour she had promised. The deep, gruff voice of the butler, Mr Wilson, answered. Lou's heart sank, expecting him to be awkward and refuse to put her through, but she was wrong.

'Ah yes, good afternoon Miss Elliott,' said Mr Wilson, respectfully. 'I believe her ladyship is expecting your call, hold the line.'

The others listened intently to Lou's responses, wishing they could hear both sides of the conversation.

'It was our pleasure, we just wanted to help,' said Lou, at one point. 'I know, I know, I understand it must have come as a dreadful shock . . . but a relief as well, I should imagine. We had a couple of others in the frame – a handful of lads in David's year at school and also the communist barman at the Bull's Head. They all appeared on both sets of CCTV footage, you see. We couldn't work out why a bunch of rough kids and a committed revolutionary would want to set foot in your place!'

'Aah,' said Lou, pulling a slightly embarrassed grimace. Really? Well who would have thought it . . . Yes, I suppose it was good for them. And the new beer should prove a good draw, as you say . . .'

Beer? What on earth were Lou and Lady Somerset talking about? The others were really puzzled by now.

'Also, on another matter,' continued Lou, 'I feel you should know about what we believe to be the theft of game birds and rabbits from your estate – which are being discreetly butchered and then sold on the quiet to local pubs and restaurants. I'm not sure if you were aware of this? . . . You weren't?'

Lou explained all that they knew and suspected of Hickman and Bounderton's activities which, the others could tell, came as a complete surprise to Lady Somerset. Lou waited patiently while she went off to find her husband to tell him. And then eventually they saw Lou smile her enchanting smile and her eyes dancing with glee. What had been said to make her look so pleased?

'Tomorrow lunchtime? . . . Oh excellent . . . that would be lovely, I'm sure they would be delighted.'

'What would be lovely?' whispered Jack to David. 'I do wish Lou would hurry up.'

Eventually, Lou ended the call and span round to the others, grinning broadly. 'How do you fancy being guests of honour at a huge Boxing Day banquet at Chumley Towers tomorrow? And this *will* be a banquet, Jack, not just scampi and chips. Lord and Lady Somerset would like us to join them for dinner to say thank you for all that we've done – along with their five children Thomas, Sophie, Hugo, Giles and Rupert. They're all our sort of age – plus another couple of dozen guests.

'Whortlebury must have called her more or less as soon as we'd left. He was apparently blubbing pitifully on the phone and Lady Somerset was very shocked to hear his confession. He's faithfully promised to return what he took tomorrow morning. They're sending Wilson round to his place first thing to pick everything up. He's had to explain to Lady Somerset why he can't immediately give back the trinket box but he's vowed to

win Pippa's auction even if it costs him hundreds of
pounds. He's "dreadfully sorry" and has pledged to
donate all the proceeds from the book he's writing about
the history of Chumley Towers towards its upkeep, to
help preserve its future.'

'Are they going to call in the police?' asked Mr Johnson, looking shocked.

'No,' said Lou. 'They say the police made little effort
to investigate the matter properly and see no reason why
they should now take any of the credit for the case being
solved. They have decided to accept Mr Whortlebury's
fulsome apology and offer to make amends. Lady
Somerset pointed out that he is a great asset to the
community and she can't see what good it would do to
brand him a criminal and shame him in public. Also, I
pointed out that he had very honestly handed me back
that twenty-pound note which he spotted me dropping in
the churchyard. I think that counted in his favour.'

'What did you mean when you said something was
good for them, and all that about beer?' asked Jack,
mystified.

'Ah well, we were a little wide of the mark in our as-
sessment of the schoolboy gang and, in fact, Colin
Drayman. The boys went in twos to the Towers in their
own time on a mission to find out historical facts about
the place to complete a school project they had been set.'

'Really? We haven't been required to do that in our
class,' said David, 'and we're in the same year.'

'You wouldn't have. This was extra work set as a punishment for the four of them because they were involved
in vandalism during autumn half-term holiday. They
were caught smashing windows and daubing graffiti on
the school walls and nearly got expelled. They were
given permission to visit Chumley Towers under the
strict supervision of Mr Wilson, who doesn't take any
nonsense!'

'Really!' said David. 'I wondered who had been responsible for that damage. I might have guessed they would be involved.'

'As for Colin, he didn't show up at the Towers to steal anything or to start a revolution – he was there to discuss various means of supplying the Towers tearoom with the Bull's Head's new cask-conditioned ale from its microbrewery. It's proving so popular, they are considering selling it to visitors at Chumley – they hope it will help to bring in more revenue.'

'That's an excellent idea,' said Mr Johnson, licking his lips, 'Bull's Gold – it's a lovely pint of very hoppy, refreshing ale.'

'All that Colin was doing, was talking things through with the head chef at Chumley and handing him a few bottles of beer as free samples,' said Lou. 'The reason he turned up on December 12th and 21st was actually *because* the weather was bad, very few people were drinking in the pub and the landlord could spare him. So Colin's in the clear – for now anyway. Although I still think he needs watching by MI5!'

'So long as he can pour a good pint, that's the main thing,' said Mr Johnson, to a frown from his wife.

'What about the poaching racket going on under their noses?' asked Jack. 'I take it they didn't know what Hickman and Bounderton were up to?'

'No, not a thing,' said Lou. 'They were utterly astounded that Hickman should be coolly supplying game without permission from their estate and without paying them a penny and that an apparently respectable businessman like Bounderton should be running his own secret butchery business using their produce.

'Lady Somerset said that it had to be Hickman at the centre of it all because only he would have access to the stock cupboard containing the vacuum packs with the Chumley crest on. She said that all game birds and poultry shot on their estate was supposed to be prepared by the village butcher Hans Fleischer and only sold in their farm shop and tearoom. Hickman is to be sacked when he next reports for work and all pubs and restaurants in the area notified that the meat Bounderton supplied was stolen. So his freezers will soon be looking pretty empty.

'And for now, at least, the Ninth Marquess of Chumley has resolved to remain at Chumley Towers and do whatever it takes to bring in more income. He's planning to appoint a decent, trustworthy estate manager to help achieve that. Anyway Lady Somerset said we better make sure we have good appetites when we turn up tomorrow because there will be some wonderful food on offer,' said Lou. 'She hopes we'll have a great day with them and their children. She also said that the return of their missing possessions will make it the best Christmas ever and they were incredibly grateful to us.'

'This has been the best Christmas ever for us too,' said Emily, giving her hand a squeeze.

'And for me,' said Lou, 'although that wouldn't be difficult, of course!'

'I'm so glad you came, Lou,' said Jack. 'We all are. And we've still got a couple of days left together. But do you know what, I can't wait for our next adventure, can you?'

'Right now,' replied Lou, sipping her tea, 'I can't wait for that banquet.'

LOU ELLIOTT MYSTERY ADVENTURES:

1. Smugglers at Whistling Sands
2. The Missing Treasure
3. Something Strange in the Cellar
4. Trouble at Chumley Towers

George Chedzoy works from home as a novelist and freelance writer. He lives in North Wales with his wife and two young children. He's always pleased to hear from readers and you can contact him directly on email or Twitter (see below). All books in this series can be ordered from bookshops or from Amazon.

George's blog is at
http://georgechedzoy.blogspot.com
Twitter: @georgechedzoy
Email: georgechedzoy@hotmail.co.uk

Printed in Great Britain
by Amazon

26854465R00148